I0596612

From the Darkest Corner

By
Sidney Reetz

Megan E. Vaughn

Kira Shay

FSF Publications

Cover art and design by Keith Decesare
Interior art by Keith Decesare, Scott P. "Doc" Vaughn, and TJ Geisen

e-Book ISBN: 978-0-9961485-5-9
Print ISBN: 978-0-9961485-4-2

Manufactured in the United States of America.

FIRST Edition

First US Printing: 2016

www.fivesmilingfish.com

Also by...

TO HADES!
Because it really pisses off Zeus.

Kira Shay would like to thank:
Nate and his pet ghost, Steve. Thanks for the inspiration. PS- Nate, Steve really misses you, you should talk to him more.
Will for, well, everything.
Keith for the cover art. Truly phenomenal work.
Doc for the art inserts- they really make the stories complete.

Sidney Reetz would like to thank:
My artist, TJ Geisen, for selling his soul to some dark demon for his amazing artistic talent.
Also, a special thank you to my manager — I mean — mother, Dawn Wagner, for her continued support.
Al would like to thank himself. Because, really, where would Sidney be without him?

Megan E. Vaughn would like to thank:
Uncle David, Uncle Gary, and Aunt Paula, for the hours of family ghost stories around the kitchen table. It warped my mind in the best way possible.
Doc, for the art and for giving me back my nose.
Matt, for staying up going through edits, even when I begged for sleep.
That guy in the red car I cut off the morning after edits. I'm sorry. I was tired.

Table of Contents

Dead Proof
by
Kira Shay

Part One
Reflections of the Dead

"It took a long time to realize I was dead. Not as long as some others I've met, mind you, but long enough to be embarrassed by it. Believe me when I say that there's nothing more pitiful than a spook that don't know he's dead. All of that moaning and groaning. It's like they are begging for chains, am I right?" the ghost chuckled a little even as his companion checked his train pass for the umpteenth time.

A voice boomed over the intercom of the station, "Now boarding platform three bound for Washington, D.C. Now boarding for Washington, DC."

The very much alive teenager picked up his bag and hoisted it over his shoulder with ease. Clasping his ticket firmly, he strode purposefully towards platform three. He didn't so much as spare a backwards glance at the ghost that had been talking at him for the last hour.

The ghost shook his head sa as he adjusted his fedora and adjusted the trench coat draped around his shoulders. He scanned the waiting area, wondering if maybe he wasn't trying hard enough. Here he was, almost fifty years dead and he still couldn't communicate with the living. No matter what he tried, he couldn't get his message to them. Was there something wrong with him?

He rose from the bench and wandered over to a man who was shuffling through a briefcase full of papers. Making himself comfortable, the ghost removed the fedora from his slicked back black hair and began again.

"Hey there. Name's Max. Maxwell Samuelson." He proffered his right hand out of habit only to pull it back as an afterthought.

The man continued going through his papers without even a blink. "You, sir, are a very lucky man, yes indeed," Max said, determined to make this one hear him. "There aren't a lot of us ghosts out here, let alone any that would willingly talk to a living person."

The man put down his papers and sneezed into a handkerchief. After wiping his nose, he went back to reading through one of the typed pages scribbled over with anxious blue pen marks.

Max considered his new companion for a long moment, nostalgia rising up inside him. Completely undisturbed that the man couldn't hear him; he said wistfully, "You know, I used to be like you. When I was alive, I was so concerned with my work that life just kinda passed me by. You should be careful that doesn't happen to you."

They sat in comfortable silence for a long while. As the man shuffled papers in his briefcase, Max eyed him carefully.

One thing he couldn't quite adjust to was how quickly things seemed to change. For instance, how his new companion—obviously a business man—was dressed. Instead of the three-piece suit, as was customary in Max's time, the man simply wore faded corduroy trousers and an ill-fitting short-sleeved button down shirt.

Also, the leaps in technology! Just the previous week, men had landed on the face of the moon. The moon!

"For all of your knowledge and advancements, you still can't communicate with the dead. You still don't know what happens after you die." The ghost stood dejectedly as he donned his old fedora. Giving his friend a solemn nod, he wandered away again.

He positioned himself out of the way against a wall and indulged in some self-pity as he sulked at his most recent failure. Max watched the people meander around the station like bees, bumbling and haphazardly flitting from window to seat to platform.

He hated them for not being able to hear him, or for not *wanting* to hear him. It was hard to tell which it was. He hated them for being alive. For a brief moment, that hate warmed him. It flushed through his soul as if it were flesh. For one glorious moment, he could almost feel like he had when he was alive and too stupid to appreciate what he had. The moment faded quickly and all that remained was the bitter cold of death.

"I used to be like them," he muttered to himself. Had it really been almost fifty years since he had breathed? Since he had eaten, smoked, or been with a woman?

With a certain amount of sadness, the realization dawned on him that he'd been dead far longer than he had been alive. Max folded his arms and let the wash of memories take him back. He had been thirty when he passed and each one of those years wasted. How in the hell had he gotten himself killed so young?

Part Two
An Unexpected Meeting

The noise of the crowded streets was like an angry cacophony in his ear distracting him from the mission at hand. The door to the American Society of Psychical Research was closed. Max came to a halt in front of the building and rested his hand on one of the wrought iron banisters that lined the edges of the stoop.

Every week he made the trip from East Brooklyn to upper Manhattan to make his case to join the Society and every week he was turned away. Well, not today. Today, he had a good feeling he would be welcomed with open arms. He shifted the paper bag from one hand to the other and adjusted his hat as he screwed up his courage. It was now or never.

His shoes clicked on the concrete steps with purpose. Taking in a deep breath, he lifted the large brass knocker and slammed it down three times. After a moment of tense waiting, a stoic looking elderly man in a modest black suit answered the door.

There was only enough time to smile widely before the door was shut on him.

Max stuck his foot in the door just in time to stop it from slamming in his face. "Hey there careful, Rudy. How are you today?"

When he realized that he wasn't going to be able to

shut the door against the menace, the butler opened it just enough to address the man on the stoop. The smile he gave his guest was thin and just hinted of condescension. "Maxwell." Inwardly, he braced himself. Maxwell Samuelson often made a scene when he made his weekly visits to the Society's main office.

"Is Walt in this morning?" Max smiled affably as he shifted the bag from his right arm to his left. He ignored the pain from the door closing on the side of his foot and kept it stubbornly in the door jam.

Rudolph's gaze flicked to the bag and back to Max. "No, Dr. Pierce is not in at the moment. Do you have a message?"

Max frowned. He hadn't counted on the president of the Society to not being there. "Do you know when he will be back? I've got some important information to share with him."

Rudolph considered what to tell him. He decided to keep the answer brief. "Dr. Pierce will be back next week. If you like, I can give him a message for you."

"Yeah. Would you tell him that I came by again? Would you make sure he gets this?" Max handed the crinkling paper bag to the man who accepted it hesitantly.

The butler handled the bag carefully. "May I?" he asked as he went to peek inside. Max nodded his consent and Rudolph reached into the paper bag and extracted a stiff, dingy clump of — well he wasn't entirely sure what. "What on earth is this?"

Max beamed proudly. "Ectoplasm. Got it just the other night during a séance with a gal down in the Bronx. Let me tell you, that was an interesting evening."

Holding the mass of so-called ectoplasm up to the light of day, Rudolph squinted at it closely and gave it a careful sniff. "Maxwell, this is not ectoplasm."

Max stuck his hands into his overcoat pocket and

cocked his head to the side challengingly. "I saw it come out of this woman's mouth as we communed with spirits. I saw it with my own eyes. Are you calling me a liar?"

Rudolph knew better than to rise to the challenge. He recognized Maxwell's stance and sought to diffuse the tension that was mounting in the air. "I'm not necessarily calling you a liar, Maxwell. You could have seen the woman you spoke of expel this from her person. Have you not examined it for yourself? This is, in fact, cheesecloth." He replaced the material into the bag and gave it back to Max. "Perhaps the woman was a charlatan."

Max had to bite back his immediate response. He had to remind himself that punching the old man in the face wasn't the best way to gain a membership to the Society. Clutching the paper bag with one fist, he swallowed his anger and tried to make light of his embarrassment. He forced a chuckle and said, "Come on, Rudy. Give me a break, would you? What can I possibly do? What evidence do you need to accept my application?" Without meaning to, Max was on the verge of begging. He hated to beg, but if that is what this sallow faced butler needed, then that is what he would do.

Rudolph sighed. "We have already told you, several times, Maxwell. Memberships into the Society come with a yearly fee of twenty-five dollars. You would also need to provide empirical evidence of your research. Again, only verified psychical researchers may join."

"How do you expect me to get the type of evidence you need if you won't let me into the library? How can anyone get evidence if they don't know what they need to get?"

Rudolph had enough of Maxwell's presence. As briskly as he could he told the man, "I will inform Dr.

Pierce that you called once again." He then kicked Max's foot out of the door jam and, after retreating inside the building, slammed the door.

Max was left cursing at the pain in his foot and staring stupidly at the brass knocker. He had dropped the paper bag containing the cheesecloth he had soaked in tea, vinegar, and wood pulp on the stoop. When the pain eased a bit, he bent down to grab the bag. After giving one last glare at the door to the Society, he pulled the brim of his fedora down low on his brow and limped down the steps.

"Excuse me," he said after his shoulder bumped into a man. He kept his eyes on the ground and simply tried to move on. There wasn't much time before he had to report to the construction site for work.

"Excuse me," the other man echoed. "Say, can you tell me, is this the American Society for Psychical Research?"

Max eyed the couple curiously. "Yes it is."

The tall man wore a sharp suit and a nice hat. His overcoat looked as though it were meant for much colder climes. The most prominent feature of his face was his long, straight nose followed closely by his large ears. The woman on his arm was attired in an expensive looking blue satin long coat trimmed in fur. A matching fashionable wide brimmed hat covered her short, curling brown hair.

"Excellent," the man smiled and extended his hand.

Max accepted it as he puzzled out what sort of accent the man had.

"My name is Harry Price. Are you part of the Society?"

It took a moment for the words to sink in. When they finally did, Max's eyes widened and his jaw dropped open. He pushed his hat up, away from his eyes so he could really look at the man. "Harry Price?

The Harry Price?"

The man's smile faltered just a little. "Yes, that's right. And you are?"

Pumping the man's hand vigorously, Max stumbled over his words. "Max. I am Max. I mean, Maxwell Samuelson, sir. It is such an honor to meet you, Mister Price! I am an admirer of your work! Your séances with Stella C. are amazing! Honestly, you are the reason why I started researching the paranormal!" Glancing over his shoulder at some passersby, he shouted, "Look! It's Harry Price!"

Harry extracted his hand from the firm grip of the exuberant young man. "Yes. Yes, I am."

"Is this her?" Max gestured to the woman accompanying Harry. "Are you Stella C.?"

Laughing, the lady shook her head. "No, no my name is Lucy, Lucy Kaye. I am Mr. Price's secretary. It is a pleasure to meet you Maxwell." She extended her hand delicately.

Max was compelled to kiss the top of it like he had seen the fellas in the pictures do when they met a pretty lady.

"Likewise. Boy, I'd never thought I'd see the day that I met the great Harry Price! I never dreamed you would come to New York!"

"Neither did I," Harry agreed as he peeked at his pocket watch. "Come, Lucy. We are running late for our appointment with Dr. Pierce." He gave Max a curt nod and took Lucy's arm as they ascended the last few steps.

"Say, Mister Price," Max called out making the man turn back around to face him. "Walt isn't in at the moment. His butler told me that he was out of town until next week."

Surprise registered on Harry's face. "Really? That is strange since I received a telephone call from him at the hotel just this morning. Perhaps I will talk to the butler myself. Thank you, Maxwell."

Still more than a little star struck, Max watched from a distance as his idol knocked on the Society's door, exchanged a few words with old Rudy, and then was admitted inside. Lucy gave a little wave to Max before she entered the building. Max waved back only to be met with the cold stare of Rudy before the door clicked shut.

Harry Price! He was really in New York! Harry mostly operated in England and Europe. The fact that he was in America was completely unexpected. Max had spoken with him, shook his hand! The pure joy and excitement threatened to overtake him as he danced his way down the street, oblivious to the stares of other people. Max was so elated that he didn't even stop to think why the president of the Society would have an appointment when he was supposedly out of town.

He had been following Harry's work ever since he had first read the interview with the medium Stella C. in a filched copy of the Journal of the American SPR. That was two years ago. Max knew someday he would prove that there was life after death and he would bring his evidence to the great Harry Price himself.

He stopped in his tracks, a realization dawning on him. This could very well be his only chance to impress his hero and prove to the ASPR that he was worthy of joining them. All he had to do was find evidence of life after death and present it to Harry before he left America.

He clapped his hands together and exclaimed loudly, "It's as simple as pie!" This earned some curious glances from the people sitting next to him on the train. By way of explanation, he said "I'm gonna find me some ghosts!"

Part Three
Gathering Evidence

Max skipped his shift that day at the construction site. He reasoned that there was too much to do and not enough time to do it in. This once in a lifetime opportunity to impress his hero was more important than renovating some old houses in Brooklyn.

First thing first: he had to find out how long Harry Price was going to be in New York. He doubted that anyone at the ASPR would tell him. Max had found out the hard way that they didn't like to give information to those not of their ranks. Maybe he could manufacture another "chance" encounter and ask Harry himself. That seemed more than unlikely though. Max knew he had been extremely lucky to bump into Harry on the street like he did, but in a city with hundreds of thousands of people, it wasn't likely to happen again. No. He would have to be clever. He would have to do some detective work, perhaps find the hotel where Harry was staying.

His mind spun with ideas when he climbed the steps to his fourth floor apartment in his Bay Ridge neighborhood. He could hear his neighbors fighting over the wail of children. There was the ever pervasive smell of old world cooking mingled with the sweat-stink of the working class.

The tiny studio apartment that Max called home

was cramped and cluttered. Papers littered every available surface. Their topics ranged from profiles on local mediums to ghost sightings with plenty of suspicious news stories that he was sure were more than what they seemed. Of course, he also had information on all of Harry Price's case studies to date.

After closing the door and locking it behind him, he removed his trench coat and flung it over the back of a chair. Immediately, he went for his bedroom to retrieve his journal. Something as momentous as meeting Harry Price deserved an entry. It took him a moment to find the old, leather bound book that his father had given him.

The thought of his father brought a familiar lump to his throat. His father, Torbjorn Samuelson, was the hardest working Swedish immigrant in all of New York. Or at least that was what he and his brothers thought when they were younger. His mother explained to her children that their father wasn't home very much because he was too busy trying to scrape together a living for his ever growing family. It wasn't until he was older that he realized his mother had lied. Their father had abandoned the family long ago, leaving Max and his nine siblings to be raised by their Irish mother.

Max put the memories of his parents aside. He had more important things to think about. He sat at the table and shoved the piles of papers away to give him space to set the book down. He wrote diligently about that afternoon trying to describe every detail about meeting the great Harry Price.

A delicate knock sounded on his front door just as he got to the description of Miss Lucy Kaye. Reluctantly, he set down his pen and called out, "Who's there?"

"Max? It's me, Sarah. The laundry carriage is here and I wanted to make sure you got your clothes down in time."

Sarah was his neighbor, a sweet girl who lived with her aging mother and aunt. She was forever looking out for him. Their friendship was strong, even though her mother often gave him foul looks and muttered curses under her breath.

Quickly, Max unlocked the door. "Sarah! You will never in a million years guess at what happened today!"

Sarah came into the apartment with a shyness that belied their years of friendship. She was a short, comely woman with bobbed blonde hair in the latest fashion. Her clothes, though worn and obviously homemade, had the same look as the ones in department stores. "What is it, Max? What happened?" She smiled as much in anticipation as a reflection of his infectious good mood.

"Well, I went to the Society this morning."

She folded her hands in front of her. "Did they finally let you join?"

Max shook his head, the smile stretching even wider. "No, even better!" He paused to get the full dramatic effect of the moment. He liked how Sarah's eyes widened with curiosity and excitement. Finally, he threw his hands up in the air and exclaimed, "I met Harry Price!"

Sarah gasped, her hands flying to her mouth in astonishment. Anyone who talked with Max for any length of time knew how much he idolized the British paranormal researcher. "No," she whispered, her eyes big as plates.

"*Yes!*" Max lowered his hands and strode towards Sarah. His arms wrapped around her in an embrace that made her flush, though she tried to hide it. "Can you believe it? Harry Price! *The* Harry Price here in New York, and I ran into him!"

Max released her and she beamed, truly happy for him. Impulsively, Sarah grabbed his hand and exclaimed, "This is so exciting! Tell me everything. What did he say to you? What did you say to him?" She realized that she grasped his hand in hers and abruptly dropped it as a deep flush of red colored her usually pale features. She hoped that wasn't too forward of her.

Max, for his part, didn't notice Sarah's sudden embarrassment. "Well, he was coming up to the Society just as I was leaving. He asked if the place was indeed the Society. I told him it was. I met his secretary, Lucy and I was such a dunce! I thought she was the infamous Stella C.!" A sound more like a guffaw than laughter came out of his mouth. "Boy that would have been something, wouldn't it? Harry Price and Stella C. in New York together?"

"I think just meeting Mr. Price today was something." Sarah couldn't help but smile at Max's excitement.

"But you see what this means, don't you?" Max asked as he pulled himself back. His hands grasped her shoulders as he peered intently into her eyes.

Her smile faltered just a little as she struggled to understand. "You met your hero. What more meaning could there be?"

Max turned away, his hands going to his mouth. Could she really not understand? When he spun back around to face her, there was a strange gleam in his brown eyes. It scared her a little bit.

"Don't you see? This is my chance! I can prove that there is life after death! I can bring my evidence to the great Harry Price himself! That will show those jerks at the Society that I matter. They will be begging me to join then. Everyone will know me as the man who conclusively proved that there was life after death!" He took hold of her hand and said, "It means that I can finally be someone important. Can't you understand that?"

Sarah was no longer smiling. Her mouth was set in a sad line and her eyes searched his intently as though trying to convey more than what she was able to say. She gently touched Max's cheek. "You are important though," she protested quietly.

Her words caused him to grimace and step away from her reach. "No, Sarah. I want to be something more. I want a better life than being alone in this shitty apartment. I want to do more than work on old houses. There's so much in this world that we can't explain. I want to find the reasons for them all."

She bit her lip and gave a hesitant nod. What she truly thought she couldn't bring herself to say out loud. Focusing her gaze at the cluttered floor because she didn't want him to see her feelings, she stayed quiet. He wasn't going to listen to her anyway.

Max didn't notice her reticence; he was too busy coming up with a plan. "Harry isn't going to be here long. I don't have a lot of time to gather my evidence."

"How are you going to do it?" Sarah asked, trying to cover her doubts. "How are you going to prove that there is life after death?"

He paced as he thought about that. It was going to take a lot of ingenuity.

An idea struck him suddenly. He swiveled to look at Sarah. "I know how, but I can't do it alone. Sarah, can I count on you to help me?"

"Me?!" Sarah blinked, her heart fluttering in her chest. "You want *my* help?"

Max wasted no time in getting onto his knees in front of her. He took her hands in his and gazed up at her. She looked flustered and confused. "Sarah," he said softly, convincingly, "I can't do this without you. Please. Will you help me achieve my dream?"

There was nothing to say except, "Yes, of course I will help you, Max. What do you need me to do?"

Max kissed her hand. "Thank you, Sarah. This means more than you know."

A kind of exultation filled her heart; a kind of fluttering breathlessness over took her. Could it be that he was finally seeing her as she hoped he would?

Max sprang to his feet and grabbed a piece of loose paper and his pencil. As he spoke, he scribbled instructions for Sarah furiously. "The first thing we have to do is to see how much time we have. I need you to make some calls to the big name hotels in Manhattan. Harry's probably staying somewhere real swank. We need to know where and how long he will be there. Then, call the ASPR and find out when Harry Price will be giving a lecture. He doesn't visit other countries without giving some sort of speech." He handed the wrinkled piece of paper to her before starting to write on another sheet.

"Of course," Sarah said eagerly. "I'll go right now." She made for the door as though she were walking on air. She paused in the hall before closing Max's door behind her and looked back at the man. He was so busy making notes and plans that he didn't even notice her leave. A giddy excitement was lodged in her heart as she silently wished him luck and shut the door behind her.

Max's mind was whirling with plans. He had to find a medium somewhere that was reliable and authentic. All of the ones he had investigated in the city had been frauds and not even decent ones at that. No, he had to do something that would capture the imagination of Harry and the rest of the ASPR.

As he thought about it, he scanned over the papers around him. His eyes caught on a letter from his Uncle Augustus. Augustus was his mother's brother. Recently he had taken a trip to Africa where he had gone hunting elephants. From the description in the letter, it sounded like he had the time of his life. Max laughed a little. He remembered telling his uncle that he had better chance of hunting an elephant in a zoo. Uncle Augustus proved him wrong. He had taken down two of the giant beasts, plus a zebra and a gazelle.

Max could hear his uncle's voice in his head saying, "Sometimes, my boy, you have to get out in the thick of it. Nature doesn't like to be caged, so if you want a piece of it, then you will have to step out of your own cage."

The sudden realization of what his uncle was trying to tell him struck Max like lightning. There were all sorts of cases of mediums and séances. What if you could capture evidence of spirits outside of the cage of the séance room? What if he could hunt down proof that ghosts exist the way that Uncle Augustus hunted elephants? Was it possible to catch ghosts unawares?

Exhilaration pumped through him as he once again started scribbling half-formed notes on the scrap of paper before him. He would need decent hunting grounds— places where the spirit world would be easily accessed. The problem was that there weren't many haunted places in Brooklyn. People were too busy trying to get some hooch and making a living to be concerned with the dead. That meant he would have to expand his territory to Queens, Staten Island, and maybe even Manhattan. Somewhere in the biggest city in America there had to be a haunted place. It would take some investigating and it all hinged on how much time he had.

Tossing his pencil aside, he strode to his chair in the small living space and sorted through the piles of paper next to it. He knew he had a map of New York somewhere. "Aha!" He exclaimed when he found it. There weren't any tacks, so he pinned the map on the wallpaper next to his front door with a piece of hastily chewed gum.

He stood back and folded his arms as he contemplated the map. It wasn't all of New York; just Brooklyn and some of Queens, but it was a start. Max decided he would ask some of the fellas at work. Some of them had moved to Brooklyn specifically for the work and some still lived in Queens. Maybe they had some stories to tell.

Then there was, of course, the list of things he needed to put on a full-scale hunt for ghosts. Naturally, he would model his kit after Harry's. A newspaper over in London had published an article listing all of the tools Harry had in his investigation kit. Max had been working on getting similar items for his own kit, but it took a lot more money and space than he had at the moment. If he wanted to get the proof though, he would have to make some sacrifices.

Max's kit was currently a small suitcase half filled with odds and ends such as rope, a pad and pencil, a box camera that his mother had given to him years ago, and some chalk. What more was needed?

Furthermore, what sort of evidence would prove without a doubt that there was life after death? Usually a hunter would have a trophy from his kill. Hunting ghosts wasn't going to give anything of the sort.

His front door opened and Sarah came running in with a pad of paper clutched in her hand. "Max! I did what you asked and you won't believe it! I found out where Mr. Price and Ms. Kaye are staying on the first try; the Plaza Hotel."

Max snapped out of his musings and returned his attention to his surroundings and Sarah. "Excellent. Do you know how long they are here for?"

Sarah grimaced, knowing that he would not like her answer. "They are leaving in three days, right after the speech he is giving for the ASPR. Apparently, he is accepting the appointment as an honorary Foreign

Research Officer. Then he has to get back to England and to his work."

"Three days," Max murmured. "That's not enough time."

Sarah felt bad for Max, but she knew from experience that when he fixated on something he didn't let it go easily. "Perhaps this is for the best. We can see about attending the speech and—"

"No, they wouldn't allow me inside unless I had proof," Max cut her off. "This has to happen now."

"You said there wasn't any time," Sarah protested in confusion. "How are you going to give them proof if you can't get it?"

The decision was easily made within Max's mind. "It's simple, really. I have to be the medium. I have to give the proof, even if it isn't real."

"No, Max," Sarah protested.

He ignored her. "Once I pull this off I will have access to the ASPR files. When I am a member, I can take my time to prove it. This is just a stepping stone to greatness."

When he smiled at Sarah, her heart sank and she shook her head as she frowned. "This is not going to end well, Max."

He had turned back to his plans without hearing her.

Feeling a deep dread, she whispered, "Be careful," as she quietly left the apartment.

Part Four
Show Time

It was a quarter until eight the night he arrived at the Plaza hotel. The banquet for the ASPR and Harry Price had already begun and was being held in the new ballroom. Max stood nervously on the street in front of the main entrance with his kit in hand. He hadn't wanted to go alone, but when he asked Sarah to accompany him, she refused.

The traffic from Brooklyn had been more than he anticipated and it caused him to arrive fashionably late. He stood at the entrance to the hotel, frozen in place. This was it. This was the point when his life would irrevocably change.

It had been two days since he had met Harry Price and since then he had been working every waking second to prepare for this. Faking a visit from the spirit world was a lot more work than he thought it was. He had read everything he could on the subject and he invested in transparent fishing line and props for his performance. He practiced and practiced, spending hours tilting tables with his toes and chewing paper and rigging it so it would come out of his nose. It hurt, but through it all, he kept his main goal in focus. He kept imagining the roaring applause and Harry Price wanting to shake his hand when it was all over. The last two days seemed to crawl by even as they sped past. Now he was here, ready to give the performance of his life.

"Show time," he muttered under his breath as he mustered up the courage to walk past the doorman and through the double glass doors.

As soon as he stepped over the threshold, it was like a waking dream with all of the opulence that surrounded him. The lobby was all glittering crystal and a warm golden glow.

"May I help you, sir?" A man inquired from behind a large desk off to the side. He wore a suit and tie of much better quality than Max. In comparison, Max felt shabby in his long coat and fedora hat. He wondered if he should have found something more suitable to wear than his brown suit.

Attempting to hide his sudden discomfort, Max responded briskly, "Uh, yeah. I am here for the American Society of Psychical Research banquet. I understand it is in the new ballroom?"

"Ah, yes," the man said. "It is down the left corridor. The ballroom will be just past the Oak Room."

"Thanks," Max waved to the man as he set off down the corridor. The rooms were labeled with golden plaques next to the doors, so despite the vague instruction, Max was able to find the ballroom with little trouble. One of the double doors was propped open just slightly enough that he could peer inside. There was the sound of many people chattering intermingled with the soft clink of glasses and cutlery scraping against china plates. Large round tables were set up around an empty dance floor that sat in front of a raised stage. On that stage sat a long banquet table where the leading members of the Society were seated. Among them were the infamous Harry Price and his secretary, Lucy Kaye.

Just then, the president of the ASPR wiped his mouth with the snow white linen napkin and rose to his feet. It took tapping his champagne glass with his knife several times to quiet the room enough for him to speak.

"Ladies and gentlemen, now that we've had some refreshment, I would like to take this time while we are awaiting the main course to introduce to you the American Society of Psychical Research's new foreign research officer, Mr. Harry Price."

Harry stood, giving a slight bow in the process. "Thank you, Walt. It is a pleasure to be here tonight among you fine people."

"This is it," Max whispered to himself. Boldly, he opened the door fully and strode into the room with his head held high. People turned and whispered as he made his way up to the stage where his hero was still talking.

"Ladies and gentlemen, I humbly thank you for your hospitality. These last couple of days I have learned so much about what America is contributing towards psychical research."

Max had just reached the dance floor when he interrupted Harry by shouting gruffly, "And tonight you will see a lot more than that!"

There were a few gasps and annoyed, yet curious mutterings from the audience. Harry himself paused for a moment, glancing back at the president of the ASPR who was staring at Max with a stunned disbelief. His jowly face slowly flushed a hideous shade of red as the disbelief transformed into rage.

"I'm sorry," Harry said, loud enough for everyone to hear. "I don't believe we have the pleasure of your name, sir—?"

"The name is Maxwell Samuelson and I am here to prove conclusively, once and for all, that there is life after death." He felt the fishing line slide further down his throat and he worried that he would accidentally swallow the cloth attached to it by accident if he kept this up for too long.

His proclamation caused a stir among the crowd and it propelled the president to his feet. "Now see here, Maxwell. This is outrageous. You can't just—"

"Hold on a moment, Walt," Harry interjected. "If this man says he has proof of life after death, it is the Society's responsibility to investigate his claim, is it not?"

When all the answer he received was a furious sputter, Harry gestured to Max. "Please continue."

With his heart thudding in his chest, Max inclined his head graciously towards Harry in thanks. He moved to the center of the dance floor and turned to face the guests. "Ladies and gentlemen, tonight, I entreat you to behold something spectacular! Tonight, I will be making contact with the spirit world. All of you will see with your own eyes proof that our spirits do live on after our bodies die."

"How will you perform this feat?" Harry inquired from the stage.

Max permitted himself a small smile. He certainly had their attention. "I will speak with the dead in this very room, with everyone who is in attendance tonight acting as my witnesses. Would someone be so kind as to dim the lights please?"

It took a moment, but his request was granted. With only the candles on the dozen or so tables to light the room, he felt a bit more at ease, but his throat was parched. He didn't dare risk asking for water now though. Mindful of the eyes upon him, he took an empty chair from a nearby table and placed it in the exact center of the dance floor. In a single grand gesture, he removed his coat and draped it over the back of the chair. His hat followed, being plopped indelicately on the top of his kit. After unbuttoning a couple of buttons on his suit jacket, he sat down and put his hands on his knees.

"Now then. Are we all set? Are you ready?" Now that he was in the moment, he was confident. He could pull this off. Everything had gone according to plan so far.

"Wait just a moment," Harry Price's voice rang out loudly in the hushed room. "It is customary for the medium to undergo an inspection of sorts before he performs." Harry stepped down from the stage and approached Max seriously. "Do you mind?"

A thin sheen of sweat formed on Max's brow. "An inspection?"

"Of course. Just to ensure the authenticity of the events to follow. Don't you agree?"

Max couldn't do anything but nod and stand as Harry Price started his inspection. He looked in Max's pockets, the inside collar of his shirt, his shoes. Just when Max thought he would get away with it, Harry looked at his face. Specifically, the almost invisible fishing line that was trailing out of his mouth and gently draped over his right ear and lead under his collar and down his arm to be attached around his pinkie finger. The other end of the fishing line had been tied securely to the edge of a small piece of cheesecloth that was at that moment, carefully held in his throat.

"Oh, Maxwell," Harry tsked. "What is this?" He gingerly picked up the fishing line with his forefinger and thumb and tugged on it. This caused Max to gag and choke as the cheesecloth moved from his throat and out of his mouth. As he jerked backwards, his hat, attached to a separate fishing line hooked to his other hand flew off his kit.

When the cheesecloth was finally free of his mouth,

he dove to a nearby table and grabbed someone's glass, and chugged the contents to clear the itchiness away. He was fully aware of the peals of laughter all around him. No! This wasn't supposed to happen. He had to get control of the situation again. There was still time to salvage this.

When he turned back to Harry, the man regarded him seriously even as he brandished the fishing line and discolored cloth for all to see. No trace of amusement was on his face. "What is the meaning of this, Maxwell?"

"I'll tell you what the meaning of this is," bellowed the president from his seat on the stage. "This man is a menace. A pest! For far too long he has darkened our doorstep, trying to gain access to this Society with the very tricks we are trying to debunk! Someone get security and get this man out of here!"

"Is this true?" Harry asked. "Have you tried to trick your way into the ASPR before this?"

"No," Max said automatically, "I mean, I've tried to join, yes, but never with tricks."

"Sir, you are lying," a familiar voice came from the audience. A couple of tables down, an elderly man stood. "Just the other day you came to the office and tried to give me a piece of cheesecloth, claiming it to be ectoplasm from a medium. If you recall, I pointed out your error immediately."

Damn it, Rudy, Max thought. *Why are you making this worse?* A titter of laughter circulated around him from the guests in the room. Harry Price just looked at him with disappointment.

"Ladies and gentlemen, this is a perfect example of what I mean," Harry said, taking control of the room once more. He gingerly folded the piece of cloth and stuffed it unceremoniously into Max's jacket pocket. "This Society needs to be focused on finding the truth, not with spiritualistic notions that are pure folly. Calling out these charlatans for what they are will further the cause to scientific enlightenment. We will prove life after death. We will prove the existence of telekinetic and telepathic abilities, but only if we make an effort to understand the difference between authenticity and illusion." He gestured to Max, who could only stand there, mortified. "This man represents everything we should be fighting against as a unified front."

There was loud applause and several people stood as well. Max couldn't hear a thing except Harry's last words ringing in his ears. Harry, his idol, his hero, saw him as an enemy? Or worse, something to be pitied? Max's world crumbled right before his eyes. Harry went on talking, but it was just a dull roar that was indecipherable. The individual faces of the Society members melted together into oddly shaped colored blobs. The lights got brighter and brighter as he tried to understand what had happened.

Firm hands grabbed hold of him and steered him away from the noise, the colors, and the light. He was shoved roughly out of the doors and into the bustle of the city nightlife.

This is the end, he thought despairingly. I have failed. There is nothing more I can do with my life. The one thing that I wanted in this world stripped away from me because of a bit of fishing wire, cheesecloth, and most of all, Harry Price.

The name crystallized in his mind, turning to something bitter and hate filled. Yes, Harry Price was to blame for this. If he hadn't insisted on looking so closely, if he had just sat back and watched the performance, why, Max would still be inside, being toasted as the break-through authority on mediums and the spirit world. His life wouldn't be this sickly, broken thing that it had suddenly turned into if it hadn't been for that damnable Harry Price. He took one last baleful look at the Plaza Hotel and turned his back on it and all of the shattered dreams it now contained.

Part Five
Drunken Despair

The afternoon sun shone fiercely against his eyelids. To combat the assault of light, he tried to shift out of its way, but it was to no avail. His arm flopped over his face in a vain attempt to shield it from the insistent rays. The movement just made him uncomfortable, which made him shift again which resulted in more painful positions. Finally, it was impossible to stay asleep any longer. He succumbed to the pressure of the day and opened his eyes.

Immediately, he regretted his decision.

He had been curled up sideways on his living room chair, still fully dressed in his best brown suit and with his shoes still on his feet. He didn't realize he was hung over until he tried to sit up. The room tilted and swirled around him and he sank back into his previous position, trying not to be sick. A sad moan escaped his lips without him being aware of it. It took several more minutes and more than one try to finally achieve a sitting position that was stable enough for him to get his bearings.

Max didn't remember how he got home, but he must have stopped at a speakeasy or something on the way because there were four bottles of gin sitting on the top of his paper strewn kitchen table. Two of them were empty and the other two were full. When he looked down though there was a fifth bottle with about a quarter of gin left sloshing at the bottom.

He squinted at the clock hanging next to the small bare window that had conspired with the sun to wake him. It was two o'clock.

Normally, Max never slept past four in the morning; working construction had him used to being an early bird. If he hadn't been so hung over, he would have cared that he missed another day of work. That was three in a row. It was almost guaranteed that he didn't have a job anymore. Even if they hadn't replaced him already, the foreman wouldn't take him back after three days of not hearing from him.

That realization should have affected him more than it did. He didn't really care about the construction job; he would find another soon and he had enough in savings to last for a while. No, what concerned him more was the disturbing dream he had about being made the laughing stock of the entire ASPR and Harry Price to boot. It had been a dream, hadn't it?

With as few movements as possible, he removed his jacket and tossed it onto the ground. A wadded up piece of cloth bound in fishing wire fell out of the pocket and onto the floor.

At the sight of the small bundle, something akin to heartbreak stirred in his chest. As the pain grew, the memories of the night before came to the surface of his thoughts. It hadn't been a dream after all.

An uneasy desperation gripped him. He had been ridiculed and made a laughingstock. Harry Price had called him the very thing they were fighting against.

Now he had nothing. Everything he had built his future on had disintegrated in that ballroom to the sound of laughter and the soft clink of crystal champagne glasses.

The pain of a shattered dream was too much to handle right then. Max picked up the quarter full bottle of gin and took a large guzzle. The sting of the hooch dulled the pain in his head and in his heart. He kicked off his shoes and undid his belt. Getting to his wobbly feet, he lurched through the small apartment to his bed. It was dark in there due to the curtains Sarah had helped him hang when he had first moved in. His bed was littered with extra cheesecloth, fishing line and his research papers. The sight of it all made him angry so he threw it all violently against the wall of the room, blanket, and all.

Stripping down to nothing, Max finished off the remaining gin in the bottle and collapsed on to the bed face first.

Sarah came to check on him the next afternoon. When he didn't answer her persistent knocks, she let herself in. The apartment was in even more disarray than usual. There was also a certain odor, a foul stench that reminded her of her father that permeated the air.

"Max?" she called out. "Max, it's me, Sarah. Are you alright?"

There was no response. She followed her nose and discovered Max lying despondently on his bed, completely naked and covered in vomit.

"Oh my God!" she cried out and rushed over to him. He was alive, but out cold. "Max!" she shouted, patting his cheek. "Max, wake up now!"

He wasn't going to wake up any time soon, she realized. She checked his breathing again and sighed when it was slow and steady. He would be all right. The only thing she could do was to wait for him to wake up.

Taking stock of his condition, she knew she would have to do more than wait. With a heavy heart, she gently laid him back on his bed. There was much work to be done.

The smell of bacon infiltrated his dreams. The aroma of eggs and toast made his stomach roil and growl at the same time. He was afraid to move lest the pounding headache started again and risk more nausea than he could handle.

Finally, he did take a chance and opened his eyes. He was in his bed and it was bright, which threatened to cause his head to explode. Something was different. He could tell that much, though he couldn't quite pinpoint what it was.

A sudden thirst overtook him. Man, was he parched! Still, the thought of water made him slightly green.

As a further experiment, he wiggled his toes to see if he could move without incurring the wrath of God. Not only did he discover that his toes were functional, but that they were covered in a sheet. A clean sheet at that. Wait. When had he washed his sheets?

Gingerly, he shifted his foot, then his leg. So far, so good. In addition to the sheet, he discovered that he was also draped with a quilt. Using his hands, he tugged on the bedcoverings until they slid down his chest. He was naked except for a pair of clean underwear. This only added to his confusion. The last thing he remembered was vomiting on his floor. He had missed most of the floor and instead had thrown up all down his front and his bed. He remembered that he intended to clean it up, but that must have been when he passed out.

So then why was everything so clean?

The answer came as a shadow came over him holding a tray and accompanied by an overpowering smell of breakfast. Max could only assume that on the tray were things meant to make him vomit up whatever booze was left in his system.

"Good!" a cheerful voice shouted. "You're awake. I've made you some breakfast."

Max was speechless with confusion. "Sarah?" he whispered.

"Of course," she replied altogether too loudly. "Who else would it be?" She set the tray of food on the foot of the bed and went towards the curtains. Before he could warn her not to, she threw them open, letting the brightest light New York could possibly produce right onto Max's bed.

The pain was excruciating. He shut his eyes and yanked the blankets up over his head. He might have whimpered.

"Oh, stop it," she scolded him. "Come on. You need to eat something."

The thought of eating made him want to be sick. "No," he moaned from under the covers. "I can't."

Sarah sighed. "Yes, you can. You must." She pulled the edge of the blanket off Max's face. "It's been days. It's time for you to get up and stop this nonsense."

"Days?" Max repeated blankly.

"Yes. You should be thankful I found you when I did. Had you been left in that state, I don't think you would have survived." Sarah picked up a tall glass of water and handed it to him.

Max struggled to sit up without letting the dizziness take him over. She was patient and waited for the room to stop spinning before handing him the cup. He sipped it slowly at first, then drank, then gulped, then guzzled until it was all gone. He handed the empty cup back to her and Sarah raised her eyebrow in approval.

"Good." She picked up a piece of dry toast from the tray. "Here. Try to eat this, alright? I'll go get you some more water."

He accepted the toast with two fingers, eyeing it suspiciously. Did he dare try to eat it? His mind balked at the prospect of being sick again.

Sarah returned with not only a glass of water, but an entire pitcher as well. "Why haven't you eaten?" She asked in a tone that warned him not to cross her. Max had never known Sarah to be so forceful. Truth be told, it frightened him more than the thought of getting sick, so he nibbled on the edge of the toast and prayed that it would stay down.

She watched quietly as he ate. What had happened to get him in such a state? "Max," she started, unsure of how to phrase the question. "What happened the other night?"

Max sat in stony silence, chewing a small bite of toast. It tasted like ashes on his tongue.

Sarah was a fairly perceptive woman. She took his hand in her lap and gently asked, "They laughed at you, didn't they? Those men at the Society?"

He didn't want to cry. He didn't want to remember that night and how his entire world had been ruthlessly shattered. He wanted to bury it deep inside and keep it in the dark so as never to look upon it again. Still, there it was, being dragged out into the light of day.

"I don't want to talk about it," he said. Even to his own ears it sounded peevish.

Sarah knew better than to say she told him so. Instead, she poured water from the pitcher into the glass and handed it to Max. "Drink this."

He did as he was told, maintaining his brooding silence. Sarah made him eat as much as she could. Despite his insistence that he would only throw it back up, he had to admit that the food was doing him some good. As he sobered, the memories of that night persisted in his thoughts.

Everywhere he looked, he saw the laughing, jeering

faces of the audience in the ballroom. As much as he tried to block it, the images of that night haunted him. How could Harry have done that? Why would Harry have embarrassed him in front of all those people? He wasn't ready to face them again. He didn't want to remember.

There was one way to block the memories, but it required a lot of gin. "I need a drink," Max said to Sarah as she was cleaning up after breakfast. She had helped him move from his bed to the big chair in the front room. He marveled at the changes she had made; his whole apartment was transformed. Surfaces of tables he hadn't seen since he moved in had been freshly dusted and all of his papers, all of his research, neatly organized in a file she had found somewhere. Instead of the old musty smell of dust and aging paper, there was a subtle scent of lemon and mint. It seemed brighter, more hospitable than he remembered.

"There's water on the table next to you," she replied without even stepping out of the kitchen.

"No, I need some booze." Max got to his feet and cast a glance down at his appearance. "Where did you put my clothes?"

Sarah appeared from the kitchen, her apron damp from dishes and wiping her hands on a cloth. "You don't need any more alcohol, Max," she warned him. "Why don't you just sit and relax for a little while. Later on, when you feel more up to it, we can go for a walk."

He rubbed his hands over his face. The stubble on his chin scraped against his palms. "No, I need to get something to drink. I can't keep reliving that night in my head and the booze is the only thing that can block it out."

"Block what out?" she asked. "Please, just tell me. Maybe it will make you feel better to just talk about it."

"Talk about it?" Max shouted and winced at the

echo it caused in his head. He had reached the end of his patience with her and her meddling ways. "What do you want to hear, hmm? Do you want to hear about how I was made a complete fool in front of the entire Society? Or how they laughed at me! My sad and pathetic attempt to prove myself was mocked! Do you want to hear how Harry Price himself said that I was everything that the Society should be striving against? Do you want to hear how they threw me out of the Plaza? Yes! Security tossed me right out of the front door and onto the street. Is that what you want to hear from me, Sarah?"

"I . . . I had no idea," she whispered, clutching the towel against her chest. "Oh, Max, I am so sorry."

Her expression was pitying and he hated her for that. He didn't need pity. He needed to numb the pain. He continued to shout, unable to stop the tide of emotion that was cut loose. "Of course you didn't know. You didn't come with me. You promised that you would help me and in my time of need, you were nowhere to be found! So tell me, how does me talking about any of this make it better? How can any of this be made better?"

Out of sheer spite, he took the nearest thing— a picture of his mother and father— and threw it against the wall. The glass shattered and the wooden frame broke apart as it fell to the ground.

"I'm sorry," Sarah cried. Her tears glistened as they rolled down her cheeks like fat raindrops. "I'm sorry I wasn't there. Max, listen to me, alcohol isn't going to help either. It's just going to make you sick. It can't erase the past. It will still be there when you sober up."

His lip curled in anger. "What the hell do you know? Who are you to tell me what I can and can't do? You don't know what I'm going through. You don't know anything about this. You're just a homely spinster lady that nobody wants. That's why you live with your mother and aunt when you should've been married long ago."

Her hand against his face was something unexpected. The painful sting that followed was accentuated by another blow. The ringing in his ears subsided a bit and his own hand covered his cheek as though to contain the pain. When he looked back at her, the pitying expression had vanished and in its place something akin to loathing.

"How dare you?" she hissed at him. "I have been here for you more than anyone else has. I've spent the last two days taking care of you and putting your apartment in order and you dare speak to me like this?"

"I didn't ask you to clean the apartment, Sarah!" Max roared. "I wish to God you had just left me alone."

"If that is what you want, fine! Go on! Go get drunk! How many bottles do you think it is going to take to change what happened? Shall we keep count? I bet that there's not enough alcohol in the world that can cure you of your foolishness!" Never before had she screamed at him so much. Sarah knew that rising to his challenge wasn't going to help much, but she was so incredibly irritated that she couldn't help it.

"Drinking is still better than dealing with you! You know, there's a reason you aren't married yet, Sarah. You pester people. You pester me with your silly ideas and puppy dog eyes. Go and pester someone else for a change. I am sick of dealing with you."

Sarah took his insults with a stoicism that would make a statue proud even though on the inside she was breaking. She had stopped crying, though her face still showed the flush of the hurt she felt. She opened her mouth to say more, to fling more insults and barbs at the man she had cared for. Instead of screaming out the hurtful things that came into her mind, she composed herself and left the apartment without another word. The door slammed behind her.

When she was gone, all of the anger faded and Max was left stunned and deflated. He shouldn't have said all of those hateful things. Sarah hadn't deserved any of that. He flopped back onto his chair, his head in his hands. "What is wrong with me?"

Suddenly the cleanliness of his apartment seemed stifling. The walls, all freshly cleaned seemed to press in on him. He could almost hear the laughter of the ASPR ballroom echoing from the walls. Fed up, he stomped around searching for some clothes and his shoes. He had to get out of there.

It took only a few moments to find his clothes, which were neatly hung in the armoire and folded in his dresser. His shoes were placed with care next to his bedroom door. He dressed quickly, placing his hat atop his untidy hair and slinging his jacket on without tucking in his shirt. He was out the door and bolting for the stairs in record time, taking care not to look at Sarah's door across the hall.

It was early afternoon and Brooklyn was bustling. Max blinked at the sun as he got his bearings. There were a couple of places that may be open this early, but he couldn't quite remember where or what the password would be. He decided to go to the one place he knew well and wait for them to open their doors. It was in a tailor shop downtown. He hadn't been there often, but it was enough that he felt comfortable there.

He started walking, keeping his head down. The memories were coming faster and mingled with the fresh argument he just had with Sarah. All of it made him feel wretched and that quickened his steps. The sooner he got there, the sooner he could drink and that meant the sooner he could forget for a while. In the back of his mind, he knew that soon he would have to confront what happened; he would have to deal with all of it. But not now. No, right now he needed to not think and be as numb as possible until he had enough courage.

The tailor shop was empty except for the shopkeeper. He glanced at the newcomer questioningly. Max gestured to the trap door. The response to the unasked question was a brief nod. Max approached the wooden panel next to a rack of fabrics and knocked three times.

"Password," a voice asked from the ventilation grate near the floor.

"Coolidge is a Rube," Max said quietly.

There wasn't any response except for the click and scrape of the false paneling swiveling inwards. The stairway was dark and the bouncer filled most of it. He sidestepped around the great hulking man and descended the narrow circular stairway into a cramped, but comfortably furnished club. The lighting was dim, and there was a radio in the corner playing jazz. A few other men sat around tables chatting amicably and smoking cigars. Max went straight for the stylized bar along the side of the room. A man stood behind the bar, cleaning a martini glass. He watched Max approach stoically.

"Gin, straight up," Max said as he leaned against the bar.

"Two," responded the bartender.

Max dug into his coat pockets and found a few coins. He set them on the wooden countertop with a clink. The bartender left them there as he turned to pour the drink. Within seconds, Max had a glass in his hands.

The burn of the gin going down his throat was like a balm for the anxiety building in his head. In moments, he downed his glass and placed it firmly on the bar in front of him. "Another please," he said and pushed the remaining money he had towards the bartender. "Keep 'em coming."

The bartender gave a brisk nod and obliged the request easily. Max settled into one of the tables in the back, away from the laughing and joking men on the other side of the room. Now that he had the initial drink, he took his time with the second, taking small sips while staring at one of the paintings on the wall. He couldn't tell you what the painting looked like; it just gave his eyes somewhere to stare off into while he focused on shoving the memories of what happened away.

He hadn't been there long before a man came up to him and asked, "Is this seat taken?"

Startled, Max glanced up to find a man about his own age with two drinks in his hand. Even though he didn't want company right then, something told him to let the man sit. "Go ahead," he said, waving to the chair next to him. The man set the two drinks on the table and made himself comfortable.

"Name's Ben. Ben Porter," the man said and offered his hand.

"Maxwell Samuelson. It's nice to meet you." He accepted the man's hand and then resumed gazing at the painting.

"Here. It looks like you could use another drink," Ben said and pushed the second glass of gin towards Max.

The gesture caught Max off guard. "Oh, well, thank you very much." He raised his own drink and Ben raised his in a salute of solidarity. "Cheers." Each man brought their cup to their lips, Max taking a large swallow and Ben simply sipping a little.

They sat in amicable silence for a long moment before Ben inquired, "It's quite a city, Brooklyn. Are you from here?"

"Yeah. I grew up in Baywood Heights. What about you? Are you from around here?"

At first Max resented the attempt at a conversation, but the more he thought about it, the more he warmed to the idea. This man wouldn't ask about what happened two nights ago. This man wouldn't look at him with pitying eyes. This could be the chance he needed to reconnect with some form of reality and to start forgetting that the incident ever happened.

"No, I'm from Long Island originally. I moved here a few years ago with my old lady. She wanted to be closer to her sister." Ben rolled his eyes exaggeratedly. "I swear, when we first met, she didn't want anywhere near the old hag. Now they are inseparable."

"Oh," Max sighed in spite of himself. He thought of Sarah and her reactions that morning. "Women are odd creatures, aren't they?"

If he noticed Max's melancholy disposition, Ben didn't show it. Instead, he lit a cigarette and continued trying to get to know his newfound friend a little better. "You a family man, Max?"

This drew a chuckle out of Max. "Uh, no. Never had the pleasure to meet the future Mrs. Samuelson. Not to mention I never had the time or inclination to look too hard either."

"I wish that was my case. Nah, instead I was a fool and got married and had a kid. What do you do for a living, Max?"

"Construction, mostly. But I am between jobs at the moment. Too many days off chasing ghosts." Max cringed even as the words came out of his mouth. Had he really just said that out loud?

Ben gave a brisk nod, "I feel you. I'm a rail man myself. Sometimes it's hard to keep it consistent. All day, every day was never my style, but having kids changes you." He took another sip of his drink and seemed to ponder what he wanted to say next.

Max was relieved that the ghost comment had been passed off. He took a drink.

Ben chose that moment to lean forward and ask, "So, do you believe in ghosts?"

Max almost choked on his gin. "What?" he sputtered after setting his glass safely back on the table. "What did you say?"

"Ghosts. Do you believe in them?"

A million warnings and questions went off in Max's mind. Was he a member of the ASPR come to ridicule him? What did he want? Was this some sort of trick? He settled for a safer inquiry and asked cautiously, "Why would you ask me that?"

Ben could tell that he hit a nerve. "Hey, I was just being curious. You said you were out chasing ghosts, it made me wonder."

Max stared at him suspiciously for a long moment before reluctantly nodding. "Yes, I believe in ghosts."

"Oh, I am really glad to hear that!" The smile that lit up Ben's face alarmed Max. There was no time to figure out exactly why before Ben admitted, "Look, I got this problem. My little girl, Dorothy, she's six, about to turn seven. She says things, things she couldn't possibly know about. My wife and I . . . we are at our wits end. That's the real reason why we moved out here. Things started happening back home. Strange things. We thought if we just moved it would stop." He glanced up at Max who was watching him with a mix of fascination and suspicion. "I promise I am not crazy. I just need some help. We don't know what to do anymore."

"What do you think I can do?" Max asked.

"I don't know. You grew up here. Do you know anyone that can help my daughter? Anything at all, please."

It was a combination of the alcohol hitting his system and the slight glistening of tears in the man's eyes that moved Max. Things must be really bad for this guy to ask a complete stranger for help with such a sensitive matter.

Max gulped the last of the gin, mulling it over in his mind. "I may know some people that would be able to help you. But, I need more information. What sort of strange things are you talking about?"

Out of sheer relief, Ben spent the next two hours detailing all of the strange happenings around his daughter Dorothy for the last year. Things had been witnessed floating towards her. She claimed to have a friend named Henry who was about her age, but looked really pale. Henry would tell her things, things about the past and sometimes the present that she couldn't possibly know. Once, back in Long Island, she had wandered off and didn't return for three days. There was a frantic search for her; the entire neighborhood looked night and day. Finally, on the morning of the third day, she was found in an open grave, all dirty and her dress torn. Dorothy told the men who found her that Henry tried make her like him. She said that Henry wanted her to be his friend forever.

That was six months ago and the incident that prompted the move to Brooklyn. At first, Ben and his family thought that was the end of it. Now, things were starting to happen again. Henry was back and this time things were escalating. Dorothy's health was deteriorating. The doctors couldn't tell what was wrong with her. It was like she was fading away right before their eyes. She would have violent fits of temper and was becoming increasingly dangerous not only to herself, but to others as well. Some of these fits resulted in her trying to kill herself so that she could play with Henry. She would curse at her mother and then cry so despondently that it would break your heart.

Max listened attentively to the stories of objects moving on their own accord, to the sounds of a child yelling Dorothy's name. Mirrors shattered in the night. Dorothy would disappear from her room at night and then would be found hiding in her parent's room with a knife or some other dangerous instrument. Max had never heard of such a concentrated account of paranormal activity around one girl. It was most certainly a haunting more in depth than he had ever witnessed.

When there were no more stories to tell and his terror-filled life had been bared to this silent stranger, Ben asked, "What do you say? Can you help us?"

"I can and I will." The words were out of his mouth before he knew what he was saying. The second they were uttered, part of him immediately regretted his commitment. What was he thinking? He was just made the laughingstock of the whole ASPR, what made him think he could help this man? The other part of him, however, was salivating for the chance. This was going to give him the proof he needed. This case would launch him into the lime light. Harry Price and the ASPR would be begging him to join their little Society once he got proof.

Ben heaved a sigh of relief. "Thank you, so much."

"I'll need a few things first," Max said.

The man tensed a little. "If it is money you need, we have a little bit, but not much. Most of our savings was spent on the move. "

Asking for money had never occurred to Max. "Oh no, you don't need to pay me," he assured Ben. "I have my own reasons for helping you. I just meant that I would have to gather some equipment and I'd like to meet Dorothy before we get started."

"Of course." Ben pulled out a pen from his shirt

pocket and made some scribbles on a napkin. "Here is my address. Please, come for dinner tonight and meet the family. Then we can discuss what needs to be done."

"Thank you," Max smiled at Ben as the man got up from the table. He shook his hand once more.

"No, thank you, Max. My wife is going to be so relieved. I'll see you tonight, seven o'clock." Ben donned his hat and his coat, looking younger than he had when he walked in. Such a weight had lifted with this simple conversation with a stranger. Hope had returned to him after he had all but given up on it.

Max watched him leave the speakeasy, excitement welling in his chest. This was exactly what he needed! It was just in time too. He had started to believe all of the hogwash that Harry Price had said about him. Max finished the gin that Ben had bought for him and prepared to leave as well. Now that he had a clear purpose and something to focus on it was easier not to let what happened with the ASPR take over his mind.

It was with a spring in his step that he returned home. Harry Price would eat his words, Max thought as he ascended the steps to his fourth floor apartment. Once Max showed the world proof of little Dorothy's ghost friend, the whole world would look to him as an authority on spirits and the afterlife.

He didn't even look at Sarah's door, however the cleanliness of his apartment was the slap in the face reminder of the fight he'd had with her that morning. He allowed himself to feel annoyed. Why had she messed with his stuff? Now he wouldn't be able to find anything.

As he started rummaging around his apartment for his kit items, he plotted how he would go about this opportunity. He would meet the family, examine the girl, and then he would launch a full-scale investigation. It would take some time, but he would be victorious. He had to be. Too much was riding on this last chance.

His box camera was placed inside of a seldom used cabinet. He pulled it out with a huge grin and checked the film. It was ready to go.

"Henry," Max said the name like an oath. "I look forward to meeting you."

Part Six
Dorothy

Ben lived in east New York near the Broadway junction. It didn't take Max long to find the address. He had scrounged up a few cents to get a bouquet of flowers. His mother always taught him that when he was invited to someone's house for dinner, you always bring something for the woman of the house. Flowers were the standard.

The Porter family lived on the third story of a seven story building. The apartments were run down, but well kept. Max had certainly been in worse places. By the time he knocked on the door, his nerves were jangling with excitement. He held his kit in one hand and the flowers in the other.

A short, plain woman answered the door. Her hair was pulled back though several loose brown strands had escaped their binding. She wore a simple, homemade floral printed dress that was too big to fit her properly. A stained apron was tied about her waist.

"You must be Mrs. Porter," Max said with a smile on his face. He proffered the flowers and introduced himself. "I'm Maxwell Samuelson. I met your husband earlier today."

The woman took the flowers silently, never taking her eyes from the man at her door. She made no outward appearance of welcome; she just stared.

"Martha?" someone called from inside the apartment. "Martha, who is at the door?" A woman appeared then, slightly older than Martha and much better kempt. Her brown hair was cut short as was the style and her dress was modernly sleek. She peered around the younger woman curiously. When she saw Max, a large smile stretched across her lips. "You must be Maxwell. Ben has told me so much about you. I'm Cynthia, Ben's wife." She grasped onto Martha's shoulders and shifted her out of the way. "Martha, darling, please go tell Ben that our guest is here."

Martha did as she was told; only reluctantly pulling her gaze away from Max.

Cynthia watched her shuffle off with a mix of concern and exasperation in her eyes. She caught herself though as she turned to Max, her worry vanishing in a blink. "Please, come in. Don't mind my sister, she's just a bit odd, but completely harmless."

"Not a problem," Max said as he stepped over the threshold. He did his best not to look disturbed, though it was hard. Martha certainly had the power to unnerve someone with her blank stare. Still, he couldn't help but ask, "Is she alright?"

"Martha?" Cynthia asked. "Yes, she is quite alright. She's always been a bit slow. When my mother passed, my father wanted to put her in the sanitarium. I wouldn't stand for it. So, now she stays with us. Ah, here is the rest of the family." Cynthia guided him into the small living room where Ben sat reading the paper and a small girl, no more than seven, played with her dolls at his feet.

"Ben, Max is here," she called to her husband. He looked up from his paper with a relieved smile on his face. Immediately the paper was set aside and he rose to his feet. Careful to step over the playing girl, he reached out to grasp Max's hand.

"It's good to see you, Max," he said as they shook hands. "Did you have any trouble finding the place?"

"No, not at all," Max assured his host. He glanced down at the girl who had stopped playing with her doll and was looking at him with a peculiar expression. "Who is this?"

There was a slight hesitation before Ben reached down and picked the girl up. "This is my daughter, Dorothy. Dorothy, this is Mr. Samuelson. He is going to help us."

"Hello, Dorothy. It is nice to meet you."

The child smiled shyly and turned her face into her father's shoulder.

"Now, Dorothy. That's not polite. What do you say to Mr. Samuelson?"

The girl looked back at Max and said quietly, "How do you do, Mr. Samuelson?"

"You can just call me Max," he responded with an easy smile.

She grinned back even as her father put her back on the ground.

"Alright dear. Go help your mother with supper." The girl scampered off towards the kitchen without so much as a glance backwards.

"She's cute," Max said.

"She is, isn't she? Please, won't you sit down?" Ben gestured to one of the three chairs in the living room.

Max sat in the one closest, a tall wing backed affair upholstered in a subtle pastel floral fabric. The padding was lumpy and uneven, leaving only the fabric between his thigh and the wooden frame of the chair. Max knew better than to comment on the disrepair of the seat, so he said instead, "Ben, I can't promise you anything except that I will do my best to help."

"Of course, of course," his host assured him.

"Believe me when I say anything will help."

Max reached into his coat pocket to pull out his pad of paper and pencil. "Alright then. I'll need to ask you a few questions."

Ben shook his head. "No."

"Beg your pardon?" Max blinked at the man, confused.

"No," Ben repeated. "I promise you, my wife and I will answer your questions, but not now. We want you to observe her at supper. Then, once you have seen what it is that we are dealing with, we will answer whatever questions you may have."

"What makes you think that she will act oddly tonight?" Max asked. As far as he knew, there was no way to tell when a haunting would happen. It was random.

"Because," Ben sighed and Max could hear the man's exhaustion for the first time, "it happens every night."

Before Max could even form a response to that, Cynthia came into the room. "Ben, Mr. Samuelson, supper is ready."

"Coming dear." Ben smiled and got to his feet once more. Max followed suit. Ben stopped short of the dining room causing Max to halt behind him. "One thing before we go in there," he warned. "Whatever happens, don't react to it. You can watch, but don't react. If it sees you react to what it does, it will only get worse."

This warning only served to confuse Max even more. Nevertheless he screwed up his courage and followed Ben into the dining room, unsure of what he would find.

The table was set and both Martha and Dorothy were waiting politely. Cynthia brought one last dish of food to the table. "Supper is ready. Please, won't you sit down? What would you like to drink?"

"Coffee, please," Max answered as he went to take the seat next to Dorothy.

"No! Don't sit on him!" the little girl screamed at the top of her lungs.

Max jumped away from the chair, startled and looked questioningly at Ben.

"Henry sits there," his host explained. "Here, sit next to me."

Max did as he was told and walked to the opposite side of the table, all the while staring at the seat where Henry apparently sat. He couldn't see anything besides an empty chair. Max took the place at his host's right. This put him directly across from Cynthia and next to Martha. Sitting beside her mother, Dorothy acted as though nothing had happened.

How peculiar, Max thought, but as Ben had warned him, he acted as though nothing was amiss.

Before any food was scooped out of their serving dishes, Ben invited the family to hold hands so that grace could be said.

Max's family was old world Catholic, but he didn't hold to the Church much as an adult. It was odd to him to hold hands with Ben and Martha as everyone bowed their heads to pray. The Porters seemed to be some sort of Protestant based on the way Ben said grace. The prayer was just similar enough to Max's childhood that it brought on a sense of nostalgia for him.

The rattling of the china made Max open his eyes before the prayer was completed. There, in Henry's place of honor, the plate shook, smacking the china beside it. The edges of the plate chipped off when the shaking became more aggressive. The serving dishes it clattered against suffered damage as well. Glancing around the table, he noticed that no one else was troubled by the noise. Indeed, no one else had even looked up.

Don't react, Max reminded himself. It was with great difficulty that he bowed his head again, though he kept his eyes trained on the flatware. With every word, the shaking grew more and more violent. He was sure that something would shatter at any moment.

Just as he was about to get to his feet and run for his camera, Ben's prayer ended. Almost immediately the clanking of the china ceased.

"Mommy, Henry wants some potatoes," Dorothy said matter-of-factly. "He doesn't want any peas and neither do I."

There was a catch in Cynthia's voice as she responded in a falsely light voice, "Well, Henry can have what he wants, but you are still a growing girl and you need to eat your vegetables." Her hands shook as she spooned out food onto both her daughter and the invisible guest's plates. Max took only a little bit of food, as he was far too excited to eat anything. Instead he watched the family and made idle conversation.

What really interested him was the activity at the supposedly empty spot at the table. The silverware shifted on its own accord. The food that was mounded on the plate moved, influenced by invisible hands. Nothing was eaten; just spread around the china in sticky, messy swirls.

At one point, something flew across the table, straight at Ben's face. A clump of mashed potato slid down his cheek and plopped onto his lap. The only sound was Dorothy's peals of laughter and an echo of something else. Was the ghost laughing?

"Henry got you, Daddy!" she proclaimed between fits of giggles.

Ben wiped the food from his face, careful not to show any fear or annoyance. "Eat your peas, Dorothy," he said.

Max stared, dumbfounded as more food was flung

around the room. It happened too quickly for him to figure out how it was done. One thing was clear; it all originated from the empty spot at the end of the table. The family ignored the happenings around them, eating even as they wiped the splatters of the flung food from their faces as calmly as they could.

Max could feel the tension rising though. A couple of times, Ben had subtlety kicked his shin under the table, a sign for him to not be so obvious in his staring. He ignored the warning and garnered enough courage to ask Dorothy a question or two.

"Dorothy. Is that Henry throwing his food?"

She didn't answer him. Instead she looked towards her father, who shook his head ever so slightly. She was not to answer any questions at the table. That was what he had told her before Max had come to her house. Conversation ceased with everyone struggling to maintain composure in the face of a ghostly food fight. Soon enough, the food stopped flinging through the air.

He thought it was over. He thought the food throwing was the main event. He was wrong.

Right before his eyes, dishes stacked on their own. Not just one plate on top of another. No, intricate towers were constructed with plates balancing on silverware and glasses. The food was sculpted as he watched in disbelief.

"Stop it, Henry," Dorothy scolded thin air. "It is rude to play with your food." She said this so decisively that Max wondered at her composure. Could she see him? Hear him? This was certainly not what he had expected. There had been children mediums before, but most of them had been hoaxes discovered by anyone who bothered to examine them too closely.

Then, the entire food and flatware structure was flung forward towards the living, breathing humans at the table. Everyone flinched away from the crashing china and cutlery. The tower of dishes shattered as it hit the table. Shards of china and glass along with globs of uneaten food acted as shrapnel. Martha and Cynthia screamed as they tried to cover their faces with their hands. Max stumbled backwards, over his chair, away from the table while closing his eyes against the projectiles. Ben ducked under the table. None of them acted fast enough. Once the tremendous noise of the crash subsided, the grown-ups cautiously raised their heads and opened their eyes to see what had happened.

Dorothy was sitting on top of the wreckage, perfectly perched on her chair. Somehow it had gotten placed on top of the table among the broken shards and food. She wore a crystal bowl on her head that had previously held the Jell-O salad. The green goop dripped off her face. She wore an expression of frustration that was almost cute if it hadn't been for the circumstance.

"Dorothy," her mother gasped.

"I told Henry not to play with his food, Mommy." She crossed her arms angrily.

Cynthia just stared in horror at the mess her daughter was in. Small angry red cuts started to bleed on her arms and hands.

It was Martha who gathered her wits first and silently reached up to assist the young child down. Together, the two shuffled off. Max assumed it was to clean the child up and to check for any injuries.

It was another long moment before Ben straightened his shirt. He picked the chair off the table and set it firmly on the ground. Cynthia, spurred by the movement of her husband, began gathering the larger shards of china into a manageable pile.

Feeling slightly responsible, Max helped to clean up the dining room. He hadn't sustained any cuts from the glass flying through the air, though both Cynthia and Ben did. He couldn't explain why.

"I'm sorry," he said quietly as Cynthia took a pile of dish pieces to the kitchen. Max and Ben picked up the remains of the meal. "I reacted."

Ben sighed. "It's all right. It would have happened anyway. It isn't really something you can't react to. It's taken us awhile to learn to ignore it. It was unfair for me to ask you to do the same."

"This happens every night, you said?"

"Not quite like this, no, but similar things, yes." Ben took the tablecloth edges and folded it over the mess, wrapping it up into a neat bundle, ready for the garbage. Cynthia returned from the kitchen, with a damp rag and a bottle of antiseptic.

"Ben, you are bleeding," she told him. Her voice trembled and her hands shook. Ben noticed her distress and went to hold her tightly.

"It's alright, dear. Just scratches. Nothing to be concerned about."

As he hugged her close, she started shaking even more, and then crying softly. Max felt very much like an intruder to witness such weakness between two people.

Once her sobs had quieted, Ben pulled away from his wife and told her softly, "Why don't you go get cleaned up and check on Dorothy, hmm? It's about time she went to bed. It's been an eventful night."

As though in a daze, Cynthia nodded. "I'll have Martha clean the food off of the walls and the floor once Dorothy is tucked in. Why don't you two go into the living room to discuss what needs to be done? I'll be there shortly once I've freshened up." The woman wandered away from her husband and hesitantly towards the back half of the apartment.

Ben watched her go, concern etched on his strong features.

"Need any help?" Max asked.

Ben turned to look at his guest, confused. "What?"

"She said you were bleeding," Max gestured to Ben's arms. "Do you need any help cleaning those cuts?"

Ben glanced down at his arm and saw the blood. He picked up a relatively clean napkin. "I've got it, thanks. Let's go sit down." Together they returned to the living room and sat in uncomfortable silence.

Dorothy had left her doll on the floor. Max stared at it, trying to gather his scattered thoughts. Its painted eyes seemed to laugh at him as though the toy knew his secret. He was scared. More than scared, Max was absolutely terrified. Besides the quaking knees, there was something else mingled in the fear. There was a thrill, an excitement that made him thirst for more. He liked this feeling. He liked knowing that everything he had ever thought about life could be ripped apart at any moment. It was also the realization hitting home that he was that close to proving there was life after death.

After what seemed like hours, Ben spoke. "So now you've seen what we have to deal with."

Max wasn't expecting it; he was too wrapped up in his own thoughts to see it coming, so he jumped slightly when he heard Ben's voice. Words failed him right then. He wanted to say something encouraging, but everything he thought of sounded so hollow and fake. Instead, he just nodded and kept his eyes on the doll.

At last, Max finally gathered his wits enough to start asking the questions.

"Have you ever seen Henry with your own eyes?"

"No. I've never heard him either. Sometimes though, Dorothy will be in her room alone having a conversation with him. She can see him, plain as day. Do you know how terrifying it is to have your daughter seeing and talking with someone that you can't see or hear? It makes you wonder if you're going crazy or something."

"When did Henry first show up?"

Ben rubbed his face with his hands as he thought back over the terror of the last few months. "I'm not sure. We moved here from Long Island a little over six months ago. I already explained why. Prior to that, there was just a bunch of little things. We didn't pay much attention to it back then. Things would go missing and then wind up somewhere unexpected. Then gradually, it got worse and worse."

"When did it start? How long has this ghost been hanging around?"

"I don't know. Maybe two years? There would be weeks without anything happening. Just enough time to make us think we had made it up or we were imagining it."

"This time, you thought the move put a stop to it. How long ago did the activity start up again here?"

"Three weeks ago. Dorothy said that Henry was back. That he was upset for us leaving him like that." The man's voice trembled and his hands shook. "I'm worried about my daughter. This thing . . . It's attached to her and I don't know if it will let her go." Ben looked Max straight in the eye even as his unshed tears watered his vision. "Max, if it hurts my little girl, I don't know what I'll do."

"Don't worry," Max said sounding more confident than he was. "He won't hurt Dorothy. Ghosts usually can't harm the living."

Ben held his bleeding arm up incredulously. "Like hell they can't! Did you see what happened in there?"

Max flushed. "Yeah, I saw. I think this Henry fellow wants something."

"Yeah, my daughter."

"No, beyond that. I think Henry is reaching out to the one person that can see him. I think he needs help moving on to the next life. That's what all ghosts need, right?"

"How can my little girl do something like that? She's only six years old."

"Well, she may not be able to, but I can."

"You can?"

"Yes. It is going to take some time though. I'll need to ask your daughter some questions. With your permission, I'd like to start immediately."

Ben regarded Max with a mix of amazement and reservation. "You really can help us? How?"

"My plan is to make contact with Henry myself. I'll communicate with him to see what it is that he wants—no what he *needs* to move on. Then Dorothy will be left alone and your family will be at peace."

"What if you can't find out what he wants?" Ben asked, not daring to put the hope into his tone.

"I will. You just gotta have some faith."

The man nodded, accepting Max's assistance. "Dorothy's in her room. It's the last door on the left."

"You don't want to come with me?" Max asked.

A shudder went through Ben and he hung his head in his hands. "God help me, no. I don't think I can go in there right now."

Max gave the man a consoling pat on the back. "I understand. I won't be long."

He went down the hall, noting the old wallpaper and a few paintings mingled with a few photographs. Most of them were what he assumed family photos. At last he came to Dorothy's room. The door was ajar and the girl was sitting alone in her bed.

Max paused outside of the room at the sound of her childish voice.

"What you did at supper was bad, Henry," she said angrily. "You hurt Daddy and scared Mommy." There was a pause before the six year old said fiercely, "I don't like it when you say things like that. Go away. I need to go to sleep now."

Max took the opportunity to poke his head in and knock on the bedroom door. "Hello? Dorothy? May I come in?"

The child peered at him suspiciously before she nodded reluctantly. Max stepped into the child's room feeling at once awkward and out of place. "That was some supper, wasn't it?" Dorothy just watched him silently. Feeling the pressure to get to the point of his visit, he asked politely, "May I sit?"

Dorothy nodded and Max settled into the wooden rocking chair in the corner of the room. He struggled to keep the creaky chair steady so he would be able to write. When he felt reasonably sure that he wasn't going to fall backwards, he flipped open his notebook. "I would like to ask you a few questions about your friend Henry. Is that alright?"

"I'm mad at him." Dorothy said strongly.

"Oh? And why is that?"

"He hurt Daddy and made Mommy cry. That isn't nice."

"You're right. It isn't very nice. Has he ever hurt Mommy or Daddy before?"

She shook her head, her brown hair swinging wildly with the motion.

"Can you tell me where you first met Henry?"

"Mommy and Daddy don't like me talking about Henry," the girl said.

"It's okay. You can talk about him with me. Your daddy said you could. Do you remember when you first met him?"

Dorothy thought about it. "It was the day Mommy and I went to say hello to Grandpa Tom. We brought him flowers. Mommy says Grandpa Tom is dead, but he would like the flowers we brought to him. She said he is in Heaven looking down on us and watching over us. Do you have anyone in Heaven watching after you?"

Max gave a soft laugh. "No, not really. So, you met Henry at the cemetery?"

"Yes. He wanted one of the flowers for himself."

"Did you give him one?"

"Yes. I asked if he wanted to play hide and seek with me."

Max nodded, becoming more and more intrigued. "What does Henry look like?"

"Didn't you see him at supper?"

"No, sweetheart, I'm afraid he was too quick for me."

The girl looked crestfallen. "No one sees him. No one but me. I wish someone else could see him. Then maybe everyone wouldn't be so mad at me all the time."

Max's heartstrings tugged at the sound of her utter sadness. "Oh, sweetheart, no. Nobody's mad at you. They know it is Henry doing these things, not you."

She sniffled, her tears coming down in silent rivulets down to her pointed chin.

"Listen," Max said, desperate to get her to stop crying, "I want to see Henry for myself, but I need your help. Can you help me, Dorothy?"

She looked up at him with a sort of wonder and trepidation in her blue eyes. "You— you want to see Henry?"

"Of course. I'd like to help Henry out. The thing is, I can't help him if I don't know what I am looking for. So, what do you say? Can you tell me what he looks like so I know if I run into him on the street?"

The little girl thought for a moment, tilting her head to the side so that she looked more like a confused puppy than a girl. "He's taller than me. His clothes are dirty and old."

"Excellent," Max murmured as he scribbled hasty notes in his notepad. "What color is his hair?"

"Like yours," she answered, indicating Max's black

hair. "But his is longer and curly."

The information was duly noted as he asked his next question. "His clothes. You said they were dirty. Can you tell me more about what they look like?"

"They're gray."

"Yes, more than that. Does he wear clothes like other little boys?"

Dorothy shook her head, but didn't elaborate.

"Alright." An idea sprang to his mind. "Do you think you could draw me a picture of Henry?"

The girl brightened at the prospect and nodded eagerly. Max flipped to a clean page in his little notebook and handed it along with his pencil to the six year old. He tried not to peer too greedily at the wobbly lines. It took her a long time to produce an odd, lumpy looking stick figure with ill-fitting trousers that were rolled up to his knees. The jacket was long and his feet were bare. She had drawn the boy's hair in wild curls framing his round face.

Possibly the most disturbing part of the child's picture was a dark splotch behind the stick figure. It looked as though it could have been Henry's shadow, but it more resembled some sort of a beast rather than a boy. Parts of the shadow were darker, giving the appearance of limbs and other appendages that didn't necessarily belong. Max could just make out a leering face.

"Dorothy," he asked as nonchalantly as he could. "What is that black thing behind Henry?"

The girl shrugged as she continued doodling on the page, filling in some background details like a sun and some grass beneath Henry's feet. "It's a monster."

"A monster? Is it Henry's monster?"

Again the girl shrugged. "I don't know. He's not around all the time. I only see him sometimes." She finished her detail work and handed the pad of paper back to Max with a yawn.

He knew he didn't have much more time before the poor thing was asleep. He studied the picture thoughtfully. The clothes looked familiar, but he couldn't quite place where. "Dorothy, what do you and Henry do together?"

The girl settled back against her pillows. "We play hide and seek. He tells me stories, but sometimes I can't understand him."

"What do you mean? You can't understand him?"

"He talks funny."

"Funny? Funny how?"

"Really, really slowly," she drawled in an apparent imitation of her southerly ghost friend.

"Does he talk a lot?"

She nodded but added, "He doesn't like to talk about his ouchie though."

"His ouchie?" Max asked.

Dorothy sat up again and reached for the pad of paper. Max held it out, but instead of taking it, she pointed to what would have been the stick figure's stomach. "He bleeds from there sometimes. He said he got hurt and the doctors couldn't make it better. I am not supposed to ask about it."

"I see," Max made some notes on the picture. *Southern. Boy. Wounded stomach.* "Well, I'll let you get some sleep, okay?" He got up and smiled at her as she leaned back into her bed. "I'll send your mommy in to tuck you in," he promised.

She nodded sleepily, her eyes half closed already.

He left the room, his mind buzzing with theories and even more questions. Ben and Cynthia were waiting for him in the sitting room.

"Well? Did you get any information?" Ben asked.

Cynthia just watched him, eyes wide with hope.

"I got some leads that I can look into."

"Really?" Cynthia gasped. "Mr. Samuelson, can you end this?" He could hear the pleading in her voice.

This time, Max was confident in the answer he gave. "Yes. I do believe that I can."

Part Seven
Making Friends with the Dead

The next morning, Max arrived at Ben's apartment bright and early. He had barely slept from all of the excitement. He had a case! A case that, if he worked it right, would make him famous. Most of the night was spent coming up with a plan to capture evidence of Henry. The best option he had was to get a picture or to convince the specter to appear in public.

Either plan required getting the ghost to communicate with him. That, he reaffirmed to himself as he stood on the apartment's doorstep, was the goal of the day.

Martha opened the door. She looked much the same as the night before.

"Hello, Martha. It is nice to see you this morning," Max said with his best smile. "I'm here to see Dorothy, please."

Wordlessly, Martha stepped aside to let Max in. He slid past her with his case and removed his hat. Martha shut the door and pointed him in the direction of the family room. Max took his cue and made his way fully into the apartment.

Cynthia was sitting on one of the chairs and Dorothy was playing on the floor in front of her. Cynthia had a lit cigarette and stared at her daughter with a sort of fearful distaste. So wrapped up in her thoughts, she didn't even notice Max come in.

Dorothy noticed, however. She looked up from her doll and gave Max a large smile.

"Good morning, little lady," he said.

His voice broke Cynthia's spiraling thoughts and she looked up at him with an expression of surprise. "Good morning, ma'am," he said giving her a nod. "I was hoping to spend some time with Dorothy today. Maybe take her to the park or something. Is that alright?"

There shouldn't have been the look of relief on her face. There shouldn't have been the eager tone to her response of, "Absolutely. I'll make sure lunch is ready when you get back. Dorothy, darling, go get your coat. It is cold outside."

The little girl abandoned her doll and scampered back to her room to do as her mother said.

Max took the opportunity to tell Mrs. Porter, "I'm going to see if Henry will show himself to me. If I can do that, then there is a good chance I can get him to leave your daughter alone. But you need to know that this is going to take some time. There isn't an easy fix."

Cynthia nodded and took a drag off her cigarette. "I understand, Mr. Samuelson."

"Max. Please, call me Max."

"Max. I just want my little girl back. Ever since Henry showed up she's been... different. Sometimes when I look at her, I can't even recognize her. Do you have any idea what it is like to be terrified of what your child might do?"

He shifted on his feet uncomfortably. "No, I can't say that I have. You know, this isn't Dorothy's fault though. She's not the one causing all of these things to happen. You know that, right?"

The woman gave a shrug. "She's the one attracting whoever Henry is to this house. She is the one that everything is centered on."

Her answer broke Max's heart. "I promise, Cynthia. I will do what I can to make sure that Dorothy is safe."

"I'm ready, Max!" Dorothy called out as she came into the room. She had her coat on and went directly to pick up her doll. "Can Amelia come too?"

For a split second, he thought there was another ghost besides Henry. "Of course she can," Max said when he realized that she was talking about her doll.

The little girl held her doll firmly under her arm and took Max's hand. "Goodbye, Mommy," she said and tugged Max towards the door.

The two of them made their way out of the apartment; Martha closed the door behind them solemnly. They left the building and stepped out into the light of day.

They had made their way about half a block before Max asked, "Is Henry with us right now?"

The little girl shook her head. "No. He will come later. It's too early for him."

"Oh," was all Max could say to that. "Well, where do you and Henry usually play?"

"We play anywhere. But our favorite spot is the tree with the swing."

"The tree with the swing?"

"Yeah. Henry pushes me sometimes."

"Can you show me?"

Dorothy let go of his hand and turned back the way they had come. "It's this way."

"I'll follow you," Max assured her when she glanced back uncertainly.

The girl led him around the block and into a large field where a little picket fence surrounded a small cemetery. The tombstones were weathered and old. Weeds had reclaimed most of the graves and tree limbs had grown low to the ground. By the looks of things, no one had been buried there in recent years.

Max was surprised to see that the six year old didn't even hesitate to forge her way through the maze of nameless headstones. He had a little trouble keeping up with her as she could maneuver underneath the low slung branches and the tall grass covered her passing. In the middle of the cemetery was a small hill with a giant tree. Max couldn't tell what kind it was. Someone had made a makeshift swing from a couple of old ropes and a plank of wood.

With the familiarity of hours upon hours spent here, Dorothy gleefully ran to the swing and perched her doll, Amelia, onto the seat. She then began swinging it back and forth. Max hung back a bit, taking in the scene. She seemed like such a happy little girl, just playing with her doll on a swing. It was hard to believe that she had a dead boy as a friend. Not just a dead boy, but one that was powerful enough to manipulate the things around her. He wondered if she realized how terrified her parents were of her because of her unconventional friendship with Henry.

With these musings rattling around in his head, he set up his tripod and camera, aiming the lens at the swing and the little girl with her doll.

When his equipment was set up, he called out, "Dorothy, do you think you could call Henry? Would he come if you asked him to?"

The little girl looked doubtful. "I don't know. Mommy and Daddy don't like it when Henry is around."

"It's all right," Max assured her. "Remember what I said last night? I really want to meet Henry. I want to be able to see him. The only way I can do that is with your help. I give you permission to talk about Henry all you want."

The little girl was hesitant, so Max decided to get the ball rolling with some questions. Perhaps she would feel more comfortable talking about him if he asked her about the ghost boy. "Do you see Henry every day?"

"No. Sometimes he doesn't come out for days. He gets tired and needs to rest."

"He gets tired?"

"Yeah. Sometimes he tires himself out and he won't come out to play for a long time."

"Did he tire himself out last night?"

"I don't know. He was really angry at me after dinner because I told him he shouldn't have done all of that. He was showing off."

"Showing off? Why was he doing that?"

"Because you are new." The matter of fact way she stated this was somewhat disturbing.

"Henry was showing off because I am new?" The reasoning didn't sit well with Max, though when he remembered Ben's warning before dinner, it made a bit more sense.

Dorothy sat on the swing, her legs dangling and running her fingers through her doll's flaxen hair.

"Dorothy," Max said, "I would really like to see Henry, to speak with him. Do you think you could call him out here? Do you think he will come?"

The six-year-old thought about his request for a long moment, biting her lip in the process. After what seemed like forever, she said, "I'll try."

Max watched in avid fascination as the girl closed her eyes and moved her lips. She was whispering, "Henry, come out. Henry, come out." She did this for a good five or six minutes straight before lapsing into a contemplative silence.

Finally, Max couldn't handle the silence or the stillness of the child. He asked her, a little anxiously, "Well? Is he coming?"

Dorothy frowned at the man. "No. He isn't answering. Will you push me?"

It took effort for Max not to look disappointed. If he wanted to get results, then he had to be patient. He forced a smile onto his face and replied, "Of course, sweetheart."

There was no sign from Henry for two weeks. Still, even with the memory of that fateful supper dimming into doubt, Max arrived every day at the Porter residence to spend time with Dorothy. It was his hope that the girl was the key. Even though there was no apparent progress as of yet, Max was faithful to the newfound routine. And each day, he held on tightly to the belief that today would be the day he had been waiting for. Today Henry would finally show himself and he would get the proof he needed to show those ASPR jerks.

The routine that had formed between Max and Dorothy was fairly simple. Every morning at precisely ten o'clock, Max would ring the doorbell to the Porter's residence. He would have his kit at the ready. Martha would let him in. Dorothy usually was sitting in the living room, dressed and ready to go out to play. Together they walked through the cemetery to the solitary swing hanging from the large, weepy tree. Max would take pictures, hoping to capture the elusive specter.

The two would then settle into a question and answer contest; Max would drill Dorothy on anything and everything regarding Henry. When he had gotten as much information from the girl on her friend as he could, he switched tactics and asked her about ghosts in general. He asked if she saw any other ghosts besides Henry. He asked for specifics on what happened to her on Long Island. He asked anything and everything he could. Her answers were short, simple, and not enough for Max's determined curiosity.

On this particular morning, Max arrived at the Porter household with some flashcards in his kit. It was his intent to see if Dorothy had any other skills as a medium. Truth be told, he was running out of ideas, not to mention time. Two weeks without a steady job was taking its toll. He made enough to cover his rent by doing some odd jobs around the apartment building for the landlord. Sarah was speaking with him again as well. She kept him fairly well fed with the leftovers of the meals she cooked for her mother and her aunt.

Max didn't understand Sarah at all. On one hand, she disapproved of what he was doing as far as Dorothy was concerned. Sarah seemed to think that he was using the child, which, in her mind, was morally reprehensible. No matter how many times Max tried to explain that he was, in fact, helping the girl, she would argue. On the other hand she still did what she could to take care of him. She cleaned his apartment, brought him food, and even helped him develop the rolls of film he took during his mornings with Dorothy.

He had just resigned himself to the fact that he probably would never understand women when the door to the Porter's apartment opened. Usually it was Martha that answered, but this time Cynthia was there to greet him with red-rimmed watery eyes.

"Good morning," Max said, taking in her disheveled appearance. "Cynthia, are you alright?"

"He's back," she whispered, panicked. "He's back and I don't know what to do."

A flush of excitement raced through Max. "Henry, you mean?"

At her barest of nods, Max moved her to the side of the hall so he could get past her. "Where?"

Trembling, the woman pointed in the direction of the living room. He heard Dorothy laugh as he approached. Not wanting to startle the girl or the ghost, he peered around the archway.

Dorothy sat in the middle of the floor, her feet splayed out in front of her. A large, red rubber ball rolled towards her from the corner of the room that Max couldn't see. Giggling, the little girl caught it and rolled it back to where it came from.

Her giggling was cut short and she said seriously, "No, Max isn't like the other grown-ups. He really does want to be your friend."

The ball appeared again, rolling steadily as though it had been pushed. Dorothy caught it and made a face. "Max is nice. You'll see." Again the ball was rolled. Henry must have said something because Dorothy's face became severe and she scolded her playmate. "Don't you be mean, Henry!"

Unable to stand back any longer, Max entered the room fully. He was just in time to see the red ball come to a complete and abrupt stop and then sent rolling in the exact opposite direction by an invisible source.

Dorothy saw Max and froze; her mouth and eyes open wide. The ball rolled into her lap and she caught onto it out of reflex.

Max tried to act nonchalant. "Good Morning, Dorothy. How are you today?"

The girl looked across the room where, presumably, Henry was sitting and then back at Max. He pretended to ignore the glance, choosing instead to smile benignly.

"I'm alright," Dorothy answered. "Is it time to go already?"

Max removed his hat and took a seat. "Well no, not if you don't want to. It looks like you are playing just fine right here."

Dorothy cast another glance at the opposite side of the room as though in askance.

When she didn't answer, Max stood and started to

shrug off the large trench coat. "Well, if we are staying here, I might as well take off my coat and get comfortable."

Just as he had draped the coat over the side of one of the chairs, Dorothy announced, "No, wait. Henry wants to go outside. He says we should go to the swing in the cemetery." She set the ball aside and got to her feet. Her own coat was on the floor. She picked it up and put it on.

"Henry. He's here right now?" He asked, feigning mild curiosity.

The girl nodded. "Yes, but he's not sure about talking to you yet."

"I see. Well, what can I do to convince him otherwise?"

She cocked her head to the side as though listening to someone. It made Max antsy to watch her. At last she pronounced, "He said he will decide after today if he wants to be your friend."

Max didn't know what to think about that. Should he just act like it was any other day? Maybe he should stop Dorothy right now and insist on taking pictures of the room. But would Henry even be in them?

Playing on a hunch, Max pulled his coat back on and donned his hat. If he wanted to get irrefutable proof, then he would have to befriend Henry and get him to appear in front of the ASPR.

Cynthia hovered in the entrance way of the room, looking fearfully at her daughter.

"It's alright," Max assured the terrified woman. "Dorothy, Henry, and I will be going out today. I'll bring them back in time for lunch."

The woman nodded bravely, trying not to cry.

Max took Dorothy's hand and together, presumably with Henry following somewhere behind, they went to the cemetery.

It was hard for Max to contain his excitement. He didn't even know where to begin with his questions or even if he should ask them.

Thankfully, Dorothy didn't share his hesitance. She and Henry conversed the entire way. Even with hearing only half of the conversation, Max learned more about Henry and his relationship with Dorothy in that afternoon than he had in last two weeks spent asking the six year old about it.

Henry, apparently, liked to boss Dorothy around quite a bit. He would tell her to do things and she would argue with him. For one so young, she had a good head on her shoulders when it came to less than good ideas. For the most part, she had learned to discern which of Henry's orders were very dangerous and which were benign.

The girl, for her part, treated Henry like an annoying older brother. The ease with which she interacted with the ghostly child astounded Max. From their previous conversations, he knew the girl understood the difference between the living and the dead. More specifically, she understood that Henry was dead and some of the things he could do, she simply couldn't.

The girl had a genuine talent with spirits.

When the trio reached the tree swing in the cemetery, Dorothy immediately ran for it. She was about to hoist herself onto it when she was briskly pushed onto the ground.

She whined at the thin air, "But I wanted to go first!" The response she got was another hard shove that flung her face first into the patchy grass and dirt. To her credit, she didn't cry; she simply brushed the dirt from her dress and glared at the swing. "That wasn't very nice, Henry."

"Dorothy," Max hazarded a suggestion, "why don't

you push Henry on the swing and I will take some photographs?"

The girl nodded obediently. Max set up his camera as she started pushing the empty swing.

Before he actually started taking pictures though he called out, "Henry, is it okay if I take a photograph of you?"

There was no indication of an answer except for Dorothy piping up. "Henry says that if your silly contraption can catch an image of him, then you can." She laughed. "He doesn't think you can."

Max allowed himself a chuckle. Yes, he thought, let's see if I can catch him.

The time with Dorothy and Henry simply flew by. Max had gone through all of the film he brought with him that morning. Despite Dorothy chattering incessantly to an invisible boy, there was no other evidence of the spirit. Still, Max was certain that at least one of his photos would show something.

Finally, there was a break in the childish talk and he seized the chance to ask his own questions. "Dorothy, why can't I see or hear Henry, but you can?"

She was playing in the dirt, digging holes with a stick she had found. There was no sign of the ghostly Henry, but that didn't mean he wasn't there. In response to his question, the girl shrugged. "He doesn't want you to."

Max blinked at such a simple and obvious answer. "Why doesn't Henry want me to see or hear him?"

"Because he isn't sure about you yet." She said this matter-of-factly as she scooped a handful of dirt out of the way. Then, she tilted her head up, smiled at Max, and said ominously, "He will decide soon."

After Max returned Dorothy to her aunt and mother, he rushed back to his own apartment. He had to get those photographs developed! Sarah was in the hall, her hands full of parcels, when he came up the stairs. "Sarah! Quick! I need your help. I think I got my evidence. Henry was there today."

Sarah's eyes widened at the news. "Let me put the groceries away and I will be right there." She unlocked her apartment and disappeared inside. Max rushed into his and set about getting the developers ready.

His mind was whirring and it took extra concentration to set things up correctly. He drew the curtains shut on the small windows and filled the gaps of light with extra sheets. He lit the oil lamp waiting on the table. The chemicals were removed from their shelf and set in a row on the table. He pulled a couple of pans from the kitchen and poured the contents of the bottles into them.

Sarah opened the door and closed it firmly behind her. "Do you really think you got it?"

"We will see in a few minutes. Grab the film from my bag."

Sarah did as she was told; taking her customary position off to the side, ready to hold the light to expose the images.

They worked in silence, the anticipation building. Slowly the pictures became clearer and clearer. The hazy images in the developer had Max peering intently at them, trying to discern if the ghostly boy was indeed there. He had to remind himself to be patient.

Just as he hung the last one to dry, a loud, horrible ripping sound and a flood of light filled his apartment. His curtains had been ripped from their hangings. He cried out as though it would stop the light from ruining his images.

Sarah moved quickly to replace the drapes, but it was too late. The sunlight had blackened the images to beyond recognition.

Through his frustration, Max thought he heard the

sound of a child's mischievous laughter.

"What in the world was that?" Sarah gasped. There was a tinge of fear in her voice. She was still trying to block the sun as best as she could, but when she saw the damaged photographs, she allowed the fabric to drop to the floor.

Max strained to listen in case it happened again. When there was nothing but the sounds of the apartment building, he said, "I think that was Henry."

"Henry?" Sarah asked in disbelief. "Do you really mean to tell me that a ghost did all of this?"

Sarah's look of incredulity grated on Max's already frayed nerves. "Yes, Henry! That is what I said. And now there is no proof!" In sheer frustration, he threw down the tongs he had been using to handle the developing pictures into the basin with the developer. The chemicals splashed over onto the table and a tense silence grew in the room.

Giving into the frustration, Max folded his arms and threw himself into a chair. Sarah quietly and composedly folded the curtains and set them gently aside. When she began to clean up the spilled chemicals and what was left of the photographs, Max's frustration ebbed and he reached out to touch her arm. She froze at the contact.

"I'm sorry, Sarah. It's just—"

"I know," she assured him. "You were so close. You can't let this set back stop you. You have to use it."

"Use it?"

She sighed as though explaining something incredibly obvious. "Think. You heard the laughter. I know you did. Henry was here. He could still be here."

The light went on in Max's brain. He almost catapulted out of the chair. He grabbed Sarah's arms. "You are right! He could still be here! Help me get the camera loaded."

The two of them photographed every inch of Max's apartment, all the while calling out to and entreating the ghost to make himself known. There was no indication of anything else in his home other than them, much to his disappointment. Still, there may be photographic evidence that he just couldn't see yet. Sarah promised to develop the film at her place as well as mend the ripped curtains. Max was never more grateful for the woman. He went to sleep that night more hopeful than he had been in a long time.

Part Eight
Careful What You Wish For

Max was woken by the sound of glass shattering. He jerked up and out of bed, still halfway between dreaming and waking. The moonlight coming through his bare windows made the glass shards on the rug glint. It was hard to tell what had broken. There was no breeze in the apartment, so he didn't think it was the window. He strained to hear anything that would indicate what happened and why there was glass all over the floor.

"Hello?" he called out.

Silence answered him.

He was just about ready to give into the urge to just go back to bed and deal with the mess in the morning when he heard it; ever so faintly there was a voice that echoed. "Hello?"

Instantly he was awake and on full alert. "Is someone there?" he asked the room again.

Again, nothing but silence.

Max bent down to inspect the glass. Even in the moonlight he could tell it was one of the highball glasses he had left on the table.

A prickling sensation on the back of his neck gave him the unshakable feeling that he was being watched. No matter how still he kept, there was simply nothing to hear or see. Oh, he could certainly feel it, whatever it was. It gave him a sick apprehension that made him want to run straight back to bed and not come out from under the covers until the sun was firmly in the sky.

It took a lot of willpower to stand his ground and boldly ask the room, "Henry? Is that you?"

Max strained all of his senses, trying to divine a response from the quiet apartment.

There was nothing however the apprehension intensified. There was a subtly different feel to it now, the feeling of growing danger.

Finally, the urge to run back to his bed and bury his head under his pillow overcame him. He would deal with the broken glass in the morning, he promised himself. With as much dignity as he could, he scampered back to his bed and flung the covers up over his head. It was a long time before sleep came.

When Max finally regained consciousness, the shadows in his apartment had grown long. It took him several minutes to adjust himself to the time and remember the occurrences that had him up all night and frightened.

He wiped the sleep from his eyes and made his way into the living room. When he flipped on the light switch, what he saw made him gasp.

His belongings were piled high in the middle of the room. Things from books to plates to shoes to lamps and even pictures from the walls. It was as though someone had thrown all of these things onto the ground with the intention of throwing them away. There was no order to it, just a haphazardness that suggested it was done in a hurry.

"What the . . .?" He could hardly believe his eyes. "Who the hell did this?" he shouted at nothing. Very faintly, a child's laughter echoed around him.

"Max?" Sarah asked as she came through the front

door. "I heard you shouting. Are you—?" she caught sight of him standing before a large pile of things, his fists balled at his sides and a wild look in his eyes. "Are you alright?" she finished softly. Her gaze shifted from the pile to Max a couple of times, not really comprehending what she was seeing. "Max, what's going on?"

"Sarah, I am so glad you are here. Look! Look at what Henry did!"

She cast a doubtful glance at the pile of objects. "Henry did all this?"

"Yes! I was asleep and when I woke up just a moment ago, all of this stuff had been thrown here. It had to have been Henry."

Sarah considered his disheveled state with uncertainty. "Are you sure you didn't do this? I heard you earlier. It didn't sound like you were asleep."

"Of course I didn't do this. You must have heard Henry. I was fast asleep."

Sarah thought it better than to argue with him. Instead, she sighed deeply and handed him a thick envelope. "I developed the pictures. There's nothing that would indicate any sort of ghost."

"What?" He snatched the envelope from her hands and clawed it open. Briskly he flipped through them. She was right about there being nothing out of the ordinary in the photographs and nothing that would prove that Henry had been there. "Damn it!" he cursed.

"There's something else," Sarah hesitated. "Max, how old were those curtains?"

He was still looking through the pictures as he answered, "I don't know. Why?"

"Because when I went to mend them the fabric was extremely threadbare and frayed in areas."

"So what? What do curtains have to do with ghosts?" Max regarded Sarah seriously. He let his hands drop to his sides, his fingers still grasping the photographs.

"I'm saying that I think the curtains fell on their own. I think the fabric simply gave way."

He allowed the photographs to drop to the floor as what she said sunk in. "You don't think Henry pulled the curtains down?" Max asked. "I suppose since there's no photographic evidence, you don't think it could have been him at all? Sarah, are you suggesting that I am making all of this up?"

The woman flushed. "No, I'm saying I'm sure there's a perfectly reasonable explanation for everything that's happened."

"What about this?" he exclaimed, gesturing at the pile of his belongings.

"Max, I heard you earlier. You told me not to come in. How can you not remember this?"

He couldn't stand the pity in her eyes, couldn't tolerate the concern in her voice. He wasn't going crazy. He wasn't.

"You heard him," Max said, fighting for composure. "You said you heard a child's laughter."

Sarah shook her head. "Do you know how many children are in this building? It's old. Voices carry. It could have been anything."

Max ran his hands through his hair. "I'm not crazy, Sarah."

"No, you aren't," she said as she reached out to him. He jerked away from her touch. "You're not crazy," she repeated, allowing her arms to drop to her sides.

"Leave!" Max shouted, unable to stand it any longer. "Get out of here, Sarah. If you think I am making this up, I don't need you in my life anymore. If you can't believe in me, in what I am trying to do, get out now."

He turned his back on her, not sure if he wanted her to stay or go.

Sarah, for her part, stood there awkwardly, unsure what she should do. She loved Max; she admitted that much to herself, but this was a destructive path that he was on. She couldn't stop him, but she couldn't help him either. He wasn't willing to listen to reason.

She didn't say anything as she left; there was nothing to say. She made sure to close the door behind her gently, her tears the only evidence that something was amiss.

After Sarah left, Max was more determined than ever to get evidence of Henry. It was not only pride at this point, but proof of his sanity. That very night he set up his camera in the corner with the best view of the apartment. With that done, he settled down to wait with a pen and a pad of paper in his hand.

"Alright, Henry. I know you are there. Show yourself!"

There was nothing but silence.

"Fine," Max said, shifting in his chair. "I will wait. You will show yourself sooner or later."

Hours passed without the slightest thing happening. Max caught himself dozing off a couple of times. To keep himself up, he took quick nips off the bottle of gin he kept in the cabinet. When the sun rose, he watched the patches of sunlight travel across the room until they disappeared completely.

A whole day had passed and night had once again fallen. Max was tired, exhausted in fact. It had been a long day of doing nothing but listening intensely to the silence and trying not to think too much about the fight with Sarah.

He was about to call it quits and head to bed when the lights flickered in his apartment. He looked around, wondering if he was going to be out of power for the night. He turned his head and suddenly, he was face to face with a small, pale child with dark hair who couldn't have been more than eight or so.

Max couldn't believe his eyes. "You," he said, terrified, even as he marveled at the apparition. The child was just as Dorothy had described him. He must have been close to eight or nine when he passed. His skin was a pale, ashen shade of gray. The clothes were torn and dirty, as though he had crawled out of a grave. There was a sickening bloody gouge in his left sign. Blood dripped from the edges of the wound, congealing to the fabric around it.

The child spoke, his voice like an echo in an empty room. The sound of it came from everywhere and nowhere all at once. "You know none of this is real, don't you?"

"What? What do you mean?"

The child ghost gave a mysterious half smile and something shifted under his skin, as though a mask were being adjusted. His face rippled and Max thought he caught a glimpse of something dark, something otherworldly just below the surface.

Henry laughed, his childish voice pealing amusement.

Max woke suddenly with the sun shining in his face and the echoes of a child's laughter ringing in his ears. The dream was still with him and it made his cluttered apartment seem strange.

A crash sounded on the other side of the room. In a flash, he was out of his chair to investigate, his disorientation subsiding enough for him to grab the camera.

The nightstand had been shoved over and the blankets from his bed were strewn across the room. Otherwise, there was nothing.

"Henry?" he addressed the room in general.

There was no answer and he was left to wonder if

it had all been nothing more than a dream.

Part Nine
Witnessing the Light

Over the following days, more strange occurrences happened. Things were thrown to the ground without any provocation; he heard the sound of a child's laughter throughout his apartment at all hours of the day and night. A child's handprints were left for him in spilled flour only to be mysteriously smudged out right before his eyes. He wanted to tell someone what was happening. He desperately wanted Sarah to see what he was dealing with, but after their fight he couldn't bring himself to face her.

Max sent a message to the Porters telling them that he was following another lead. He didn't want them to worry, but he didn't think he could be around Dorothy in this state either.

He was beginning to buy into the thought that he just might be crazy; that all of this could just be coincidences that were conspiring against him. He hadn't left his apartment in three days.

Enough was enough. Max decided to take a walk out in the world and get some much needed air and perspective. When he woke up, he would get dressed and go out.

However, with the sun the next morning, that decision changed. His bathrobe hung loosely from his shoulders and the belt dragged along the ground as he shuffled out of the bedroom. He raised his sleep blurred eyes only to come face to face with what looked to be a child standing in the middle of the room.

Henry looked the same from Max's dream a few nights ago and real enough to touch.

Max hastily wiped the sleep from his eyes and when he looked up again, no one was there.

"Good morning, Max," a strangely high pitched, yet gravelly voice greeted him.

The man spun around, terrified and hopeful all at once. There was nothing. "Hello? Who's there?"

There was laughter and the voice said, "You don't know?"

"Henry?"

"Yes."

The affirmation made Max want to dance, but he held it back. "Where are you?"

The voice didn't seem to originate in any particular direction. "I'm here."

"Will you show yourself? Will you let me take your picture?" Max knew it was a long shot, but it was still worth the asking.

"No," the ghost said simply. "Not yet."

"Why not?"

"It's not time yet."

"What do you mean, it's not time yet?"

A dark giggle was the only response he got.

Max decided to take a different approach. "Why aren't you playing with Dorothy right now, Henry? Why are you here?"

"Dorothy's boring," the invisible child sighed. "You're much more interesting."

"Oh? Why is that?"

Without warning, a book flew off the shelf and straight at Max's head. He ducked just in time to avoid being hit in the face, but the pages flapped violently as they grazed the top of his head.

Peals of childish laughter echoed through the apartment.

"I see," Max said grudgingly as he got back to his feet and straightened his robe. "You find me amusing. Well, if you're gonna get a laugh out of me, then you can do me a favor."

The laughter stopped. "You want me to do you a favor?"

Max allowed himself a small smile. The ghost's interest was piqued. "I want you to come with me to the ASPR and appear in front of them. I want you to help me prove that there's life after death."

Whatever response Max was expecting, it definitely wasn't the all-out laughter of the child specter.

"What's so funny?"

"That's not how it works, Max."

Max frowned. "What do you mean? How does it work then?"

All he could hear was the noise of his neighbors through the thin walls of the apartment.

"Oh, come on, Henry!" Max cried.

The ghost boy didn't speak again.

Over the next two days, Max was always on alert, always listening for the phantom laughter. He scraped by with whatever food was left in his cupboards, but mostly he was too busy trying to distinguish the sounds of his neighbors from any noises that a ghost would make. It was a hell of a way to live. Finally, just when Max was seriously starting to doubt his sanity, Henry made himself known again.

"I've thought about your offer," the ghostly voice woke Max out of a fitful slumber.

"Wha—?" Max started. His sleep-blurred eyes opened wide, searching for the merest hint of where the voice was coming from. It took him more than a moment to get his bearings. "My offer?" he repeated, sitting up.

"I will do what you ask," Henry's voice ricocheted in the small room. "I will appear before whomever you wish, but I will do it on my own terms."

The meaning of the words Henry said completely dispelled whatever sleepiness was left in Max. He grabbed his blanket from the foot of the bed to combat the sudden chill in the air. "What terms are those?"

"It's simple, really. I want to show you something—something that very few living people have ever seen."

"What is it?" Though he tried, Max couldn't keep the eagerness from his voice.

The ghost child laughed. "I can't tell you. It's a secret. You have to go see it for yourself."

Max was out of bed in an instant, already pulling on his trousers. "Go where?"

"Not yet," Henry chided. "I'll come for you when it is time. Then, after you see what I have to show you, then we will go to your ASPR president."

Max had no choice but to agree. "Alright then. I'll be ready."

There was a rustling as papers fell from their surfaces and onto the floor and Max knew that Henry was gone.

It was impossible for him to return to sleep after that, regardless of how tired he was. Instead, he used the time before dawn to gather his supplies and prepare himself for what he was sure to be the most important day of his life.

Waiting for a ghost is a terribly boring activity. To pass the time, Max tried a number of things; he read, he prepared a statement for after Max appeared to the ASPR, he checked, rechecked and triple checked his supplies. Finally, he simply sat in his armchair, stared into space, and just waited.

The hours slipped by in agonizing slowness. Max had to force his anticipation into submission. He didn't realize he had fallen asleep until Henry's voice once again called his name.

"Max. Wake up. It is time."

Max blinked himself awake. Henry stood over him, peering into his face.

"Come on. It's time to go," Henry smiled a ghostly grin that made Max's flesh crawl. There was something not right about that smile.

Still, this was the opportunity of a lifetime. Max wasted no time in getting his things and sliding on his trench coat and hat. "Where are we going?"

"Follow my voice and I will guide you." The boy ghost faded from view. "Get to the corner of 8th street and Lewis. I'll meet you there."

Max didn't wait to see if Henry was still with him before he headed out the door, his kit in his hand.

He made it to the corner of 8th Street and Lewis in record time. He must have slept for quite some time because the sun had sunk into the horizon long ago and the night now ruled. He had forgotten his watch, so he wasn't sure what time it was. Based on how dark the streets were and how few people he saw, it had to be very late. The corner was silent and dark, but he could see he was in a residential area. It was an older neighborhood, one that probably saw its heyday back in the previous century. The properties were large and spoke of old money. The lane that separated the looming houses stretched at least three miles into the horizon.

"You made it," Henry's voice whispered in his ear. "Good. The place we are going is the third house at the end of the road." The ghost voice faded, leaving Max to proceed on his own.

As he strode down the darkened road, every instinct in him told him to turn back, to go home, and forget all of this nonsense. He almost did just that, but then he remembered the men in that hotel ballroom laughing at him. He remembered all of the disparaging comments that were slung at him by his hero, his idol, Harry Price. And for what? All he tried to do was prove to them what he knew in his heart and to make a name for himself. It was those memories that spurred him forward. His pace picked up as his eagerness to prove them all wrong came flushing into his brain full force.

It didn't matter how dark the streets were or how shadowy the houses were that lurked in the near distance. He was going to get there and he was going to prove them all wrong.

The house Henry had indicated was the only one illuminated on the street. Lights burned in the windows of the four-story mansion. Music seemed to be playing from somewhere inside, a haunting melody on a harpsichord.

Max hesitated at the walkway to the front porch. Was he ready for this? He stared at the house, so warm and inviting against the bitter night. What secrets could possibly be in such a welcoming place?

Henry appeared next to the front door, his ghostly shimmer and pale countenance almost glowing in the dark. He waved for Max to come forward.

It was all the urging the man needed. He strode confidently to the house. Henry must have gone inside because by the time Max made it to the door, the ghost was nowhere in sight. Max grasped the brass knocker and tapped it onto the plate on the door three times.

He had scarcely let it go when the door creaked open. The sight of the entranceway was from another time. Thick carpets covered wooden floors, crystal dripped from everything from the lampshades to the edges of the doilies on the tables. The lights Max had seen from the street weren't electric; instead white taper candles were lit and placed along several chandeliers and candelabras. The glow was bright as any electric light Max had ever seen, but there was no smell of candle wax or heat coming from the flames. In fact, the house was strangely cold, colder than it was outside. He huddled in his jacket even as he gaped at the opulent interior.

"This way," Henry called from the first landing up the stairs.

Max ascended the stairs, grasping the wooden banister. The steps creaked under his weight, but the sound was muffled under the rug covering them. There was an odd smell in the home, like dust and mold and so much rot.

"It's on the top floor," Henry's voice egged him onwards and upwards.

Max gained speed, taking the steps two at a time in his eagerness to see what Henry hinted at. Four flights of stairs left him winded once he made it to the top. Henry stood against the railing that guarded the view down to the floor below. The ghost child smiled, a little wider than was natural for a living human.

"Max, I knew you wouldn't disappoint," he said. His voice took on an odd slithering quality.

"What is it you wanted to show me?" Max demanded. The sooner this was over, the sooner he could prove that there was life after death to those jerks at the ASPR. Then life on easy street would commence.

The ghost child solidified the shimmering manifestation he appeared with dissipating. "You wanted proof that there was life after death," Henry said. "I can show you."

The hairs on the back of Max's neck stood on end.

"What do you—"

Before he could even finish his question, Henry's form changed right before his eyes. It doubled in size and contorted grotesquely. Any semblance to a human child melted away and was replaced with the most horrifying thing that Max had ever seen.

Whatever Henry turned into, it didn't have any relation to a human form. Tentacles, beaks, and unnamed appendages squirmed around what could only be called a sort of torso. Horns protruded from scaly skin that shone as if it were coated with a putrid coating of wetness.

A guttural scream could be heard over the melody of the harpsichord. It took Max a moment to realize that the scream came from his own mouth.

The monster that had once been Henry charged at him, sliding and lurching forward with thick, slime-like venom dripping from the oversized fangs in the middle of the thing's torso. Max stepped backwards, searching the pockets of his coat for something to fend the monster off.

All around him the house he thought he was in fell away, piece by piece. The fancy, plush carpet gave way to rotting floorboards. Expensive wallpaper darkened and peeled right before his eyes, leaving the bare wooden walls exposed. Holes and rot could be seen in the old wood. The furnishings decayed in seconds. It was as if time accelerated and he witnessed the complete decomposition in a matter of moments. Max couldn't tell what was real and what wasn't.

So distracted was he by the ever changing scenery and his terror that he didn't pay attention to where he stepped. His foot snapped through the floorboards, twisting painfully as he fell. His shoe was lost in the process. Faintly, he could hear it land with a crash on something below.

He couldn't get his leg free. Panic rose within him as the monster advanced. He pulled with all of his might, jumping with his other foot, trying to get loose.

Instead, there was a sharp snapping sound, a rumbling creak as the rotting floor collapsed from under his weight. Max plummeted sharply into the room below along with the broken wood flooring and remains of furniture and fabric long since abandoned.

As he fell, Max saw the monster peering down at him from the hole he had created. With every frantic blink of Max's eyes, the image of the monster changed. First it was Henry, the child specter grinning ghoulishly. Next was Dorothy, who smiled a little too widely. She was followed by Martha, then Cynthia, and then Ben. After that, the demon flickered back into Henry's form and waved cheerfully.

Max didn't feel the impalement when it happened because he blacked out for that precise moment of impact. When he came to, dust rained down on him. A horrible pain radiated from his stomach. He looked down to see a large, splintered beam sticking out of him. The old wood was coated in blood and guts.

The sight was almost unreal. For a second, Max wondered who had made such a grotesque mess. Then he realized that all of the blood and gore belonged inside of him.

Unable to bear the sight, Max looked around and tried to control his breathing. The house of opulence he had walked into was long gone. There were no candles, no crystal, no carpets or doilies. All that surrounded him was dust, decay, and rotting wood of a home long since abandoned.

He cast his gaze upward. He had fallen all the way from the top floor down to the bottom to his death.

Max understood that now. He understood the signs he had refused to see before with the enlightenment reserved for those on death's door.

Henry continued to peer down at Max from the top floor, his paleness glowing in the dank darkness. Within seconds, the ghost boy—or rather the demon masquerading as a ghost boy—was at Max's side.

The too-wide smile stretched his lips even as Max coughed. Blood dribbled from his mouth and down his chin.

"Why?" Max wheezed, unable to ask anything more.

Henry's smile stretched even farther, threatening to break the illusion's face. "You wanted to know if there was life after death. Now you will find out."

Max nodded ever so slightly as though he knew that was the reason all along and only needed the final confirmation. He closed his eyes for a moment and when he opened them again, Henry was gone. Max was alone.

The pain was horrible, but it was lessening with every second that passed. Instead, a far more frightening numbness was taking over his limbs. He was scared, terrified, actually. This wasn't how he wanted to die. This wasn't how he wanted to find out if there was life after death. A final panic set in and he tried to move, but he couldn't quite get his arms to function. After a few moments of struggling and getting nowhere, he stopped. There was nothing left to do but accept his fate.

In his final moments, Max did his best to level out his breathing. A spasm and cough seized him causing more blood to flow into his mouth. Slowly, and without dignity, Max drowned in his own blood.

Part Ten
Sylvia

"I don't exactly remember what happened after I died," Max explained to an elderly lady that waited patiently for her train. Her head was turned away from Max and she wasn't paying the slightest bit of attention.

"I tried to talk to people. I tried to make that connection to the living, but I couldn't. No one could hear me or see me. I even tried communicating with Sarah, but all she did was cry whenever I was around. She stayed in the apartment building long after her mother and aunt had passed. She never did get married either. I always felt bad for calling her a spinster that no one wanted. She deserved so much better than how I treated her. So, now I am here in this day and age that is so confusing and different than the world I lived in. No one knows I am here. There's no one that can help me. Hell, no one can even hear me."

When he looked at the elderly lady, she had gone off to catch her train. He wasn't even sure who he was talking to anymore, so wrapped up was he in his memories. With a sigh, he stood, stuffed his hands into his trench coat pockets, and turned to leave.

"I can hear you," a girl's voice said.

Max blinked and turned around. A tall, willowy girl in a sundress tilted her head at him, her blonde hair flowing freely around her face and her brow furrowed in concern. "Why do you need help?"

Max stood in pure astonishment. "You— you can really hear me?"

"Of course I can. Your story was so sad."

"You were listening the entire time?"

The girl gave a hesitant laugh and nodded. After a moment, she offered out her hand. "I'm Sylvia. What's your name?"

Out of reflex, Max held out his own hand. "I'm Max."

He wasn't expecting to make contact, but Sylvia grasped his outstretched fingers and it was like lightning coursed through the connection.

He jerked his hand back out of shock. "Wha—? You! You can touch me?!"

Sylvia gave the ghost an odd look. "I can. Haven't you ever met a witch before?"

"Sylvia! Dai! Il nostro treno èqui."

The girl nodded to the older, thin Italian woman who had called her. There was a strong resemblance between them; it made Max think that the older woman was how Sylvia would look when she was older. Sylvia picked up her bag and stood. "I have to go. My aunt is calling for me."

"Wait!" Max called out as she turned to walk away. Sylvia paused and glanced back.

He glided up to her. "Can I come with you? You are the only one that I can talk to and it's been so long . . ."

The girl smiled bewitchingly. "Of course. Perhaps we can find a way to help each other."

Ribbons
by
Megan E. Vaughn

"That child has gone mad! She murdered her own brothers and she's now after our Sue!"

"Everyone in town is out searching. We'll find her, Bill. Take your family home and get some rest."

"Rest? Searching! Don't you understand? No one will find her until she chooses to be found. There are too many places to hide in those woods."

As the two men argued, the town's children gathered close to their mothers, their eyes tracking the tree line beyond for signs of movement. At the center, a young girl, blonde ringlets framing her pale face, stared instead at her father. Spit flew from his angry lips, his arms flailing to illustrate his point. Her nails crushed the checkered pattern in the lap of her cotton dress. "She's going to get me," she whispered, her voice low and trembling. She tried to cry, to release her fear in some way. She wanted to, but could only stare.

As the mothers handed off lanterns to their husbands, they shared worried glances. Each woman played her own version of the day's events within her mid.

The Catholic Ruskoffs spoke practically no English when they moved to the quiet wilderness community in the Oregon territory. Ten years and three children later, Mr. and Mrs. Ruskoff still spoke mainly their native tongue. By that time more immigrants joined to create a smaller community of outsiders at the edge of the ever growing town.

The Ruskoff's farm hung on the outskirts of the immigrant community, preferring their land against the wooded area to the town proper. Their barn stood directly alongside the forest's entrance with an acre of crops. The land was harsh, but what they grew they used as feed for livestock. Their house, a small crooked thing with a slanted roof, stood just beyond the first patch of trees. Mr. Ruskoff was the only man in town who could successfully hunt the woods and with that the family earned their place in society.

Their three children were sent to school with all of the farmers' and merchants' children. The two boys could speak English beautifully. They blended in with the community, made friends with other farmers' sons and engaged in the typical shenanigans of any endearing, pesky little boys.

The oldest daughter spoke with her parent's thick Romanian accent. Her hair was dark and messy, covering her dusky skin in such a way that her eyes glowed from beneath, seeming to others more cat than girl. The other little girls with their rosy cheeks and smiling, pink mouths treated her as they would any unwanted stray.

Their actions were subtle, so minor as to hardly

seem malicious at all: a side comment about how she barely spoke one day; a pointing finger at her ill-fitting gingham dress the next; the occasional mean-spirited prank, like dipping the end of her hair in honey or sprinkling dirt on to her share of the noonday meal.

Their actions were often met with violent responses. She hit. She bit. She left nasty gashes in arms. Concerned parents insisted she be taken from the school. A child with such disturbed attitudes had no business being around their precious youngins'. The teacher would at times stand up for the Ruskoff girl, insisting that her problems were not so dire, all the while setting the girl in a corner each time she failed to use English correctly. Eventually, the Ruskoff's eldest stopped speaking entirely.

Only one student could occasionally put an end to the wicked behavior. Susanna Schofield was the apple of her parents' eye. An only child, she received all she could ever want out of life, including nice dresses patterned after catalog pictures, shiny shoes, and red velvet ribbons her father would often order all the way from New York. The other students adored her because she shared her riches with all of them. Her latest doll would be fussed over by the other girls and her shiny new marbles would rattle against the boys' dull, cracked toys.

Susie said when it was time to stop picking on the Ruskoff girl. The others instantly obeyed for fear of falling out of favor. It was not that Susanna particularly liked the girl. At times she would start the harsh whispers herself. The power to end the behavior as quickly as it had begun only added to her charm.

Only once did Susanna receive one of the Ruskoff girl's angry outbursts. When one of the strange girl's little brothers threw a dirt clod at Susanna and her friends, Sue lashed out at the boy. She chased him down and slapped him harshly across the face with her jacket. The buttons left a scrape below his right eye. Before she realized how she must have been harming the boy, his sister had leapt upon her back. She yanked the velvet ribbons from Susanna's hair, taking a few golden curls wrapped around her fingers. She cast the ribbons into the mud and spat down. The school mistress gave her a sound lashing. After that she lost all protection from Susanna Schofield until the following autumn.

When fever swept through the town, the immigrant community was the first to fall ill. Many people blamed the most recent family to arrive, although they were not the first to pass away. Mr. and Mrs. Ruskoff were. The three children were left alone for several weeks. No one made them go to school. No one ensured they were fed save for an elderly Italian neighbor.

It was she, with her pleading grandmotherly eyes, who made the public request that Sunday at church for someone to take the children in. The Ruskoff children were the third order of business after fencing for the Smith cattle and whether the town could afford to serve lemonade at the next picnic. Several people offered to take the boys, not minding some extra help on their own farms. However, no one wanted that strange, anti-social girl.

Then, the Schofields stepped up. Mrs. Schofield's eyes gleamed with the thought of a new challenge, a new project. "We can take all three children," she announced with an air of superiority. And that was that.

At first, the most difficult part was catching the children. Each time a member of the small town arrived at their door, the girl and two boys were nowhere to be found. They scattered to the darkness of the woods at the edge of their farm, hiding in ominous places other children would not dare to go. Stories of wolves and cannibalistic witches haunted the gnarled trees. The Ruskoff children slipping in and out like shadows on the wall unnerved some of the more superstitious "good Samaritans".

In the end, Mr. Schofield himself declared that his family would find the children and bring them home. They stood at the end of the crooked house Mr. Ruskoff had built ten years earlier. Sue clung to her mother's hand against the chirps and rustling of the forest.

"Papa, what if they just don't want to live with us? Why are you trying to force them?" She had spent the last week watching her mother move her possessions to make room for three extra beds. Some of her toys had been cast upon the new beds as an act of continued charity to their new wards. Meanwhile, her father planned happily about the extra help and life the two boys would bring to their home.

The experience had left Susanna bitter and sulky. During the search, she complained about their intrusion into her life. The idea of sharing her perfect existence forced un-Christian sentiments to escape under her breath. Her pouting reached only deaf ears. Eventually, she seemed accepting of her fate and stopped complaining until her father announced that they would fetch the Ruskoff children that morning.

One of Susanna's older dresses hung on Mrs. Schofield's arm as a potential offering. "Do not be silly. They can't live out in the woods like savages," she said, smoothing the pink stripes to make the garment more enticing.

Mr. Schofield rapped his fist upon the door. No answer. An animal rustled in the bushes nearby, the awful scraping filling the void as they waited. A second round of knocks. Still no answer. Then Mr. Schofield turned the knob and entered the house uninvited.

The house was in shambles. Chairs lay broken and

overturned. Cream spread across the floor from a toppled butter churn. The white trail flowed into a congealed puddle of pink, becoming darker as it wound toward the bodies of the two Ruskoff boys. One lay sprawled upon his stomach, having bled out from jagged hacking wounds across his skin. His brother's wounds were more horrific, his face nearly unrecognizable. Deep gashes remained filled with velvety crimson along his features. Both displayed defensive cuts across their arms. Nearby lay a hatchet, light yet sharp. Red, youthful fingerprints grasped the handle.

Mrs. Schofield screamed. Susanna buried her head into her mother's side. Her blonde hair hung loose around her ears hiding her face.

Mr. Schofield stumbled back outside, heaving his breakfast into the shrubbery. As he gasped, choking back the burning acid within his throat, he declared, "Where is the girl? We need to find the girl?"

His wife followed him into the sunlight, not feeling the warmth or recognizing that her daughter had not followed. Susanna hovered inside, her eyes locked upon the floor at the horrible sight.

Mrs. Schofield scowled at her husband. "Find her? Bill, isn't it obvious? A child did this! She did this!"

"All the more reason to find her!" Mr. Schofield recovered, frantically shaking the sweat from his brow like a dog.

The world spun around the couple, reality giving into horror. A heart gripping scream called them back to the shack. Their breath stopped. Susanna backed out the doorway, her finger shaking and pointing accusingly inside.

From behind the house, the Ruskoff girl appeared. She regarded the family through tangled dark tresses. Her cotton dress had been stained with large patches of brown and a smaller spattering of bright red. The family could only stare back at her, surveying the proof of her crime on her clothes. She darted into the forest.

Mr. and Mrs. Schofield rained a barrage of questions on Susanna as they returned to the town. Had the girl tried to harm her? Susanna just shook her head and wrapped her loose curls around her fingers over and over again.

The men formed their hunting party, ready to protect their community from the little girl no matter what crimes that meant. They started within the Schofield property, then assigned sections of the forest to be combed in groups.

Meanwhile, Mrs. Schofield and her daughter lay upon the couple's four post bed, suspended between exhaustion and fear. Her mother tried to sleep. Susanna counted shadows. The moonlight moved across the wooden floor, dust glistening in its beam. She edged out of bed, squirming from her mother's arms. Her breathing grew heavy as she approached the open window. Releasing a muffled gasp, she fell to the floor and crawled to the bedpost, fingernails digging into the wood. Her whimpers occasionally took the form of "No."

"Sue? What are you doing?" Her mother sprang from of the bed on the side furthest from the window. She sat upon the floor, attempting to wrap her daughter in her own shawl.

Strangled creaks continued as Sue pawed at her own throat, trying to force herself to speak. The words continued to fail. She pointed at the dark corner.

"There's nothing there," her mother assured. "Nothing at all."

A breeze, cool and comforting, pushed against the window frame and filled the room with a pine perfume. Her mother's eyes adjusted to the moonlight just as a diminutive figure started to turn around. She had been facing the wall. A curtain fluttering settled against previously unseen shoulders. The curtain slipped over her and fell back to the sill once again, hiding the figure in darkness.

Mrs. Schofield's cried out. Her husband burst in, spilling light in from the parlor. The Ruskoff girl turned from the light, scrambling out the window. Mr. Schofield clumsily gave chase, nearly landing on his face alongside of his own house. He screamed with as a newly discovered madness possessed him. He raced across his property; the search parties were not far off.

His wife watched from the window as other men joined him in the pursuit, the girl only a few feet ahead of them. She turned to check on Susanna and discovered she was alone. She looked back outside again. Her daughter sprinted over the fields after her father and the search party, blonde curls bouncing gracefully in the blue light.

The woods swallowed Mr. Schofield and the men with glee. The normally uneven ground and confusing, dense paths suddenly became an easy the trail. They tread swiftly, keeping the Ruskoff girl in sight. Despite the transformation of the forest, they still could not quite reach her. The dried blood upon her dress kept it stiff at her side, but her dark hair waved around in a wild dance. Susanna caught up to the men as they growled threats to the Ruskoff girl in frustration. The threats could not slow her, yet they continued to holler.

Sue shouted as well. "Papa, let's go home! Please, papa. I'm afraid. You can catch her tomorrow."

None of the others heard her pleas. They trekked on as they lost the girl in a grove. Everyone stopped dead in a ring of trees. Susanna's ankle caught a root and she plummeted to the ground. The root held her to the dirt while the men approached their prey.

The Ruskoff girl had also stopped, staring at them

wide eyed, her chest rising and falling to warn of an oncoming flood of tears. Taking one final step backwards, a patch of darkness engulfed her. The men perused once more at a steady pace, arms out in front. Hands grasped at the darkness. Feet waded through the fallen leaves.

Mr. Schofield's vision strained. The ground beneath him began to squish and crutch. The air was perfumed with a foul, rotting stench. The other men backed away from the spot, holding their lanterns close to the ground

Susanna scrambled to her feet. Her body heaved with loud moans. "Papa!"

The men dug at the leaves, curiosity overtaking their minds. Their lights swung wildly, molding wicked shadows upon the trunks of the surrounding trees.

Mr. Schofield plunged his own hands into the ground, covering his mouth and nose with the collar of his shirt. Susanna cried out wildly, demanding that her father take her home. As he pulled a clump of orange foliage and mud up, she screamed, "Papa, don't!"

Sprawled upon forest floor, lay the mauled body of the Ruskoff girl. The front of her dress had been soaked through with brown blood stains, yet they could see gashes across her belly. Blows from a hatchet, the same wounds as her brothers, had been pecked at by birds and small creatures. Her eyes stared through the forest ceiling in desperation, all life having flickered out days ago. Entwined in her stiff fingers were the familiar expensive velvet hair ribbons.

The group turned to look at the perfect little girl, her delicate blonde curls framing her tear streaked face. She sniffled, the one final act of a stubborn, sad child. Then, in a voice of calm logic, Susanna explained, "I didn't want to share this time."

Dealing with Demons
By
Sidney Reetz

CHAPTER ONE

"Ninety-nine dictators' heads on the wall. Ninety-nine dictators' heads."

In Hell no one can hear you scream, because everyone is bloody damn well screaming. Your voice just tends to get lost in the atmospheric white noise, so why bother? I much prefer to sing rather than shriek anyway.

"Take one down, pass it around—"

As you can imagine, it's rather hard to gauge the passage of time down here among the sulfur and brimstone. There might have been a sun somewhere in this God forsaken realm once, I can't rightly recall. It's been far too long since I've seen the sky. If I were asked how long I'd been imprisoned in this hole in the wall that I currently call home, all I could honestly answer is: a shit long time.

"Ninety-eight dictators' heads on the wall!"

Then again, old Satan-butt makes sure that Hell is a well-oiled machine. One so predictably run that I was sitting in the corner of my dungeon, wittily prepared for the inevitable. "Five, four, three, two, and cue the prick."

Before I'd even finished, a nasally voice called, "Demon Alastor?"

The silhouette of a demon moved into view at the front of my little dungeon. A small globe of blue light followed after a moment and hung beside him, lighting his features in the dimness. He wasn't like the warrior angels who typically checked on me in my incarceration. He was shorter and mousier with a fastidious way about him that was reflected in the crisp edges of his robes. Obviously not the looker our other brothers and sisters were blessed to be, he seemed obsessive with his appearance to deter one from noticing his lack of natural charisma.

Myself on the other hand, even dressed in rags and lacking half the grace I was created with, I could turn the heads of nearly every demoness I passed. Okay, fine. Maybe they turned their heads only to mouth, 'What in the nine levels of Hell is that?' but I say, I still got them to look.

"Phenex, you perky bastard. Here for a conjugal visit again? My, my, we mustn't tell the hellhounds. Just think of the rumors that will spread."

The demon before me sniffed and narrowed his green eyes. "I will not be baited by you, prisoner. I'm here on business or else I wouldn't waste my time."

There were no bars at the threshold of my cell for old Phenny to look through, just a single glowing ward hanging suspended in the air. So I could clearly see him when he reached into his finely tailored robes and pulled out a scroll.

I groaned and bashed my head back into the stone wall behind me. "If it's more therapy sessions ordered by your betters, you can take that damn thing and sodomize your hemorrhoid ridden bum with it."

"What's with the British accent?" Someone I couldn't see piped up. He was hidden from my sight somewhere down the tunnel behind Phenex.

"I'm not sure," another faceless commenter replied. "Hasn't he been in there since before England was—"

"Yes," Phenex snapped, looking over his shoulder. "I told them it wasn't a good idea putting that Ripper guy in the cell next to him."

"Jack? You mean ole Jacky boy? Speaking of, how is the bugger? And what is this England you speak of? The land of Eng? What's that?" I moved against the ward, smooshing my face up against it. "And whoever are you speaking to?"

"I heard Jack was set back twenty years in his therapy just from spending one week in the cell next to this guy," one of the unknown voices stage whispered.

"Nonsense! It was three days . . . I think. You know, I could really use an hourglass down here. What do you say?"

"Enough of this." Phenex raised a hand to silence his minions. "Demon Alastor, I am here to inform you that—"

"That you have explosive diarrhea!"

"Here to inform you that—"

"You are currently wearing a toupee!"

"Inform you that—"

"The moon is made of hummus!"

The demon stopped and glared at me. "Are you quite done?"

I thought about that for a second, then proceeded to press my mouth against the barrier ward. I puffed out my cheeks and give the prick a good forked tongue waggle. Oh, how Mr. High and Mighty did cringe.

There came a soft chuckle from the darkness beyond Phenex. "He's repulsive, arrogant and crude. He's perfect for the job."

I pulled my head back. "Job?"

In a rush, Phenex said, "Demon Alastor, I am here to inform you that you have been granted parole. We are here to escort you to your work release program."

My head snapped back as if I'd been slapped, spittle running down my chin. "P-Parole?"

"Well," Phenex shoved his scroll back into his sleeve, "if you'd prefer to stay here, I'll report your request back to my boss." He turned, the silk of his robes swooshing across the stone floor and began to leave.

"I'll take it! Whatever it is, I will take it!" I yelled. I slammed my fist against the ward barring my path. The ward turned red in response to my hostility. Sparks shot out from the thing and an all too familiar sting jolted up my arm, numbing it instantly. "Alright, you bastard. You win."

For now at least, I tacked on.

Phenex didn't turn to look back at me, but he nodded to his companions and moved out of the way. Two of the biggest angels from the Principalities choir I had ever beheld stepped forward to block out all the light from Phenny's little orb. I eyed the silver scepters each of them bore and tried to swallow down my budding nerves. I'd heard stories of what those weapons could do. Stories were as close as I wanted to come to reality.

The one to my left held his scepter up to the ward on my cell door. With just a small tap, the ward changed from red to white and then burned itself away. Both Principalities stepped back, seeming all the more imposing now that my small shield wasn't barring them from me.

I stepped out of my hole and though I knew the air to be the same, it felt fresher somehow. Still, even though I'd longed for the world beyond my hole, the sudden vastness that stretched before me was intimidating. Some stupid part of me actually wanted to scurry back inside my cell.

Instead, I turned to look down the halls, wondering how much had changed since they'd tossed me inside.

"Right, let's be on our way," Phenex announced.

As if waiting for the cue, the two brutes took up positions on either side of me. They swooped me up from the ground, each grasping me by the shoulder as if they were palming a melon.

A second later, we were not in the bowels of Hell, but inside a human home. It wasn't the flimsy structures I'd seen when I'd last been on Earth, but the basic layout was unmistakable. The sickly heat of the underworld was slapped away and replaced with a far gentler humidity. The sudden change in atmosphere sent a shiver wriggling up my spiritual form.

My physical body had perished in the War in Heaven, leaving me with only my spirit form to flounce about in. It was in moments like this that I missed my meat suit; predominantly the feeling of goose pimples rising on the surface of the flesh. I'd always found sensations as that particularly titillating.

I'm sure I'm not the only demon who found it infuriating that my spirit could still feel some of the Earth's elements but couldn't interact with any of it. Why? Well you'd have to ask my Daddy-waddy that one and we all know how wonderful He is with explaining Himself.

Then there was the light! Gah! After so long in the pit, my poor eyes were assaulted with the stuff. Sadly, I flinched away from that overstimulation, which only gave my nose a go at taking over my senses. The first scent to strike me was that of the ocean. It wasn't far from where we were and it had the peculiar tang of swamp and fresh rainfall peppering its olfactory perfume.

I un-scrunched my face and dared to crack one eye open.

Though I was being held off the ground by a good two feet, I swear to the Saints, I felt my jaw hit the floor. The two brutes for hire dropped me while I was ogling the wood panels and painted walls surrounding us. And that grand staircase was to die for! Simply to *die* for! No, seriously, it was giving off some major mojo that someone had *died* on it. Which only made it more wonderful in my eyes.

Everywhere there was a sheer riot of sensory overload. Light, color, sound, scent and the feel of something other than cold stone under my hands and feet! (Once the Goons dropped me that is.) I fear I went a bit daft in those first few moments from the giddy high of it all.

Hearing, last in the running of my senses, tuned in next.

"—not here yet," Phenex was saying somewhere near me. "Good, we can get this started properly."

"Is he licking the hardwood floors?" Goon One said.

"I can't say much. You should have seen me when I first discovered Hot Pockets," Goon Two replied.

"Alastor!" Phenex's slipper clad foot kicked me in the ribs, which slammed me back to reality just as I was starting to claw my way up the drapes. "Bad demon! Bad! Don't make me get a rolled up newspaper. Now look at me." He grasped me by the horns and spun my face back to him as an odd honk from outside drew my attention away. "Now here is the deal. Your mission is to get the family who is moving in here today to move right back out again. The sooner, the better. Understood?"

I blinked. "That's your work release deal? Pah! You underestimate me. I am Alastor, the Demon of Torment, the Bringer of—"

Quicker than I could blink, a silencing ward was slapped across my lips. "Here are your conditions," Phenex hissed. He looked over his shoulder at the front door nervously and said in a rush, "You are not to set foot outside of this house's property line. If you do, the wards surrounding this place will kill you. You are also denied any form of demonic possession."

I screamed against my gag. *"Mfff! Mufff Murf mur muff!"*

"No," Phenex decreed dryly. "You will have limited atmospheric manipulation capabilities only. So get inventive."

I glared at the demon and proceeded to flip him off with both hands, waving both of my middle digits in the air.

"Oh, and two more conditions," he added, a smile I did not like one bit gracing his lips. "One: If the family finds out that it's a demon living inside this house, you will serve another hundred years back in your cell in Hell, regardless if you succeed in getting them out."

I had to masquerade around this place pretending I was a *human* spirit? A human! Oh, of all the undignified injustice! I'd never live it down!

"Condition number two: You have until the next full moon to get the job done. That's ten days from now. If not, you'll go back to Hell and serve five hundred more years before you're due for parole again."

I gestured at the ward on my lips and proceeded to tap my foot on that glorious, finely polished wood floor. A moment later Phenex snapped his fingers and the ward vanished.

"Phenex, I want to first thank you for this opportunity."

"And?"

"And lastly that, yes, those robes do make you look like a cock in a corset."

<u>CHAPTER TWO</u>

Truth be told, I didn't even notice when Phenny and his two goons vanished.

I was on my stomach, staring at an odd, very tiny piece of art hanging on the wall. The frame was white with two sets of holes punched through it. The top two were elongated with a small circular one just below and between them. There was a screw in the center, obviously holding it on the wall, I told myself. At least I'd figured that part out.

"But why is it so near the floor?" I mused aloud. "Don't they know art should be at eye level? Unless, this is art for the shoes? Or rats."

Reaching a hand out, I tapped it. Not having a physical body anymore, my spiritual hand passed through the wall. Instantly, a jolt of electricity zapped through me.

The scream that issued from my lips sounded far too similar to a ten-year-old human child for my comfort. Through the shock, I noticed that my body solidified for the briefest of instances. My spirit didn't become a physical body per say, but for the barest fraction of a second, I *felt* the world against my *skin*. Everything registered; from the humid damp of the air, to the solid wood of the floorboards below and silken texture of the wallpaper against my other hand.

Yanking myself away from the *floor de arte*, I cried, "Ah ha!" and pointed at it. Turning to look around me, I noted one of these devices on every wall. "This must be the torture chamber. Oh, ingenious! They now threaten their guest when they first come through the door! I must say, I like this place's sty—"

My words were cut off as the front door swung open. Well, to be more accurate, the door whooshed through my spirit, bounced off the wall behind me and stopped in the middle of my spiritual form.

"Here we are," boomed a brazen male voice. "Our new home sweet home."

I waddled around in a circle on my knees until I beheld those who were to be my adversaries.

The first in this line was the patriarch of the clan, no doubt about it. He was a rotund fellow with a bulging gut and a full beard. His features were . . . well, human is the best I can say. He was the sort of man you looked at and just as quickly forgot. Or at least to me he was and my opinion is the only one that really matters here, now doesn't it? Moving on.

Next came his mate. Or what do the humans call them, wives? Or the singular wife? Honestly, I've always been a fan of that polygamy idea. The more shagging the better, says I. Now then, if I still had a physical body, the matriarch would have been added to my list of bed romping companions for sure.

She was a lithe creature with a nymph's curves and a wealth of golden curls. She wore funny little shoes that made her stand on tip toe and were supported by a small stick coming off the back of the thing. They announced her presence with an annoying *click-clack, click-clack* as she walked across the entry.

"Oh, David, darling. It's just perfect," she shrieked; perfect being pronounced *p-oui-fect* in her nasally, soprano voice. "It's just as lovely as you described. The kids are gonna love it!"

I groaned and slapped my hands over my pointed demon ears. Addendum to my prior statement: I'd still consider keeping her on the shag list if I could find an adequate muzzle.

"Kids!" the harpy did doth harp, "Get in here and see this!"

"Children? Dear sweet haven above, it's bred already?" I groaned.

The next to follow through the door was a son. I gathered he was somewhere in his mid-teens, judging from the sporadic facial hair, general unkemptness and the volcanic lava pit that was his complexion. I snickered inwardly, suddenly very grateful that my Father had never made a single angel go through puberty. Could you just imagine a Cherubim with acne or a Seraphim with a cracking voice? Saints and sinners, just imagine a tampon aisle in Heaven!

Next came a young girl, perhaps ten or so, with mousey brown hair. She was a shy thing, looking about the house with wide green eyes and hugging a book against her chest.

I looked down at the girl and over to her mother who was fussing with the drapes, and back. "So, I take it she's not a natural blond?"

Being a spirit, no one reacted to my words.

I didn't even see the last of the clan come up the steps until a burbling giggle drew my eyes down. Wobbling on unsure legs was a toddler. He was looking directly up at me and waving his chubby little fingers in greeting. His other hand had his thumb shoved in his drooling maw, sucking furiously.

I knelt down to his level, tilting my head this way and that. He mimicked me.

"Well now this is a twist," I muttered. "You can see me."

In answer, the little beastie reached out and tried to grab my nose. Of course his hand just swooped through the air, catching nothing; which seemed to confuse him all the more.

I sat down on the floor and looked from the toddler to the rest of the family. They completely ignored the child as they moved in and out of rooms; filling the air space with something between inconsequential chatter and verbal vomit.

The toddler came over to me and tried to sit in my lap. Once more, his body fell through mine and he landed quite hard on the floor. Instantly, the waterworks and screaming started.

After a number of minutes of the siren wailing, the harpy was the first to take note. "Joey, what on earth are you doing?" She scooped the child up into her arms, fumbling with him as if she didn't have much experience.

I sat there on the floor, looking at the family that was to be my adversaries, feeling like a disapproving landlord. Lifting a talon to my chin, I mused aloud, "Now, either this is indeed a test for my parole or, and I feel this is far more likely, old Phenny boy isn't telling me the whole story. So, why would he want this family out of this particular establishment?"

As expected, no one answered me.

"Well," I huffed getting back to my feet, "I guess I should count my blessings. At least they're not Catholic."

"First thing is first, David," the harpy screeched. "Kids, go find my tote bag. We need to hang the family cross over the front door."

"Fuck," I muttered.

* * * * *

I wandered out on the front lawn as the moving of boxes into the house commenced. The world had changed so drastically since I'd been incarcerated in Hell. The carriages and wagons Jack had described to me had certainly been upgraded; though I could do without the toxins they spewed into the air. The streets were paved in one solid sheet of rock; but don't ask me how the humans managed that one. In front of the drive there was even an automatic lamppost that clicked itself on once the sun began to set.

I stood out there, mindlessly soaking in the colors of the grass and trees and flowers. It was a riot of color compared to my shadowed cell I'd called home for the last . . . My, now there was a question: what year were the humans calling it now? Exactly how long had I been cloistered away?

I'm afraid to admit that I became very melancholy and introspective at that point. So not like me, I know. Though I'm glad to admit that the mood didn't stay with me for long. For you see, in my mental musings, I happened to wander too close to the edge of the property line and, well, let's just say those wards Phenny mentioned were not a bluff.

The moment my foot edged near one, I was catapulted through the air and slammed face first into the side of the house containing the cat's claw vines. The damn blast must have rocketed me up to the second story balcony. I slammed down on the balcony's weathered floorboards with an audible *crack*.

"What was that?" I heard the daughter squeak from inside.

"It's just an old house, it creaks," her older brother snapped.

I rolled on the floor holding my throbbing head and curled into a ball. *Ouchie, ouchie, ouchie . . .*

"Aren't old houses like this supposed to be

haunted? D-Do you think that this one is?"

"For the love of Christ, Annie, there is no such thing as ghost. Have you been watching *Paranormal Activity* again?"

Ouchie . . . I stilled myself for a beat and glanced back at the edge of the property line. I didn't have a physical body. I shouldn't have been in pain. Just like with the small torture device, the jolt of energy had made me corporeal for a faction of time.

Now that was interesting.

"That was about a demon, not a ghost," the girl was saying. "And it was real! They say so right when the movie starts!"

"You are such a moron," the brother sighed on a long breath.

Peeking over the edge of the window, I saw the door to the room closing as he left. The girl, however, was looking around at the four walls of her room like they might come alive and attack her.

I was about to leave and see what the harpy was up to when the child did something peculiar. She went to one of the boxes that had been delivered to her room and began flinging clothing out of it. Garments littered the floor around her until she'd unloaded nearly everything. Leaning into the box, her tiny feet kicking into the air, she came back out holding a thin, long, rectangular box.

Passing through the wall into the room, I tried to get a good look at the thing.

"Annie!" Her father's bellow rang from the stairway. "Dinner time!"

Jumping as if she'd just been struck with a hot banding iron, the child skittered to her bed. Lifting the mattress, she shoved the box under it and arranged the bedding to hide the gap it made. "Coming, Pa!"

I stood there, stroking my chin as the child fled the

room. I turned to the bed. Well now, what was this?

* * * * *

It only took me that first evening to make up my mind about the family. They were bumbling, boisterous twats.

I watched them, endlessly bickering at the dinner table after moving their petty possessions around for the last few hours. One was always yelling to be heard over the others. It was as if whoever had the loudest voice was automatically right. The children fought like hyenas in a barren wasteland over scraps at the table, which seemed to go completely unnoticed by the parents.

Now, don't get me wrong, it wasn't like these actions bothered me. They could tear each other limb from limb and I'd have been taking bets on who came out the victor. After all, if they were to do so, it would make my job here easier.

Then again, should I have been surprised? Humans were all decedents of Adam and Eve. The inbreeding these people suffered from wasn't all their fault. Perhaps dear old Dad hadn't thought to widen the gene pool in time to correct the problem.

No, as I sat back and watched their drama unfolding, what angered, and also confused, me was how in the world my Father had chosen them over us. Back when I'd been a pure, angelic creature, had I somehow been more disappointing than what I was currently witnessing? Then again, perhaps if He had spared a moment of time for each of His children equally, maybe there never would have been a War in Heaven in the first place.

Oh, bollocks! What was getting into me?

Just for good measure, I slapped myself across the

face. Rubbing my stinging cheek, I looked up at the ceiling and beyond it, just in case He was looking down at me at that very moment. "You're a fucking 'tard is what you are and don't let any mental wanderings on my part convince you otherwise."

The sudden silence from the side room was what grabbed my attention. The oldest son was on his feet, looking out into the hall where I was. His eyes kept swinging back and forth. "Did you hear that?"

Behind him, his father grunted, "No."

"Sounded like someone talking."

"You got too much sun today is all. We're not used to this southern humidity yet." Pushing his son forward, the father added, "Now take your sister and brother upstairs and put them to bed. We've got more work ahead of us tomorrow."

The son nodded as he gathered his brother up from the floor and reached a hand out to his sister. But I could see his eyes still searching out each nook and cranny as he moved.

I kept pace behind him as he moved. Curious, I said, "Puckernuts."

The boy jerked to the side, away from me, his eyes wider.

Beside him, Annie rubbed her tired eyes and looking up at him. "What is it, Mark?"

"Just the wind," he said.

"Flim flam, skuttle doo," I yelled, waving my hands in the air. I dropped them when the boy didn't even flinch that time. "Well bother. Why did you hear me down there but not now?" I grouched. Looking down at the floor, I imagined Phenny in Hell. "Hey, you could have given me a lot better instructions."

You also could have listened when he was trying to do just that, the sliver of my old angelic self-whispered back. *Instead, you practically pulled up your robe and flashed him your arse.*

"He deserved it."

After some sort of routine of shoving a small brush into their mouths and spitting into the water basin was accomplished, the children each were settled in their respective rooms. I wandered over to the girl's and stuck my head through the door. Just as I suspected, she was at her bed, pulling that odd box out. I moved into the room and sat across from her as she opened the box and pulled out a flat piece of wood with numbers and letters printed upon it.

"Oh! That's umm — one of those spirit boards, isn't it?" I'd seen something similar to it in China once upon a time; I think they called it *fuji*.

The girl didn't hear a word I said. She sat on her knees in her oversized nightgown and pulled a small triangle shaped device out of the box next. A modernized planchette, I guessed. It was roughly heart shaped with a hole drilled into the center. She set it on top of the board, placing her fingertips lightly on the base of the device.

"Okay," Annie sighed. "Hello? Is there any spirit here that would like to speak with me?"

Clapping my hands together, I rubbed them villainously. "Well now, since you asked so nicely." Reaching out my hand, I grabbed at the planchette. My fingers passed right through it. "*What?*" I exclaimed and tried to slam my fist down on it next.

Again, nothing.

Frustrated, I leaned back and scratched at one of my horns. "Bloody Hell. Why is it that I can only sometimes affect physical objects and not others? Phenny, you cock sucking twat. Get your arse back here!"

Annie was staring at the board, biting her lower lip and waiting. "Umm, okay. How about, what is your name?" She moved the planchette around in a circle and settled it in the middle of the board, waiting.

"Son of a demon's turd fart," I snarled. "Alright, Alastor, let's think this through. You're not corporeal anymore so how on earth do you interact with corporeal mortals?"

At that, my mind drifted back to the strange little piece of art on the wall I'd been looking at. Which, after watching the family stick numerous cords and devices into it, I found out it was called an 'outlet.' It was some kind of power source that brought their various 'electronics' to life. There had also been the wards at the edge of the property which had zapped my arse a good one.

Rubbing my chin, I looked around the girl's room until I found another of those outlets. "Well, it's worth a shot." On my knees I waddled over to the thing as the girl asked another question. "Here goes nothing." I shoved my hand through the device.

Once more an electrical shock jolted through my body, but this time I held onto it. The illuminating device on the ceiling flared to life, flickered and suddenly popped, sending the room back into darkness.

Annie screamed and jumped away from the board, eyes fixed on the ceiling.

I released my hold on the outlet, shaking out my arm. "Right," I spat through gritted teeth. "Here goes nothing."

I reached out to the planchette again and experimentally flicked it with a finger. This time, it moved! Just barely a wiggle, really, but it counted.

"Ha!" I crowed in victory. "Did you see that?" I looked at Annie whose eyes were wide and swinging from left to right. "Hey!" I yelled. "I'm doing some damn amazing paranormal shit here! Look!" I slammed my fist down on the board, causing a loud thump and the pointer to jump a good six inches into the air.

The girl saw it that time. She leapt back, screamed her head off and ran from the room. She threw the door open, crossed the hall and started pounding on the door of her older brother's room. "Mark! Maaaaark!"

A moment later the boy came out dressed only in his underclothes. "Dammit, Annie, what—"

The girl grabbed the boy and dragged him into her room. "I told you! This house is haunted! It made the light break and then it threw the board at me!"

"I did no such thing!" I scoffed.

"Then I felt it chase me out of my room!"

"You lying puss bucket!"

"Stop it, Annie." Mark looked at the board and planchette on the floor. "Where on earth did you get that?"

"Yard sale," the girl sniffed. "You have to believe me! There's a ghost in this house."

"There are no such things as ghosts!"

"Boo," I yelled at them. "Ooga booga!" Standing up and waving like a maniac, I accidently stepped on the board, kicking it out from under me as I moved. The damned thing slid across the floor and under the girl's bed. I heard it *thwack* against the back wall.

Annie jumped behind her brother, pointing at the bed. "See! See!"

Mark's mouth hung open, completely stunned. "What the fu—"

"Ah, I meant to do that," I declared. "Yes, that was completely intentional!"

"Maybe it doesn't like the board," Annie whispered. "Mark, I'm scared."

"Yes! Fear me, humans!"

"Who the fuck are you?" Mark yelled. "What do you want? What, you get your jollies from scaring little girls, you sick freak?"

"Sick freak?" I crossed my arms over my chest and stepped up to the boy. "Don't you understand how this game is played, testosterone for brains? I'm the one who insults you puss-filled, pimple on a troll's ball sack."

Mark stepped back from me suddenly, goose pimples rising all over his arms and chest. "Did you feel that?"

"It got really cold in here all of a sudden," Annie whimpered. She wrapped her hands around her brother's wrist and tugged him back towards the hall. "Mark, let's go before we make it angrier. Can I sleep in your room tonight?"

Ignoring her, Mark puffed out his chest. "I'm not afraid of you, you hear me? This is our house now. You have to leave."

"I would be very happy to leave, if I could!" I dropped my hands to my hips. "But that's not going to happen until you and your dimwitted family leave first."

In frustration, I kicked at the planchette still on the floor. There must have been a good deal of residual energy in me from the outlet. My foot connected with the small device, which rocketed through the air and hit the ceiling above Mark's head.

This time, both humans screamed and ran from the room, slamming the door behind them.

<u>CHAPTER THREE</u>

That night, after the frightened mice had barricaded themselves in Mark's room and finally settled down to sleep, I decided to play with my newfound ability. It seemed that energy was required for me to manipulate physical objects, so I moved around the house looking for all the sources of this electricity I could find. I cackled manically at discovering more and more of these outlets and little cylinders I'd heard called 'batteries.' It appeared that the humans were completely dependent on this resource.

All I had to do was tap the device to absorb the shock of the energy and *POW*; I could channel that energy into momentum. It took some control though. In the kitchen, I accidently used too much and blew up a bag of rice, a glass jar of some kind of red sauce, and a couple of odd looking, metal containers labeled Dr. Pepper. I learned the hard way that those sinister contraptions were pressurized somehow and very sensitive. How the humans opened them, I had no clue.

It was close to three in the morning before I got bored with the kitchen and wandered into the living room. Taking advantage of the family being asleep and out of my way, I nosed through the unpacked boxes.

Testing myself, I used a bit of power to pick up a

small flat object and pull it out. It was a portrait of the family, crafted by a very talented artist; I couldn't even see any of the brush strokes! However, the subject matter was far more frightening. The family that I was coming to loathe was grinning up at me from the frame. I grimaced, sticking out my forked tongue. Just then, I lost grip on the power and the damned portrait fell from my hands. It hit and glass shattered from it, tinkling around the living space.

"Oh bother," I muttered. "This is a lot harder than I ever would have guessed."

I flopped back onto the couch as I'd seen the father figure do many times that afternoon. My rear end landed on something hard and I jumped. Simultaneously, the large black box hanging on the wall across from the couch came alive. Light exploded into the room along with a cacophony of sound, music burst from out of nowhere.

Fearing that I'd just hit some sort of panic alarm, I dove behind the couch looking about for any weapon I could use for defense. (My Celestial Blade had been confiscated from me when I'd been incarcerated and not returned upon my parole.)

After a moment of heart pounding panic, I realized that no one was coming for me. Curling my claws around the edge of the couch, I peeked my head around the side of it, my cheek inches from the floor.

The black box was no longer dead, but alive with images of humans. They were talking to each other, yelling mostly. The scene before me was of two sisters fighting over who got to wear what shirt. Curious, I came closer and tapped at it.

I huffed as the purpose clicked for me. "It's like the frame holding the art. But the pictures on this one move and talk. What a curious invention."

Looking back to the couch, I discovered the thing

I'd sat on. It was palm sized and covered with small, colored buttons. Feeling emboldened, I reached out and tapped it again. Behind me, the box changed from showing the fighting sisters to a bustling kitchen. It now showed people everywhere cooking frantically as one blond man dressed in white shouted orders at them. Whenever one of the cooks failed him in the slightest, he berated them left and right, nearly bringing every one of them to tears.

"Now there is an upstanding fellow!"

I slapped the device next to me again, beginning to find this amusing.

However, a nightmare greeted me for my folly. Now, I'm well aware of the fact that humans came in a wide range of skin tones. However, I never once thought to see them with orange pigments. The girls were dressed in the skimpiest outfits mine eyes had ever seen and though they were firmly on my highly fuckable list, each one of them had that same nasally, high pitched voice of the harpy!

"Don't you talk 'bout my family that way," one carrot colored girl was screeching at another.

"I'll talk however I want, yah muff garbage," the other shrieked.

Both girls screamed and began pulling the other's hair. They tried to kick at each other while doing so, using what I assumed were footwear created for warfare. Each shoe covering their foot had a needle like dagger on the heel that they used to try and pierce their opponent.

I screamed myself, slapping at the image changer frantically. "Go back to the nice evil man!" I yelled at it.

Just then the lights in the room flared to life, momentarily blinding me.

"What the Hell?"

I looked up to see the father figure standing in the

room's entry. He had on what I was coming to refer to as 'the stupefied human face.' Looking about, he came over to the couch and picked the changer up. Not seeing me in spirit, his hand reached right through my groin area.

I tried to slap his hand away. "I do say, sir, be kind enough to buy me a drink first!"

Oblivious, he lifted the device, pressed something on it and in response the black portal box turned off.

"Pardon," I snapped. "I wasn't done with that."

The buffoon put the changer on the table and turned to leave. Lifting my foot, I slammed my heel down on the thing. The portal box flared back to life; showing the screaming man holding up a bowl of slime and almost shoving another human's nose into it.

"Finally!" I crowed in victory.

Instantly, it turned itself off again.

Snarling, I turned to see the moron with my new favorite toy in his hands again. He was slamming it against his palm and checking some compartment in the back of it.

"Stupid kids. They must be messing with it again," he muttered. He set it down again, but stared at it this time.

"Bloody wanker." I hit it again, making the thing bounce a little on the table. "And if you touch it again, I'll castrate you."

The man jumped away from me, eyes wide as he looked from the device to the portal box and back. A trickle of sweat beaded at his brow, growing as he struggled with the adrenaline pumping through his system. With slow, measured, movements, he moved over to the portal box, reached behind it and yanked at something. The screen died once more.

"H-Hey!" I stamped on the changing device again and again.

Nothing happened.

"Technicality!" I bellowed. "I still get castration rights, you pig-bodied, sack of shit!"

As he turned to leave, the idiot glanced back into the living room. He stood there as if he expected something, but after a moment he snapped the lights off and went back upstairs.

I chased after him and shouted, "The wrath of—" What had the chef's name been? "—Sir Gordon Ramsay will be upon you!"

Steam trickled out of my nose as I watched him go. "So be it. It's personal now."

* * * * *

In Hell all I had to do day in and day out was verbally annoy whoever happened to be my lucky neighbor for the week. Considering they seldom lasted longer than that, I always had to come up with new tactics to get under the next one's skin. I guess that's where I developed my clever wit and slashing comebacks.

But here on earth, now that I had discovered ways to interact with my environs, I found I had the soul and skill of an artist!

Using a small tube of something labeled Monistat, I squeezed out the white substance within and added grotesque amounts of pubic hair to my drawing. Stepping away from my mural, I held out my thumb and tried to look at it in the way I imagined Da Vinci examining the Mona Lisa would have.

"No, no, the tits are all wrong on that one," I admonished myself. Leaning over the water basin, I focused and picked up a small black cylinder. I found that if I twisted the base a coloring stick came out. It was rather handy and labeled 'punish me pink.' What can I say; it had me written all over it.

Just as I was completing the perfect pair of artistic knockers, the door to the small room was thrown open. My concentration lost, the coloring stick dropped from my clawed fingers and clattered onto the counter.

Annie's mouth hung open as she surveyed my work.

"I know. Wonderful isn't it? I particularly like the way I captured your parents shagging in a lava pit. Oh, yes, that is your father and not a pig though I see the resemblance now. And yes, your mother is the harpy he's boinking because, let's face it, that's what she is."

Annie turned and bolted down the hall, screaming at the top of her lungs, "Mommy!"

"Yes! Call the family! Share in the wonder of my work!"

Moments later the whole family was crowded around the door peering inside with slacken jaws.

"Annie, what did you do?" the harpy did doth harp.

"It wasn't me!"

The harpy elbowed her husband. "David, what is going on here?" She turned to her oldest son. "Do you know anything about this?"

Mark shook his head. He pointed at the mirror. "Is that supposed to be a Minotaur slicing someone in half with a saw?"

"No, it's a field of flowers," I said in falsetto. "It's *the saw*! Honestly, parents, why are your children not educated about medieval torture techniques? I bet they've never heard of the Judas Cradle or the Devil's Fork either. Pah!" Crossing my arms over my chest, I added, "Oh, and the Minotaur is killing you. Just for your information, Mark."

The mother gasped and pointed up. "Are those arrows?"

Annie ducked behind her mother's nightgown.

"Why are they pointing to the air vent? Does it live in there?"

"Do I look like I could fit in there?" I jabbed a claw at the vent. "That vent is filthy! You need to clean it!"

"Mommy, I'm scared!"

"I'm scared of the fungus growing behind that thing!"

David pushed his son inside the bathroom and nodded to my art. "Just clean it up for now."

Mark braced his hands against the doorframe. "Are you crazy? I'm not going in there!"

"I told you, this place is haunted!" Annie shrieked.

"Did you not see the rice and spaghetti sauce jars in the kitchen? They looked like they exploded!"

I looked between the four of them as complete panic broke out and the yelling commenced on who would and would not do what.

"Hmm, maybe I've finally found the chink in your armor, dear unwanted family. Ha, Phenny old boy, just you wait and see. I'll have them packing their bags and out the door within the week."

"Marjorie, just calm down!" David was yelling.

"I will not calm down! I'm calling the priest right now!"

"The *what*?" I screamed.

* * * * *

After the bathroom gallery incident, I proceeded to run with the theory that the stranger the things I did, the more the family ran around like chickens missing their heads.

As they were all upstairs cleaning Monistat, lipstick, and toothpaste off the walls and mirrors, I slipped downstairs. David had hung all of the family photos on one of the living room walls that morning. I took each one down and carefully constructed a perfect replica of Stonehenge out of them on the area rug.

Immediately following the priest announcement, I knocked the family crucifix down from above the front door with a broom. I used a potholder from the kitchen and proceeded to try and shove the damned thing down the garbage disposal. (I'd seen the family use it the previous day.) Sadly, it only danced around in a circle making a horrible racket when I flipped the switch.

But, I will admit, the scream dear Marjorie expelled when she saw old Jesus boy spinning in the sink was one for the record books!

I went outside, being very careful to mind the property line this time, and looked at the vehicles the family transported themselves and their goods within. The wheels seemed to be balloon-like. As I stood there pondering how I could pop them, thereby hopefully preventing said Priest from arriving; the strangest sensation came over me.

Eyes. I felt someone staring directly at me.

Pivoting around, I glanced back at the house. The human larva they called Joey was nowhere in sight.

Mentally, I knocked on the door of that angelic part of my soul that was still stomping about telling me to be all holier than thou. He was a pompous ass that I typically chose to forget existed, but every now and again, I hated to admit, I needed him.

No one is home, it said in response.

"Get off your duff," I berated it. "You're the part of me that can still do tricks. So stuff a sock in that maw of yours and do a sweep of the area."

Tricks? The angel squeaked. *I am an angelic spirit! I do not do tricks. I am a messenger of our Lord and Father. I perform His will and bestow messages to those who – Oh look! There's a Hoodoo lady behind you.*

Arms flying akimbo, I screamed and spun around.

"A little more warning next time," I snapped at the angel.

I heard the bastard snickering as he slammed the door in my own mind on me.

Heart hammering, I squinted through the morning light. There was indeed a woman behind me, but much further behind me than the angel lead me to believe.

She was across the property line in the yard of the next house. Perhaps in her seventh decade of age, she had rich mocha colored skin and seemed to have kept some of her youthful physique over the years. Dressed in a simple yellow sundress, she was holding a green tube in her hand that sprayed water over her rose bushes.

Curious, I shuffled first from one foot to the other. Her eyes followed my little dance unerringly.

"Well, damn," I mused aloud. Then louder, I called, "Shall I start selling tickets or would you kindly mind shoving your peepers up your own knickers?"

The old woman gasped, raising her hands up in some complicated gesture that truly baffled me. If she was trying to ward off bad spirits, sticking her head inside an oven and demanding ice would have proven more fruitful an endeavor for her.

In reply, I threw my own hands into the air and gave her a few choice gestures back.

From where I stood, I heard her startled cry as she dropped her watering tube and ran across her lawn. Her front door slammed and moments later I could make out her figure at the window peering out from behind the curtains.

"And don't make me do it again," I called after her. "You muff garbage," I tacked on for good measure. I still wasn't sure what the term meant, but it sounded properly insulting.

That might not have been the smartest thing, the

angel inside my head said.

"Smart would be me permanently evicting you," I retorted.

The angel huffed. *You're doing well at that as it is. This room of mine shrinks every year. By the way, you completely overlooked that bracelet of hers, didn't you?*

"I did not." Though just as I said that, the thought 'What bracelet' zinged through my head.

Well, at least I know we will die together.

* * * * *

I kept my eyes on the old bat's house the rest of the day. Actually, I turned it into a bit of a game. Each time I caught her looking out her windows, I threw open the curtains to a corresponding window in the house.

For the first few rounds of the game, I gave the old hen the mooning of her life. Once that stopped shocking her, I began opening said windows and chucking cans of something labeled SPAM at her house. I must say, I still have a decent pitching arm. A few cans actually thwacked against the house's siding and fell into her precious rose bushes.

Once that began to bore me, I grabbed a bottle of ketchup from the kitchen and proceeded to write sonnets for her on the side of the house. Of course they lost their charm in this modern day tongue, so I transcribed them in cuneiform. It only seemed proper after all.

My poetic script seemed to vex her though. She stared at it for nearly an hour scratching her head. Perhaps she didn't read the language. If so, I pitied her improper and utterly incomplete education.

The day was nearing the late afternoon and I found myself sitting cross-legged on the front lawn staring at the old woman's house. She hadn't done a window peek-a-boo in nearly two hours. I began to wonder if she were dead.

Just as I was pondering what insects would feast on her remains first, the tell-tale screaming of Annie drifted up the block.

"I'm telling you, we need to call those ghost hunter guys," she was pleading to her older brother as they came into sight at the corner. "We could get on TV!"

Exasperated, Mark groaned, "For the hundredth time, knock it off. I had to hear this nonsense all day at school already."

The children had to cross in front of the old woman's house to reach their home. As they did, the old bat burst out into the daylight waving at the two of them. She called out, "Children, you come on over here. I needs to be speaking with you."

"Oh, this can't be good," I muttered, rising to my feet. I edged as close to the property line as I could, perking up my pointed ears and listening intently.

Mark looked down at Annie, shrugging.

"You the folk who just moved into old the Johnson place, right?"

Mark nodded. "Yeah, yesterday. I'm sorry, we haven't met. I'm Mark and this is my sister Annie."

"You can call me Mama Sabine." The old woman descended from her porch and grabbed the boy by both shoulders. "Now you need listen here, son. There be an awful, foul within that house with you. I been seeing it all day."

"Seeing it?" Annie squeaked.

"Aye," Sabine said sagely. "You folk been feeling it too? I heard all the commotion last night. And this morn it was out by your car, looking at it funny like. You best be careful from here on out. I'd be taking the bus if I be you."

Mark narrowed his eyes at her. "It? What did you

see?"

"A ghastly monster of a thing. The most horrendous thing Hell ever spat out."

"Beg your pardon?" I sniffed, straightening my threadbare robe self-consciously.

"Just look at what it did to the side of your house," the woman declared. She pointed behind her at my poetic prose.

Annie leaned out. "Are – are those scratches in the siding?"

I lifted an eyebrow. "Cuneiform," I huffed. Apparently the world was illiterate in this century. "Fine. I'll try Aramaic next time."

Mark just shook his head, his eyes wide. "Mom is having a priest come over tonight. This will sort itself out. I'm sure of it."

"Priest?" Sabine scoffed. "You don't be meaning Father Eugene?" She threw her hands into the air. "Of course it would be him. Who else would those fools send?"

"You know him?"

Sabine scoffed, crossing her arms. "Indeed I do and I be telling you what, you give me one day to make some calls and I'll be at your house. Then we'll get this sorted out right and true."

CHAPTER FOUR

It was half past six when the doorbell chimed.

The family was in the kitchen taking their evening meal and I was in the bedroom of the parental units digging through the lowest drawer of the cabinet they called the 'dresser.' I found that it contained the most baffling garments I had ever seen. They were roughly cup shaped with two straps and an odd hooking mechanism in what I assumed was the back. I had unloaded the drawer around the room and was wondering if they were to be worn about the buttocks when I felt *it* enter the home.

A rather peculiar sensation of dread suddenly crashed down upon me. I turned in the direction of the front door, one of the cupped garments falling from my horns as a shiver ran up my spiritual spine.

Yikes! The inner angel part of me squeaked and scuttled back into its personal room, closing and, I assume, bolting the door.

I rose and spirited through the room's wall. The rest of the garments fell off me as they hit the physical barrier. On the second story landing, I grasped the edge of the railing and leaned over curiously.

"Well now, what fresh Hell is this?" I mused.

Marjorie, the harpy, was opening the front door and ushering inside a squat, bald man dressed all in black, save for a small square of white at his throat. "Father Eugene, thank you so much for coming. I know we haven't been here long, but I—"

The priest raised his hand and smiled at her. "There is no need for apologies, Mrs. Hemlock. I am here to help, in our Lord's name of course. After all, what better time is there for a home blessing than when you first move in?"

I descended to the first floor and edged closer to the old geezer. "A home blessing?" I turned and looked at the mother. "Didn't have the bollocks to tell him you needed an exorcism, eh? Get laughed right out of the community, hmm?" Turning back to the newcomer, I tilted my head and mused, "I will never understand why Father cursed your lot with receding hair lines." Lifting a hand, I jauntily twirled a lock of my black hair about a claw.

"Thank you," the harpy shrieked in her nasally tone. "We're just finishing up dinner. Would care to join us?"

"No, no but thank you. If it's alright with you, I would like to walk the house first. But we will need everyone for the family prayer once I'm finished."

"Of course."

Father Eugene nodded to Marjorie and walked into the living room immediately to his right. I followed, noting the black case he held at his side. It had blended in with his garments before.

I flopped myself down into the armchair nearest him, still twisting a curl. "Maybe Father cursed Adam with baldness for that whole apple incident," I thought aloud, "and it was genetically passed on to you? Oh, hello! What do we have here?"

The priest had set his case down on the coffee table and unlatched it. When he lifted the lid I could see that the inside was lined in cloth with specially made indentations that cradled a number of objects. He pulled out a crucifix, which made me pull my lips back in a snarl, and a small container of liquid. Next came a jar of salt, which joined the other two items on the table.

Finally, Father Eugene pulled a purple stole from his bag of random trinkets. He kissed the center of it before placing it upon his shoulders. The last thing he did was take a tiny jar of oil and anoint the cross with it, kissing it once he was done.

"Humans have always had the oddest customs," I muttered.

He stopped suddenly, looking around him as if he'd heard me. Without taking his eyes from my corner of the room, he grasped the crucifix in one hand and the container of water in the other. He turned in my general direction and squared his chubby shoulders.

"Ohh," I cried in mock fear. "Is the little wanker going to try and scare me?"

He started muttering some prayer then and held up the cross in front of him as if it were a weapon. My lip curled on reflex, wishing I had something to stopper my ears with. After a moment, he opened the small bottle of water and started flinging drops around the room.

"I bless this home in the name of the Father, Son and Holy Spirit."

"Ahem, water spots? Please tell me you're going to clean this up when you are—"

My words were cut off as one stray drop landed on the framed picture above my head and dripped down the glass. That one tiny drop fell demons landed on my ear. It felt as if acid had been dropped on me.

A scream was ripped out of my lungs as I bolted from the chair; my hands uselessly clawing at the tip of my ear. It was no use though. That one drop had eaten cleanly through my spiritual lobe, leaving a small, reddening hole.

"You snot guzzling, babooned ass of a hemorrhoid!" I snarled.

The priest jumped at the sound of my scream echoing around the room. He lifted his cross again. A few heartbeats later, the rest of the family was gathered at the entrance of the living room.

"Did you hear that?" someone, I think it was David, whispered.

"*In nomine Patris, et Filii, Spiritus Sancti,*" the priest continued praying. He looked to the gathering family. "There is a very angry spirit within these walls."

"Angry? *Angry*? I am well beyond that, thank you very much!"

I stormed over to the nearest of the outlets and pushed my hand into the wall. This time, I channeled as much power into myself as I could hold. It didn't go as planned though. Just when I was about at my limit, the power suddenly turned itself off. Every electrical appliance in the living room suddenly died and fell silent. Even the lights around us flickered into darkness.

"Did the circuit breaker just get tripped?" David asked.

Annie tugged on her father's sleeve. "It's not the breaker, daddy. It's the ghost!"

"Ghost?" Father Eugene asked.

Marjorie bit her lower lip and nodded. "Ghost," she nodded. "I thought a blessing would be the easiest way to solve the problem."

Ignoring them all, I marched into the kitchen.

I heard father Eugene say, "My child, we can try but I fear you may need a home cleansing, not a blessing."

I stopped at the edge of the dining table, still loaded with serving dishes, full plates, utensils and glasses. Wrapping my claws around the edge of the thing, I heaved, tossing it across the room and into the far wall. The symphony of the destruction and art of the mess were not lost to me. My actions brought the desired effect.

I crossed my arms over my chest and smirked as all out panic erupted in the living room. Every human present dashed to see the cause of the noise. The larva, Joey, started screaming his head off in Mark's arms. His voice quite effectively overshadowed that of everyone else, I must say.

Father Eugene began screaming his prayer into the air, thrusting his cross into the four corners of the room and demanding, "Be gone!"

In response, I marched right up into his face and slapped the crucifix out of his hand. The old geezer didn't see that one coming! He back peddled on me until my claws caught him by the front of his robes and jerked him back.

"Now see here, you annoying, little monkey fart," I hissed. Channeling all the remaining power I had within me I began to lift him off the floor.

The priest choked something out before the collar of his garment effectively cut off his words. His plump face instantly turned red as perspiration began beading on his forehead.

Every member of the family was plastered against the walls of the kitchen screaming. From where they stood, I suppose it looked as if the priest was levitating.

"I have tried to be nice," I ranted to everyone in the room. "I have tried to, in my own polite way, ask you all to bugger the fuck off. But my messages have been ignored. All well and dandy. We've done no lasting harm to one another. But this," I dropped the priest to the floor and gestured to the hole in my ear with one hand, "is the end of my niceties." I began dragging him towards the front door. "Therefore, good evening, good day and I hope you trip on the stairs on your way out."

I must have struck a fine and dapper figure as I did this. At least I imagine I did. I was feeling very self-assured and all-powerful as I grabbed the front doors handle and flung the thing wide open.

No! My inner angel was yelling at me. *Don't! Watch out for—*

"Not now. Can't you see I'm taking out the trash?"

But he's going for the—

Mayhap, in this one particular situation, I should have let the little prick speak and take his counsel to heart.

What I had failed to notice as I'd been shoving the prune-faced, reject of a holy man out the door was the vial of holy water still in his hand. I hate to say, but a few of my claws had ripped holes in his robes as I'd manhandled him. I'd probably even nicked his skin a time or two judging by the drips of blood on the crisp white under shirt showing passed the black robing.

The little priest had managed to uncap the vial as I'd been dragging him. In one swift move, he flung the contents, which splashed across the right side of my face.

On reflex, I kicked him out the door as I screamed and fell back inside the house.

The funny thing about pain is that if it's too much for your body or in my case, spiritual form, to process, your mind tends to go on little adventures while you're writhing in agony.

It was at this time that my mind jumped back to the day before when I'd been observing the family around the black box with all the moving pictures. David had clicked onto something called a 'movie' where black, sinuously shaped, monsters were terrorizing a group of soldiers on some made up planet in space. The funny thing about the monsters, or aliens as I'd come to find out, was that anytime one of the soldiers attacked one of them, they bled acid. One poor character had actually been hit in the face and chest with the stuff.

So that was why I had, "Hicks! I know how you felt!" repeating over and over in my mind like a mantra.

I didn't pay much attention to the family. I knew they were outside helping Father Eugene up but I didn't see if the fat ass had broken a hip falling down the steps. Though I hoped he had.

I'd managed to crawl my way along the floorboards until I was able to spirit my way through a wall and land in the garden outside. It was there, under the rose bushes with my face mashed into the mud, that I finally passed out.

CHAPTER FIVE

I spent the next two days recuperating and trying to pull together my scattered dignity. Too bad for me, my only company during my recoupment was the angel in my head.

I tried to warn you, it said for the – well I'd lost count but the twat had said it a lot!

"Ummff," I replied.

The mud had dried by the first afternoon, but bully for me, the automatic sprinklers had turned on at dusk every night and dampened everything once more.

We will just have to be more careful next time. The priest himself wasn't the problem, but his bag of tricks was.

I lifted my face out of the mud and muck, tenderly running my fingers along my face. Wincing, I could feel the swollen and blistered flesh even in my spirit form. If I still had a physical body, I wouldn't want to look at myself in a mirror.

My claws moved up my jawline and fiddled with my ear. I'd expected to feel the jagged, gaping hole that had burned through it. Instead, a nub was all that remained of my left ear. When I'd taken the holy water square in the face it must have intensified the damage.

A thousand curses flew from my lips as I sat up for the first time in two days. My hands poked around the

raw stub of my once gloriously pointed and elf-like ear.
Gone! All gone!

Well, we'll save on earrings now, won't we?

"Hide," I told the angel. My voice was pitched low
and maybe a little more guttural due to the holy water
that'd dripped down my neck. "Now. Go into that little
room of yours inside my head and don't come out for a
long time."

I heard an *"Eep!"* followed by the satisfying sound
of a door clicking shut.

I pushed myself up out of my temporary shelter
among the roses. Being a spirit, I didn't have to worry
about the thorns as I walked right through them. Well,
stumbled more like.

Holy water; it was a powerful weapon against us
demons apparently. Odd that a physical element could
harm those of the spiritual world. Then again, I'd heard
through the grape vine in Hell that it was something
blessed by God. So, quite literally, God only knew what
the stuff really was.

It took a while for me to get my feet working in
tandem with my mind once more. But once that was
squared away, I moved around the edge of the house,
peeking through any open windows I could find. I
doubted the priest was still around, but sue me, I was
being paranoid.

Something had definitely changed in the aura of the
dwelling while I'd been incapacitated. I could smell
scented oil and upon closer inspection, I could see small
crosses smeared in the stuff on every windowpane.
Looking within the windows, I could see a cross in
every room now.

Rolling my eyes, I went to pass through the wall
and into the house. However, that didn't happen. My
face slammed nose first into a kind of barrier. I
stumbled backwards, eyes wide with disbelief.

Apparently there was a small mail slot in the angel's door in my mind. He flipped it open and called out, *They did a house blessing while you were face down in the muck. Did I forget to tell you?*

My temper got the better of me. "Would you kindly die already?"

Suppressing a growl, I marched around the house with my hand outstretched against it. Much to my disappointment, I couldn't find a single break in whatever blessing had been performed. In a moment of pure desperation, I even climbed the drainpipe and tried to enter from the roof. No luck.

Once back down in the yard, I tried to kick over a decorative lawn gnome. The damnable thing just grinned at my foolish attempts. I didn't have the power to affect even that currently.

"Well," I huffed finally, "we certainly have a problem here, don't we?"

The angel took a moment to respond. Disbelief peppered his voice when he finally asked, *Are you talking to me?*

"No, the gnome. But please, by all means, feel free to butt your pig nose in."

Not so snarky when you're pissed and licking your wounds, now are you? You're losing your touch.

"Oh, go boil yourself in oil." I flopped to the ground next to the driveway, regretting that I didn't have the power to properly mash the pansies growing there with my rump. "I hate Phenex, but he is the one holding the cards in the end game of all this. Cards that will spell out our future, need I remind you? If we don't get this family out of this. . . well, let's call it a fortress for now, because that's pretty much what they've made it. If they aren't gone by the time Phenny comes back, he'll have his goons toss us back into the asshole of Hell for who knows how long."

The angel actually snorted through the mail slot. *We? Our future? Now we are a united entity? Pah! I'm not that much of a fool. You are a demon. You become more of a demon every decade. And with every decade that passes, I'm fading more and more. Frankly, it would be in my better interest if you knocked off this planet, even if that would take me out of the game with you. At least then, I wouldn't have to witness your depravities.*

I gnashed my teeth. The righteous prick had a point. If I wanted his help, I was going to have to give him something. He was the last bit of purity within me. I'd been kicked out of Heaven, slowly morphing into a demon as a result, and that meant he held all my remaining angelic abilities.

"Fine," I bit out. "Here is my offer: we call a ceasefire and team up on this and I—I'll—"

Yes?

"I'll—"

Still waiting in here.

"I promise that I will—" Oh mercy! I was going to be sick just thinking of what I had to say next! "I swear upon my demon heart that I will do no malice and only seek to help others for one year. But first, you have to help me kick the living shit out of these people."

Silence responded to me.

"Are you still there? Did I finally kill you by saying that? Because I actually need you now."

Fifty years, the angel spat back.

"Fifty! Are you off your medication? A few days of your services are not equal to fifty years of mine! Two years, but that is all you're getting from me."

The angel snorted. *Fine. I hope you like your cell in Hell. Hopefully they move you to one with a view of the lava pits upon your return. Heaven knows I'm trapped here in your head no matter what happens. So, fifty, or it's no deal.*

"You little rat!" I tried to grab a fist full of flowers and throw them at the front door. My hand passed right through them, only frustrating me more. "You're trying to reverse the game on me, aren't you? Fifty years of do-gooding and you think it will make you stronger, eh? Strong enough to push me into that little room of yours and lock me up?"

My, the angel said with mock sincerity, *whatever are you going on about? I only wish to see you on the right path instead of this misguided one you're on.*

I leapt to my feet, needing motion as I contemplated. Was it worth the risk? Fifty years of servitude or potentially a millennium (possibly two) caged back up in Hell? What other options was I looking at? Granted, the angel was going to be using every second of those fifty years trying to get a hold of the reins within my mind again. If that came to pass, I'd be locked away, in my own head this time. Still, the odds were better for me with the devil I knew, so to speak.

"Alright," I said. "Fifty years. But you help me do everything you can to get those human pricks out. Even if that means getting your pristine hands dirty doing it."

Deal!

I ran my hand through my hair and looked about us. As I did so, that sensation of being watched came over me again. This time I turned towards Sabine's house unerringly and glared at her front porch. She was there, sitting in a chair and watching me. Unlike last time, she sat staring with a detached expression on her face.

"Knew Eugene wouldn't be able to get rid of you," she called out. "But it be lookin' like he did some damage, a'right."

A snarl erupted from my throat. I walked over to the edge of the property, carefully minding the barrier. "I will rip out your lungs and use them as balls to kick around this yard, human."

"Mmm hmm. Right den. Let's see you come right on over here and do that."

My eyes moved down to the small fence blocking off one houses property line from the other.

The old woman started cackling. "I knew it! You can't step one demonic paw off that lot, now can you? Wonder why that be."

I knelt down and swiped to pick up a rock to hurl it at her. Once again, I forgot I needed power to manage even that. She couldn't have missed my blunder and as a result the cackling started up again.

I pointed a claw at her and in my most vile voice said, "You are marked, human. I will see you dead."

She sobered then, but not in the kowtowing manner I wanted. Straightening her shoulders, she rose from her chair like some kind of African queen and pointed right back at me. "Mark yourself, demon. I vow that by sunrise two days from now, you will be obliterated from this plane of existence and all others."

I think her threat was better, the angel said. *And more than likely, she can back that one up. Unlike you.*

"And just whose side are you on?" I asked it.

"That of the Loa and the creator," Sabine declared, her tone high and mighty.

"Oh, shut up!" I yelled at her. "Did it look like I was talking to you? Sheesh, tell your creator not to let you butt into other creatures conversations!"

Sabine blinked, sweeping her head around the yard.

"And you," I said to the angel. "I thought we were a team now? Or did that go out the window already?"

You are a right bastard when you've been horribly scarred by Holy Water!

As we ranted at one another, a small part of my attention noted Sabine shaking her head as she watched me. "Give me strength. This thing is completely off its rocker."

I threw my claws into the air and yelled, "We're not doing this in front of an audience, you whiney little fuck! Backyard, now!" I turned my back on Sabine and walked straight through the fence marking off the front from the back part of the yard. By the rose bushes I was far too familiar with now, I stopped. Placing my hands on my hips I demanded, "Right. Truce. Work together and all that bollocks. So, first thing is first, how do we get back inside the house?"

The angel made a sound as if he were sighing in exasperation. *You have got to be kidding me. You haven't figured that part out yet?*

"We can't kick them out of the house when we're outside of it. So how, pray tell, do you plan on accomplishing our goal?"

At that, the sound of the back door opening struck my poor damaged ear. A moment later I saw Annie and Joey, toys in hand, playing in the grass. I looked to the door they'd come through.

Just slip back inside with them when they open the door, mud for brains, the angel said. *Did you forget? They might live in there but they can't stay inside all the time.*

"Oh! Well now. . . sodomize me with a porcupine! I didn't need to make that deal with you at all!"

Idiot.

CHAPTER SIX

After slipping back inside the house with the children, I spent the rest of that night taking in the new lay of the land, so to speak. The priest had blessed each wall and window of the home. The bastard had even been clever enough to bless the floors, ceilings and air vents!

A part of me was impressed. I must have scared the piss and shit right out of the fool for him to be so thorough. Granted, being as intimidating and fierce as I am, I seemed to have made things much harder on myself in the end.

The war was on, sure enough. But I had to play this right. If the family knew I was back before I had a trap to spring, then the priest would be back before I could get the crosses off the walls. My face still burned from the holy water and that was one experience I never wanted to repeat.

I spent the next full day monitoring the family as they came and went. Towards evening a plan began to form in my mind; an organized assault that would hit all my targets in a precise order of destruction.

I knocked on the angel's door and waited for him to open it. "If I recall correctly, you spent time with some fishermen back in Jerusalem, didn't you?"

Yes, he answered warily.

"Good," I said, my fangs biting into my lower lip as I grinned. "How well do you remember your rope knots?"

*****

I waited until twilight the next night to make my move. Now that I was paying attention for such things, I found that the humans had a schedule they stuck to each night. After their evening meal, the children were forced into clean up labor and then disappeared into their rooms or into the living room to watch the black portal box. They would sit in front of the box and proceed to do whatever they could to ignore each other. Once this odd dance was completed, the family would all head to bed. Usually this was all accomplished by 9 pm.

I waited to ensure my adversaries were all passed out before I headed into the garage. Grabbing a length of rope, I headed back up to the second floor and let the angel have control of my hands. The holier-than-thou fool remembered his knots very well.

We looped one knot around Annie's doorknob and trailed the remaining length of rope to her older brother's room across the hall. One more knot about that knob and we did the same down to the baby's room. Lastly was the parent's door. The effect was a chain connecting each room to one another.

I'm starting to have second thoughts about this, the angel whined.

"Well, have a third and a fourth while you're at it." I was in Mark's room rifling through his sock drawer. I must say, doing so stretched my courage to its limits. Teenage males are — how shall I put it — revolting with their hygiene and smells. "Now where did we see him stash that – Ah! Here we are." I pulled out the small lighter and felt my grin stretching my cheeks. "Let us begin."

I moved around the bed with its sleeping occupant and knelt down amongst the discarded clothes. In my surveillance of the family, I had discovered a collection of articles that were secretly stashed under Mark's bed. These were pictorials showing scantily clad women in very provocative poses. Admittedly, I was quite despondent about what I was about to do to those lovely, shag worthy harlots.

You're sure he'll be alright? We are just scaring them all, right?

I flicked the lighter experimentally. Next to me, Mark snuffled in his sleep at the sound and tossed in his bed. I froze instantly and held my breath. After a moment the boy's light snoring started again. Shaking my head, I flicked the lighter once more until a beautiful little spark produced a flame. Trying not to chuckle, I pressed the flame to the papers under the bed.

Riiiiight?

I made sure the edge of the magazine had caught before I dropped the lighter and stood. "Your plan. Not mine," I told the angel. I think he cursed at me but I'd stop listening. This whole plan was hinged on timing for the best effect.

Passing through Mark's door, I crossed the hall into Annie's room. The little girl was tucked into bed, one hand hanging over the edge of her mattress and a line of drool trickling down the corner of her mouth.

Without pausing, I walked right up to her, grasped a fist full of her blankets and ripped them away. The child woke up instantly, her eyes wide as she saw the blanket flying away from her. I didn't toss the fabric away though. Instead I flung it up into the air and over my head. The thing fell around my form, outlining my head, horns, shoulders and arms.

The child went ballistic then, screaming at the top

of her lungs.

I raised my hands in front of me and charged at her. Now I say, this was something I should have tried doing sooner. If the brat had been going ballistic before, she was downright irrational with terror now. I flung myself at her as she scrambled to get off the bed. Dispelling the energy it took to hold the blanket over me, I passed through the fabric and little Annie with no problems. Annie on the other hand became entangled in her sheet. She tripped and fell on her bedroom floor, screaming all the while for her mother.

"Right," I hissed with glee. "Next!"

I passed through the wall of Annie's room and emerged in Joey's nursery. The little larva had woken up, hearing the terrified screams of his sister next door. In fact, I could hear the whole family awakening.

I winked down at the boy who lifted his hands to me, begging to be picked up. "Luck is on your side, chap," I told him. "You I hate the least of all your clan." I reached down and tapped him on the chin. "So I'll be merciful. But just this once."

Oblivious to the budding chaos in the house around him, the boy giggled and stood up in his crib, little hand waving to me as I strode through the next wall.

I came out of the wall and into the harpy and her mate's chambers. Both were just getting out of bed and looking around in bewilderment as the fog of sleep was whisked from their minds.

Upon hearing her daughter's cries, the mother flung the covers from her and muttered, "Good heavens, what is that child doing now?" She grasped the handle of the door that opened out into the hallway and yanked. The door gave minutely thanks to a tiny bit of slack on the rope tied about the handle on the other side.

Upon realizing what was going on, Marjorie, just

like Annie, went ape-shit nuts. She screamed, wrapped both hands around the knob and pulled. "You bastard!" She screamed. "Don't you touch my babies!"

"As if," I said. "I have no interest in your children, Madame. I just want you all out and if this doesn't send that message, well—" I chuckled, a small growl rumbling out of my throat. "That just means I get to be more inventive next time."

David had thrown himself out of the bed at his wife's screams and moved to take over pulling at the door. He was stronger than she, stronger than I had anticipated. When he pulled, I popped my head out the wall and saw the handle on poor Joey's room bending, threatening to break off.

"Oops. Damn that mule and his imbecilic strength."

This isn't going to work, the angel whispered. *They are going to break free and call the Priest again and then we'll be burned with Holy Water and taken back to Hell and we'll be stuck in that cell again for who knows how long or until you finally kill me off and—*

"Would you shut the damn flap on the opening in your face?" I yelled at him.

I pulled myself back into the parents' room and marched over to the wall socket. Preparing myself, I shoved my hand into it. The lights in the room blew out as the power flowed into me.

Marjorie and David jumped and yelled as the main light in the ceiling blew, its glass falling and shattering on the floor around them.

I ignored them and moved to the large dresser just to the left of the door. Rubbing both my palms together, I braced them on the edge of it and channeled all of the power I'd just sucked up. With a herculean shove, I muscled a burst of momentum into the bulky piece of furniture. It slid smoothly and quickly across the hardwood floors, slamming to a stop in front of the door.

Both parents yelled and threw themselves away from the door. They stood there looking at the dresser, wondering if it were going to move again.

I took advantage of their lizard brains trying to process what had just happened and jumped out of their room. As I was dashing down the hall to check in on Mark, the small fire alarm in the ceiling started to scream in a long banshee-like cry. Curses were emanating from within the boy's room. I stuck my head through the door and saw him dancing around his bed, a pillow held in both hands as he used it to swat at the flames beginning to engulf his mattress.

The child was frantic, coughing and sputtering as he yelled for his parents to come and help. Finally, some sort of sanity must have bubbled to the surface of his mind and he ran for his door. Just like his mother, he pulled on it only to have the door open a fraction of an inch before it was yanked back closed. Across the hall I could hear Annie doing likewise, trying to escape her room.

I leaned back against the wall and allowed the demon within me to take in the terror that permeated the air. It was like a fine bouquet for the senses; akin to one who has just had a full meal but the scent of baking bread awakens the stomach to say, 'Hey, we have room for a little more down here.'

The flames were spreading now, beginning to reach for the curtains. Oh, how lovely they would look ablaze. . .

Enough! The angel burst out of the room within my mind and mentally tackled me. *That's enough! You've made your point!*

The little fucker must have been storing up some energy on his own side. In the mental context of things, he body slammed me out of the driver's seat and took over. I reeled off, my head spinning from the shove and the shock. By the time I came back into myself, the twat had my body outside of Mark's room and was undoing the knot around his door.

"Traitor to yourself!" I shouted at him.

I mentally rushed him like he had done to me. At the moment our two psyches collided, our spiritual form fell to the floor holding its head. Whatever power the angel had welled up to take over, didn't seem to have held out long. He screamed and ran for his room within my mind, throwing the locks as I battered against it, raking my talons upon its metal façade until sparks appeared.

"If I ever catch you out here again, it will be the end of you!" I shrieked at him.

Just as I was getting back to myself, the door to Mark's room was wrenched open and the teen emerged, sputtering and hacking. A fraction of a second later, the handle on little Joey's room was wrenched off the door as a result of David's strength. The bastard must have moved the dresser.

Marjorie fell to the floor with her oldest son as David picked up the length of rope. The man's eyes ran from each bedrooms door to the next and he visibly gaped.

Mark seemed to be the only one of the group with any sense. The boy shoved his mother towards Annie's room. "Get Annie and Joey! We have to get out of here." He picked himself up off the floor and dashed for the bathroom. A moment later he reemerged with a small red can with a black clip on top of it. Rushing back to his room, he pulled a small pin on the contraption and squeezed. A jet of white foam erupted from the thing, dousing the flames on the bed and drapes instantly.

"Hey! It took a lot for me to start that!" But I wasn't really complaining. I was dancing actually. The phrase

'We have got to get out of here' had never sounded more blissful than it had coming from those terrified lips.

Marjorie yanked open Annie's door and the little girl came out, clinging to her mother's legs like a terrified leach. Down the hall David had reclaimed some to his senses as well and had rushed to check on the larva.

And so it was, with tears, terror, smoke and sobs, the family rushed down the stairs and out of the house.

Now, there is a saying in Hell that was coined among the angels after the battle in Heaven. It goes: don't preen the blood from your feathers until there is no more to bathe in.

Unknown to me at the time, my work was far from over.

<u>CHAPTER SEVEN</u>

"I am a wonderful demon. The best demon. The brightest, actually. Even old Satan-butt himself should be bowing before me!"

I was lounging in the living room, flicking through the options on the black portal box.

It had been two days since the harpy and her clan had run out of the house and, well, I'm rather guilty of making myself at home in their absence.

"Phenny, you old cunt, underestimated me, didn't you? How long did you give me to get them out? Well now, look who got the job done with time to spare? I'm going to enjoy seeing you eat crow when you show your ugly mug back up here. In fact, I'll force feed it to you if you are not so inclined to eat it on your own."

I kicked a stack of newspapers into the air that were lying upon the coffee table; my personal confetti for my own parade.

"How would you like your crow prepared, Phenny, hmm? Broiled? Sautéed? Or, what was it Mr. Ramsay said earlier? Barbequed? Oh yes, now I think that will be the ticket!"

In my fit of self-congratulation, I did not hear the ruckus taking place at the front door. A moment later the entry was filled with bodies looking about them like paranoid mice trying to sneak under a hawk's nest.

My face fell at the sight of the harpy and her brood. It fell even further as Mama Sabine, my unrequited neighborly love, moved forward from between them.

In stunned stupefaction, I watched as Sabine strode forward and declared in a booming voice to the room, "Spirit! Hear me! You still be here, I knows. I be here to tell you that you have not won. You have not destroyed this family or their resolve. I am here to aid them in their fight against you. One way or another, this will end tonight!"

"It hears you," an unfamiliar, withered voice croaked.

From behind the family, a hunched, elderly woman pushed her way forward, her white cane clicking upon the floorboards as she moved. The cane matched the white dress she wore and the matching white turban wrapped about her head. The only adornment on her was a lengthy set of wooden beads about her neck.

She came to a halt at Sabine's side, that damn cane of hers lifting from the floor and pointing directly at me. "It's there," she declared, "watching us."

I sat up on the couch and crossed my arms over my chest. Curling my lip in disgust, I spat, "Oh, goodie. Don't tell me you're thinking of turning this place into a retirement home. The place will stink of mothballs and Depends before the week is out."

Sabine's eyes moved to the spot that the old bat had indicated and, intentionally or not, our eyes locked with one another. "Good."

"What in the name of the seven levels of Hell is this shit?"

"It's not happy we are here." The older woman lifted a hand into the air, waving it about as if she were feeling a draft before her. "The air is vibrating with its malice."

"That's just my farts, you old coot."

"You can set up in the kitchen," the harpy said. "I think there is enough room for your — things."

I pushed myself up from the couch and followed behind the group as they all made their way into the kitchen. I placed myself nearest the doorframe and watched as they made quite an odd spectacle. At the older woman's instruction, the two older males took the dining table outside and the girls cleared as much floor space as possible.

A large wooden box was dragged inside and placed in the center of the room. From within it, the old crone pulled out an assortment of glass bottles, herbs, feathers and bits of animal bone. The last item to be revealed was a —

"You kinky old colostomy bag! I wouldn't have guessed you to be rocking the necrophilia," I said.

"Is that a skull?" Annie shrieked.

Mama Sabine grabbed the girl by the back of the shirt and forced her to sit. "Yes, child. It's nothing to be afraid of. That is the skull of the great Mambo who taught Mambo Yana," she nodded to the crone. "Who in turn, taught me. There is great power in such relics even after the spirit be passed on."

As they talked, I approached the skull after it was set on top of the box. Mambo Yana had started lighting candles, then she sprinkled herbs and tobacco around the thing. They were right; there was a power radiating off the decrepit old relic. Enough power that, out of self-preservation, I stepped away from it.

Being born to a strict 'thou shall not speak with the neighbors' sort of pantheon, I was justifiably wary of the other cultures my dear old Dad hadn't arm-wrestled under his dictatorship. I'd never witnessed it first-hand, but I'd heard rumors through the incarcerated grape vine of things getting a bit *finicky* when angels and demons got too close to those labeled 'other.'

"I hate to admit it," I whispered to the angel inside me, "but we might have a problem here."

Marjorie wrung her hands in the air as Mambo Yana went about the kitchen drawing symbols and setting up what appeared to be an altar. "I don't know about this anymore," she said to her husband. "We're good Catholic folk. We're going to go to Hell for this, I just know it! I mean, Voodoo? Oh, what would my mother think?"

At Marjorie's words, and to my shock, Sabine and Yana burst out laughing.

"Voodoo?" Yana cackled. "This one gonna be seein' some Hoodoo tonight."

Marjory turned and blinked owlishly at Sabine. "I'm not following."

"Voodoo, or Vodun, is so old, no one knows where in Africa it originated or when." Sabine paused and held up her hand. "What the world also doesn't know is that Vodun is a side branch of another religion called Nudov."

"Nudov. I've never heard of that."

Yana's cane smacked sharply upon the tile floor. "And you never shall again after today. It's a religion that is kept alive only within certain bloodlines these days and I shall say nothing more to you about it than that."

My eyebrow lifted as Yana went back to her preparations. Out of the corner of my eye, I saw Sabine wave Marjorie into the hall. Nosey Nelly that I am, I followed.

"Much like the Vodun," Sabine whispered, "we call upon the Loa in our ceremonies. But we work with them in different ways."

"What does that mean?" Marjorie asked.

Sabine winked. "Oh, you'll see."

The Loa? My angel asked. *If I recall correctly, they*

*were the messengers or demigods of the Vodun supreme
God. So they are kind of like angels, right? Comrades in
arms? Perhaps they'll actually help us if they are
summoned here and not — well, you know, do whatever
these witches tell them to do to us.*

I'd never heard of this Nudov-whatcha-ma-call-it,
so my doubts were high. Then again, the two of them
could have been bat-ass crazy and doing nothing more
than talking up a good game. As I thought that, my gaze
strayed to the skull in the center of the room. Much like
certain pieces of art, I felt like the eye sockets were
watching me no matter where I moved in the room.

I walked around the red circle Sabine painted on
the white tile of the kitchen floor.

You're being very quiet. This isn't like you.

"I don't like this," I muttered. I kept my eyes on the
two Mambo in the room, wondering if they could hear
me or not. The older seemed quite tuned into my
presence but I wasn't sure how far that sense of hers
stretched. "The Vodun . . . They predate our Father?"

*Pah! Nothing predates our Father! There was
nothing before Him. That's fact.*

My glanced to the skull. "That's what all angels are
told. But are we so sure about that?"

*****

The clock on the wall chimed seven o'clock before
the family's preparations were all in order. The first
command Yana had given the family was to have all the
crosses removed from the house and the marks in oil
taken off the windows. As they did so, she went about
lighting what felt like a thousand candles all over the
first floor of the house. All were different shapes, sizes,
and colors. Some were in the forms of people. Some in
the forms of animals. The scent of incense was thick in

the night air, mixing with fresh tobacco and a few choice food offerings that were left near the now completed altar.

Symbols drawn in white had been added to the red circle on the floor as well as the walls. They all looked like chicken scratches to me. Nothing was even remotely familiar. As soon as the last symbol had been completed, it felt like an oily, unseen tar had blanketed the air within the house. It was stuffy and uncomfortable, but nothing that went beyond a mild discomfort for me.

Yana and Sabine gathered the family within the large circle on the kitchen floor and began a low ululation.

I glared at the group. "Right. Well it's not like I'm going to go out without a fight here, chaps. You win and I go back into the brimstone pit for who knows how long. You lot might colonize Mars before I'd get to come up for air again."

As the Mambo's chant quickened in speed, I went for the altar they'd carefully arranged outside of their little circle. Concentrating what little energy I had left, I threw my arms out to swipe everything off the top of the altar box.

A cane smacked across my outstretched arms with a deafening *crack* that echoed around the walls of the kitchen. It felt like a white-hot branding iron had been laid across my arms instead of a piece of wood.

I screamed, falling backward and smashing into the pantry door. The burning sensation only increased until I thought my hands would fall right off. I fell to my knees crying out and then — then the feeling was simply gone!

"It is very rude to disrespect someone's altar," the deepest voice I'd ever heard said. The aroma of tobacco mixed with the musk of road dust filled my nostrils.

Clutching my arms to my chest, I looked up from the floor to see a man sitting cross-legged on the kitchen counter; his cane resting across his knees. His dark skin was pockmarked and creased with wrinkles as he smiled down at me. The clothes he wore were thin and well-worn with colorful patches carefully stitched here and there. He was thin and gangly; reminding me of an old man I'd once seen just before he'd died of hunger.

"But then," he said, "what would you know of such things?" The wooden cane he'd used came up sharply as he pointed it down at me. "If I be remembering right, your papa is the one who gets all the reverence in your pantheon."

Perhaps it's a blessing or a curse of my character, but ever since the great fall from Heaven, when I find myself confronted with figures of authority, the filter between my brain and lips seems to take a small vacation. Yes, I will conveniently blame that on what I said next.

"You pigmy pustule of a goat raping dung beetle!" I batted his cane away from my face and pushed myself to my feet. "You nearly broke my arms! So do not get all high and mighty over me about respect. You, sir, are spiritually trespassing on *my* territory and attacking *me*! Were you raised in a barn? Didn't your mother ever tell you that counters are for glasses and not asses? Now be off with you." I waved my clawed hands at him. "Shoo. Scat now you creepy spirit of anorexia."

To my utter astonishment, he broke into peals of laughter, rocking back and forth on the countertop and slapping his cane against his knee. "You are not like the others of your kind I have met before."

"I should say that I am not! Those pompous, peacock plumaged, puss filled prattlers; I disown the whole lot of them."

"Nice alliteration."

"Thank you." I straightened the hem of my robe and sniffed. "Now if you don't mind, I have a," I waved at the humans still chanting, "*thing* I must disrupt."

"Well," the old coot said, "that is why I am here. You see, they summoned me." Not removing himself from the counter, he bowed at the waist. "The name is Papa Legba."

"Papa? I already feel sorry for your children."

"He is here," Yana cried. She held up her hands to stop the chanting of the others. "Papa Legba, we beseech you to open the gates between us and the Loa. We seek your aid to destroy a spirit within this residence that does not belong."

"That would be you," Legba said needlessly.

I scoffed.

"Papa Legba, we beseech you! Hear us!"

"Blah, blah, blah," I sneered. Turning to the old coot, I lifted an eyebrow. "I guess we can skip the middle men and—"

Legba held up his hand, one finger pointing toward the ceiling. "No. I am just the guardian of the gates. I cannot act in this particular problem. Who they need is—"

"Baron Samedi, at your service."

I jumped as another Loa appeared in the kitchen with us. This one had skin as black as the midnight sky with an artfully drawn skull in white paint masking his features. He was tall on his own, but the black top hat and tight fitting suit he wore seemed to elongate him even more. Like Legba, he also had a cane in his hand. It seems to be a requirement. Maybe they thought of them as wizard's staffs or safety blankets, I didn't bloody well know.

I rolled my eyes at Papa Legba. "And here I thought our date was going fine but noooo, you had to make it a threesome."

Across the room Yana gasped, falling back into Sabine's arms. "He is here! The Loa of the dead is with us."

"Oh, shut up," I snapped at the wailing woman. "You keep that up and I'll take the most annoying person award I gave the harpy and shove it down your gullet!" Straightening myself once more I addressed the two Loa. "Now, as I've been trying to say, I think we have a miscommunication here. You see, I need them," I hooked a thumb over my shoulder at the humans, "out of here. Trust me, lots of politics and nasty stuff you just can't be bothered to waste your precious Loa time with. So if you'll just help me t—"

Baron Samedi clucked his tongue at me and waved a disapproving finger in the air. "I'm sorry but that won't be happening. You see," he hooked a thumb over his should this time at the humans, "they are our people. You . . . well you are a Christian piss ant that should be stomped out of existence with the rest of your ilk."

Papa Legba swung himself down from the counter. With a deft flick of his wrist, he swung his cane up to rest across his shoulders; his hands hanging off it like a man in the stocks. "Pity," he seemed to say to himself. "I rather liked this one. Make it a swift cleansing, won't you, Samedi? The poor creature is completely outclassed."

"Cleansing?" I asked. I stepped away from the Loa, suddenly unsure of, well, everything. "If you want to wash the rugs I can show you where they keep the Rug Doctor." I bristled suddenly as his words sunk in. "Outclassed? Outclassed, you say! Ha! You two look as if you haven't bathed in a century. Why by comparison, I'm the epitome of class compared to your sorry—"

Before I could complete my diatribe, the Loa of

Death lifted his hand and snapped his fingers. One moment I was glaring at the Lao and in the next, a snake with a head the size of an oven was in my face.

Though I was a spirit, I felt as if the blood had just drained from my face. "Snakes. Why did it have to be snakes?"

CHAPTER EIGHT

It wasn't just a large snake. It was *the* large snake. The largest to have ever roamed the earth in fact. For the life of me, I had no idea what the humans called its fossils these days, but back in the time of the dinosaurs (no idea what Dad was thinking making those) the damned things had been large enough to eat alligators whole.

They were supposed to be extinct. I know, I'd had a front row seat to the show when Daddy dearest sent the comet out of the sky to be his magic eraser.

Then again, the Loa of the Dead was in the room, I reminded myself. Perhaps his powers extended beyond human spirits and into everything dead. That made me gulp down a lump of fear, which only lodged itself in my throat.

The snake reared its head back, its spectral eyes glowing a dull green. When it opened its maw and hissed at me, the fangs were the size of machetes and dripping gobs of yellow poison. In life, the damned thing had to have been nearly three thousand pounds and the length of a bus.

The angel in my head was screaming like a rabbit caught in a trap with the wolf only feet away. Really, I couldn't blame him. If I were in a physical body, I would have been pissing myself.

I edged backward from the beast. "Ahhh . . . I think the negotiations have broken down between us. Let us retreat and readdress our issues in the morning, shall we? Perhaps over coffee and crumpets?"

The dark skinned Baron came around the side of the snake, smacking the serpent fondly as if it were a dog and scratching around its scales. "The Loa have never negotiated with the Christian swine." He brought a thick cigar to his lips and with a muttered word, the tip of the thing ignited into flame. He puffed once then said, "Kill him, my darling. Tear his soul into bits and bring them back to me."

The snake spat. I saw its body shift slightly and then it was moving faster than I could track.

Screaming, I half pin-wheeled and half fell to my left as the beastie rushed past me. It corrected its course in one twist and hissed.

Beside me, Papa Legba clucked his tongue.

"Any words of advice here, gramps?" I huffed.

He stroked his chin and thought for a moment. "I'd run."

I gaped at him. "And here I thought we were starting to be chums."

The Loa lifted his cane and pointed. "Duck."

I fell to the floor as the snake's jaws snapped at roughly the level at which my head had just been.

Do what the old coot says and run! My inner angel shrieked.

And on those two expert opinions, I ran. Though I wasn't really sure where I should be running to. When you're trapped in a prison and being chased by the spirit of a long extinct dinosaur snake, what exactly is there for one to do? Well, for starters you can run from one end of your cage to the next screaming your lungs out and relying solely on dodge and evade techniques. But that really didn't have a long-term goal, now did it?

From the second floor of the house, I leapt out one of the bedroom windows and landed in a rough heap on the lawn below.

What do we do? What do we do? The angel was asking over and over.

I rolled to my feet and looked about for the snake's pursuit. "For starters," I snapped back, "we need to calm down and think logically. It's another spirit right?"

Right.

"And we are an angel. I mean demon," I corrected myself quickly. "Demons and angels can only be killed by angelic weapons right?"

Right. Well, technically.

I froze in midstride and blinked owlishly into the night. "Technically?"

Well, it's only said that an angelic weapon can kill us from within our own pantheon. We're dealing with a Loa; someone completely outside of our Father's realm of influence and rules.

"So what you're saying is that there is a very high probability that the snake, under that Baron so-and-so's power, could really hurt us?"

I think it's a very distinct possibility that it can kill us. One that I really don't want to put to the test.

"Right. Back to square one. How do we get rid of the beastie?"

We - ahhh!

The angel's cry was better than any alarm. Without looking behind me, I fell into a roll and dodged to my right. I was too close to the edge of the property line and that bloody barrier to move in any other direction.

Thankfully, the snake didn't know that I was confined to this specific area. It charged past me at full speed and probably would have whipped back around like it had done in the kitchen to come after me again. Well, it didn't get to do that.

The monstrosity slammed into the barrier at full speed headfirst. The force caused the entire perimeter line to flash with a white-hot light. Sparks exploded from the impact point and a sonic boom exploded out from it. One second the snake was at the edge of the property and the next, its spectral form was flung back into the house.

Recall what I mentioned before about different pantheons and powers not really being copasetic with each other? It seemed that Mister Slithers wasn't immune to my pantheon.

I leapt up from the ground and crowed with victory, "The door swings both ways!"

I felt the angel's confusion.

"It was from that movie we saw last night. Ghost Busting or something like that. Wait!" I paused and let a thought blossom in my mind. "If the wards can hurt it, then logically any weapons we possess could hurt it as well. We might just have a chance here."

Yes, the angel said, though his tone was that of a school marm talking down to a student. *But if you recall, all of our weapons, including our Celestial Blade were confiscated prior to our incarceration in Hell!*

"Well don't you just have to rain on every parade I'm trying to have?"

As we argued, I failed to feel the shift in the air that signaled another of my kind teleporting in.

"Alastor!"

I turned to see Phenex glaring at me.

"I *told* you about the barriers and not to go near them!" He came marching across the lawn, sticking his high and mighty nose in my face. "It just felt like you used a battering ram on one. I felt it in Hell and had to excuse myself from a very important meeting with demons you don't want to piss off. Now, what on earth are you up to?"

Behind Phenex, the snake's head poked itself out of the side of the house, its tongue flicking the air. It had recovered from the ward's defenses much faster than I had anticipated.

In my mind, what I said to Phenex was, 'Well, jolly good to see your pimpled arse, Phenny ole boy. You have such remarkable timing. Meeting you say? Did I interrupt your weekly licking of Satan's bum? Oh, I do apologize. You see you forgot to mention the Loa infestation before you dropped me here. Care to take care of that now? Oh, look, their pet is coming over to say hi.'

Instead, what came out of my mouth was a long, high-pitched wail that continually increased in octave as the snake came for me again.

Phenex's eyes were wide as he stared at me. "He's lost his mind," he said to himself. "The fool has finally cracked."

I pointed a talon over Phenex's shoulder, my voice singing one long held note of 'oh shit!'

Rolling his eyes, Phenex looked over his shoulder. His mouth dropped open. Just as the snake was rearing back to strike down at us, the other demon grabbed me by the front of my robes and teleported us to the other side of the lawn. There, he grabbed me by both shoulders and started shaking me.

"Alastor, what did you do?"

"It — wasn't — me," I said between throttles. "It — was — the — Baron!"

Phenex shoved me backwards hard enough that I fell on my rump in the grass. "What Baron?"

I pointed to the kitchen windows where Papa Legba and Baron Semedi were both puffing on cigars. Both dark skinned spirits lifted a hand in unison and waved at us.

Phenex turned and kicked me in the leg. "What did

you do, Al?"

I batted his foot away before it could make contact. "What you told me to do! Is it my fault the family had Hoodoo connections? I say not!"

The other demon growled as we both saw Mister Slithers darting through the grass. He reached down and placed his hand on my shoulder. "Fine, I'll teleport us back to Hell and we can regroup there."

Mister Slithers was gaining on us.

"Uh, anytime now, Phenny." I looked up at the other demon. "Beam us down? Now?"

The colored drained out of his face as he looked down at me. "I can't. Something is blocking me."

"But you just did it!"

In response, Phenex teleported us back across the yard moments before the snake stuck.

"I can teleport within, just not outside of this place," Phenex snarled. He lifted his hands and fisted them in his dark hair. "I should have known better. I should have known you'd mess this up somehow."

I got to my feet and straightened my robes. "Don't blame this on me! I did my job days ago. The family was gone. Mission accomplished. It's not my fault you didn't leave me with a way of contacting you."

Argue about it later, the angel yelled. *You two need to work together here.*

"Right," I hissed. "Like he says."

Phenex blinked at me. "Who? I didn't hear anyone."

I ignored his comment. "We need to work together. The ward hurts Mister Slithers there. It can also hurt us but it seems to be the best offensive we currently have. It's also a double edge sword that's trapping the beastie and us in a very tight spot. So," I declared, pointing at the barrier, "take it down."

"Take down the perimeter ward?" Phenex scoffed. "Do you have any idea how long it took to put that thing up in the first place?"

"Life and death here Phenny."

The demon growled. "Think, you British wanna be twat! If it took days to put up, it's going to take days for me to take down!"

"Oh," I said. "Well, on to plan b?"

CHAPTER NINE

"What exactly was plan b again?"

I dashed around the corner of the house and sprinted forward. "I'm still working on that," I yelled over my shoulder.

We were making circuits round the house like two marathon runners. The snake couldn't corner worth a damn and teleporting around the yard was starting to wear Phenny's batteries low.

Darting around the next corner, I skidded to a stop and waited for the other demon. "Swords," I panted. "Celestial Blades. You still have yours don't you?"

"Of course I do."

"Well, get your inner Saint George on and use it to slay that dragon!"

Phenex held out his hand and within it a long, curved sword manifested. His grip on the weapon was shaking though. "I — Umm, is this a bad time to say that I've never actually been in a fight?"

I was peeking around the edge of the house. At those words, my head snapped back to him. "What are you talking about? You're a demon. You fought in the battle in Heaven like the rest of us."

"I — ahh — was more moral support for our side."

I turned, fisted my talons in his tunic and lifted the

demon off the ground. "You were a cheerleader? Are you serious? You never once fought and you — you were promoted to management in Hell?"

"Secretary, actually," Phenex squeaked. "To General Remiel."

"Secretary! You mean that I've been getting pushed around by a bloody secretary all these years?" I snarled and dropped the demon, who lost his footing and fell on his arse. "Fine, let me take care of this." I reached for the Celestial Blade that'd dropped from Phenex's hands.

Stop! The angel warned. *Are you both that far gone? That is his blade. Not ours! Halt and think! Remember Angel Training 101.*

I cursed under my breath and stepped back from the weapon. Angel blades were a manifestation of an angel's soul. Should I touch it, the discord between its energy and my own would come with a pretty hefty fall out. If I were lucky, it would be a few moments of pure agony and maybe make my hand go numb for an entire day. If I wasn't lucky, well I'd heard stories about angels who had gotten their soul so scrambled from the discord's reverberations that they'd fallen into a death-like coma and come out of it a few centuries later.

"Phenex." I couldn't recall the last time I'd used his true name. I kept my tone level and dire. "I need you to pull yourself together, pick your weapon up and help me save both our lives."

That seemed to jar the demon out of his fear. He did as he was instructed, though his hands still shook as they grasped the hilt and held the weapon before him. "Right," he said more to himself than me. "Just charge and hack at it. I can do that. I can."

Our stalling had allowed the snake to catch up to us. It came around the corner much slower than it had before. The creature's brain must have finally understood to take its speed down a few notches.

"Right-e-o! Go get him!" I shoved Phenex forward.

He wobbled on his feet for a moment before planting them in a fighter's stance. The two of them stared each other down for the barest of moments before the snake charged again.

I expected Phenex to give some sort of battle cry and lurch forward to meet the attack. Maybe my backing him would allow the inner warrior to surface within him and take over, saving the day and ending this in one divine stroke.

My luck is for shit though.

Phenex, the obnoxious prick, pivoted on his heels and bravely ran away.

I stood there slack jawed for one stunned moment before the angel kicked me in my mental rump and I followed suite. "You moron! Now what are we going to do?"

"Come up with a plan c!"

"I think we already did. C is for coward!"

On the straight run down the length of the house the snake's speed increased tenfold. I must have been tiring or maybe that was what Mister Slithers was waiting for. It launched itself at me, its fangs clipping me on the back of the leg.

Pain exploded not only from my leg, but the very fabric (or whatever it's made from) of my soul. I'm not really sure how to explain it. Imagine your soul as a sheet and someone ripping into it with a scythe, then also imagine your soul as a bell and someone slamming a mallet against it. The combined tearing and gut churning resonance caused everything to suddenly go black.

* * * * *

I woke up in the house, just inside the entry. I

couldn't have been out for long though. When I cracked my eyes open I could see the Mambo and family still in the kitchen muttering their prayers.

I pushed myself up and twisted to see the back of my leg. Not having a physical body, my spirit showed the damage. A black gash was slashed down my calf and, just as if the wound was physical, I was unable to push myself back onto my feet.

I'd been scared since the Lao had shown up, but now true fear was taking root. In a fight, typically you have one of two options: fight or flight. The fight option had been pretty much out for me from the start of this, now my ability to run was off the table as well.

"Well," I told myself on a sigh, "dying is actually more preferable to going back to that hole in Hell."

"Two spirits are with us now," Yana wailed from the kitchen.

"Oh, shut it, cow," I mumbled.

I crawled across the floor towards the living room. If I was going to die and be spiritually digested by a reptile, I would make sure I was in the comfiest chair available when the beastie finally found me. I just hoped he'd managed to eat Phenex first. Where was the bastard?

"Legba, Samedi, take from us what energy you need to vanquish these foul demons!"

I froze as Yana's words sunk in past the pain still reverberating through my body. Hope kindled to life within me.

In a desperate move, I rolled until I was able to put my head out the side of the house. "Phenny, you wanker! You better not be dead! If you are, well, I'll see you in a bit I guess. But if you are not, get your cowardly arse over here!"

From the other side of the house I heard a faint scream getting closer. Phenex rounded the edge of the house, oblivious of my head sticking out of the wall. I grabbed him as he charged passed me and yanked him back within the house. His wail turned into a scream until I wrapped my hand around his mouth. With any luck the damn snake's fossil brain wouldn't suggest to it that we were back inside the house for at least another two laps.

Phenex batted my hand away. "What the Hell happened to you?"

"Shh!" I grabbed Phenex's chin and forced his head around until he could see the humans in the kitchen. "The Loa are drawing their power from them!"

"So, we get rid of the humans and the snake loses its batteries?"

"Exactly."

"We can't kill the humans," Phenex snapped.

"Why not?"

"No," he said firmly.

I snarled at him and rolled my eyes. In doing so, my gaze fell upon the circle and the elaborate preparations Yana and Sabine had laid out. The ritual of their ceremony was so precise, so painstakingly placed...

"Right. I know what we need to do! Phenny, my old boy, you are about to get in touch with your feminine side."

* * * * *

"I can't do this!" Phenex squawked at me.

I'd managed to push myself up onto one leg and was hanging onto the other demon for balance as I shuffled and pushed him into the kitchen.

"It's one of the cardinal sins for a demon!"

"You are a demon," I reminded him. "Sin is kind of how you got into this business in the first place."

"It's also the fastest way to degrade further down

the road of Demonhood!"

"Well, you will level up quicker then."

Phenex spread his hands and braced himself against the doorframe leading into the kitchen. "Alastor! Don't make me do this."

"We're out of options. Now, go lose that possession virginity of yours and get inside the old bat!"

And with that, I shoved the spirit of Phenex into the body of Mambo Yana.

The two Loa, who had strangely been absent in the room, suddenly appeared.

Baron so-and-so-what's-his-face came for me, the white mask painted on his face making him even grimmer. "What are you doing?"

I dodged the hand that reached out to grab me and in the process lost my footing. I slammed hard into the tile floor right next to Mama Sabine, who was still completely oblivious to the spiritual happenings around her. Blinking up at her through dazed eyes, I wondered if she was truly as gifted as she seemed to think she was.

"Where is the other one?" Legba asked.

Was it just me or was there a note of fear making his voice crack just a little?

Next to me, Mambo Yana gave a shriek and doubled over, her head almost slamming into the floor. Her arms were wrapped tightly about her and she groaned, spittle flying from her lips. Everyone jumped away from her, humans and spirits included. Except for me, my head was still spinning enough that I couldn't tell up from down.

Mambo Yana stiffened suddenly and sat back up. Her eyes were wide and she looked down at her fingers, flexing them demd cringing at the pain that must have been in every joint she possessed. "Oh, that's not very pleasant." Though it was Yana's voice, the pace and cadence was completely altered. "I say, I'm very happy we don't have to suffer though the aging process. Yuck."

"Phenex?" I called.

"Mambo Yana?" Sabine asked in unison.

I frowned at her. "Stay out of this!"

Phenex, controlling the old bat's body, looked down at the form he was housed within. "Great heaven above, I have tits!"

"Focus Phenex!"

Around us, the humans were on edge and getting more agitated by the second.

"And I feel as if I'm going to lose control of this bladder at any moment," the other demon moaned. "I forgot how annoying physical bodies were."

"Phen—" My words were cut off by Baron Samedi slamming a pointed boot into my gut. I doubled over into a fetal position on the floor, unable to do much to retaliate.

The Loa of the Dead snapped his cane up, placing it against Mambo Yana's throat as if it were a sword. "Out of the woman, you filthy piece of shit." He snapped his fingers once more and Mister Slithers poked his head back into the house. "Or I'll have my pet eat your friend."

Phenex narrowed the woman's eyes. "I believe you have the relationship between myself and that one completely wrong." He sniffed disdainfully. "I'd actually love to see you obliterate that fool out of all existence. You have no idea the pain in the ass he's been. I mean I give him one little job, a chore really, and look how he's managed to mess that up. He's rather useless, if you ask me."

"Going—" I gasped between words, "to — kill — you."

The Baron hissed again, shoving the cane deeper.

Phenex held up a hand. "However, in light of

circumstances and the fact that he is my only ally at this moment, I feel I must say something unto you gentlemen."

Both Legba and Samedi looked at one another and then back at the demon.

"From Hell's heart I stab at thee!"

And with that, Phenex used the old woman's foot and kicked the altar. The box flew across the room, smashing into the wall and splintering into a thousand pieces. The skull that had been reverently placed atop the display rolled off. It smacked harshly onto the tile floor, a wide crack spreading over the cranium. A tooth even flew out of its mouth and bounced off my forehead.

Things went a bit haywire at that point.

As soon as the skull cracked, a whiplash of power exploded out of the circle, throwing everyone back a good two feet. Myself, I just kind of skidded across the floor, still hunched and lame. The Loa were shouting at one another, but as the outpouring of power dissipated, they began to fade.

Before he vanished into the blackness of the night, the Baron looked down upon me and snarled something in a foreign tongue I couldn't understand.

Beside him, Legba was snickering. Before he also vanished, he used his cane to tip his hat at me and winked; almost as if he were telling me, "Well played."

I pushed myself up from the floor just in time to see Mister Slithers pop out of existence along with his master.

"Oh, thank you," I groaned.

That was when the voices of the humans around me broke through my selective hearing with alarming clarity.

Annie was crying and clutching at her older brother as her mother and father were screaming for answers. Everyone's hands were in the air and yelling at one another as if the person next to them had some clue about what was going on that the other hadn't keyed into yet.

I saw Sabine crawl across the floor towards the prone body of Mambo Yana. "Someone call an ambulance! Yana? Yana, talk to me? What happened?"

Yana coughed once and cracked her aged eyes open. I wasn't sure what had happened to Phenex when the skull had cracked and the circle had been broken. If he was still in the old coot or if he'd been kicked out, I couldn't tell.

Yana coughed and rolled onto her side. "That, fucking hurt," said a familiar, nasally tone.

"Phenex," I sighed in relief.

"Yana?" Sabine asked. "You alright?"

Phenex, turned to the woman and bit out through clenched teeth, "I just defeated two Loa and their reptile assassin. How do you think I feel?" The face crinkled into a toothy smile. "I'm fucking awesome!"

Sabine jumped back from Phenex. "You - you are not Mambo Yana!"

"She's just now getting that?" I scoffed.

"That's right I'm not." Phenex pushed himself up from the floor and grabbed Sabine by the front of her blouse. "Now, I'm only going to say this once, to all of you," he added, gazing around at the stricken faces of the family. "Get. Out. Now. Before I get really pissed."

The father stepped forward, his quavering voice betraying his bluff. "You're the ghost aren't you? The one that's been terrorizing my family?"

"No," Phenex said bluntly. He pointed at my prone form on the floor, which of course they couldn't see. "He is and he isn't a ghost, he's a lowly demon. Me? I'm his boss."

At that declaration, every face in the room went

white.

"Demon?" the harpy whispered. "We've had a demon in this house the whole time?"

Phenex puffed out his chest, which was rather comical with him in the crone's meat bag. "He's not the one you have to worry about," he said, his voice deepening into something vile. "I am." He flung out his hand and suddenly every bit of glass in the kitchen shattered.

Wide eyed, I gaped at the other demon. "Now how the Hell did you do that?"

Every one of the children screamed and rushed for the door. The parents followed suit. The last one to leave the house was Sabine, who fled hesitantly, looking over her shoulder at the possessed body of her mentor. "I'm sorry," she sobbed. "I'm not be strong enough for this, Yana. I don't think anyone is." She slammed the door closed behind her as she fled.

As soon as the room was cleared, the spirit of Phenex dropped out of the body of Mambo Yana. The demon fell to the floor like a sack of potatoes, gasping and twitching as if he'd undergone a mild seizure.

Free of the demon now, Yana stumbled forward where she stood. Her wide eyes took in the disaster around her. "Mercy," she panted. "Mercy! I know you now spirit and you are a mighty one indeed. We will go and not return, just leave us in peace." She bent and gathered a few of the key items from her ceremony, stuffing them and the skull into the wide pockets of her dress. She shuffled to the door and left.

I'm not really sure how long old Phenny and I lay there, quietly trying to pull ourselves back together. My leg was still mangled from the snake's attack, so walking was out of the question for a while. Instead, I used my elbows and crawled my way over to him.

"The windows. How on earth did you do that?"

Phenex had his eyes closed but he answered in a drained and weary voice. "That old bat has a lot more power within her than she's ever known about. Thankfully for us, I was able to tap into it when I was within her. Unfortunately, I just let her know about it. So probably for the rest of her life, she'll be gunning for us with more firepower than she's ever had before."

I snorted. "I don't think we have to worry about that. I think you scared the piss out of her, jumping her meat suit like that."

The other demon shrugged. "I guess we'll have to wait and see." He coughed, his spirit dimming slightly, becoming just a touch transparent to my eyes. His energy was dangerously low. I guess his first possession had taken more out of him than we'd both expected.

Not that we'd had any choice.

Still, I filed that little tid-bit of information away in the back of my mind for future reference.

"Don't you die on me yet, you bastard," I called. "We still need to discuss the terms of my release from Hell."

Phenex rolled his eyes towards me and harrumphed. "Release? You didn't complete your job, Alastor."

I rolled on my back and let out a groan. "Did too. They're gone aren't they? I'm still within my time frame." I held up my hand in a halfhearted cheer. "Yay, victory. Now let me sleep for . . . what year is it?"

"I got them out, not you," he stated. "Sorry to say it, but you're going back to your one roomed apartment down under once I can stand, Alastor."

"True. However," I added with a grin lacing my words, "you never once stated in the rules that I couldn't get another demon to do the job for me."

"That — that wasn't — I never— We didn't—"

"And you were the one to tell them that I was a

demon. You broke your own rule, so that doesn't count."

"I— I—"

"That's how the game is played, Phenny! Check and mate, you flatulent toad!"

CHAPTER TEN

Both of us were still exhausted and sprawled across the floor when the sun started to peek through the cracked glass of the windows. I lay on my back, glaring at the overhead kitchen light as I contemplated my situation. Phenex was out cold next to me, but once his energy was replenished, I was in no shape to take him on if he chose to drag me back to Hell.

I twisted and glanced down at my injured leg. The only way to heal that would be to have another angel do it. I doubted Phenny was going to be kind enough to do it just so I could kick his arse.

Grimacing, I laid my head back down on the hard tile floor and sighed. "Right," I said to the angel in my head, "any ideas from you on how to fix this?"

To my utter horror, a voice answered me, but not the one I was expecting.

"Actually, yes."

Craning my head up, I saw Papa Legba leaning down over me. He used his cane to tip the rim of his straw hat up to me in greeting.

I think I actually screamed. Using my elbows, I tried to scurry away from the Loa.

Legba held up his hands in placation and said, "No need for that, silly one. You stay put now and let me do my magic." He reached out and grabbed my leg. My spiritual form felt an odd combination of branding iron heat and the soothing fizz of an ocean wave wrap up my leg.

Of course I tried to kick him off me. Of course it didn't work. I was down for the count and he was at full power. If he wanted, he could have smashed me like a bug then and there without a second thought.

It was only a matter of seconds before he lifted his hand from me, that odd burning and fizzing sensation leaving with him.

Shocked, I looked down to see the tear in my spiritual form mended.

Looking down at my leg and back up to him I asked, "Why?"

Legba sat back, laying his cane across his folded knees the way I'd first seen him appear. "Because I have not seen Samedi that mad in ages. He will be after you now, my friend. No doubt about that. He doesn't take kindly to having people or spirits best him. Christians and those from your pantheon, less so."

"I don't understand."

The Loa shrugged. "You are entertaining. Like a good sitcom, I want to know what will happen next. Now stop looking this gift horse in the mouth. You're going to have company in a moment. Best not to show weakness before him."

"Samedi?" I squeaked. "He's coming back?"

I pushed myself onto my feet, taking care to test my weight on the healed leg first. Panic flared through me. I was dead. I was going to be so dead if that damned, skull faced, baron came for me again. Screw it all. I was going to force Phenex to take me back to Hell rather than face that psycho again.

I grabbed for the other demon to shake him awake when the true wonder of what Legba had done to me set in. I was grabbing Phenex with my own, physical hand. Jumping back in pure shock, I looked down at myself to see not my spiritual form in the room, but my own physical body!

"Why did you—?" I spun around to face the Loa, but found no one else in the kitchen with me.

Phenex let out a groan and blinked his eyes open. He must have keyed into the new changes about me, for he made an odd sound of surprise and rolled to his feet as well. "Alastor? Is that you?"

I was shaking inside. I was terrified and exhilarated at the same time.

Sadly, there was no time for me to puzzle out this new happening. At that moment the air pressure within the house changed, as if a great power had suddenly appeared out of nowhere. A moment later it descended and the front door opened.

The angel who stepped inside was one I recognized instantly, though I'd only glimpsed him once during the war in Heaven. He wasn't someone you easily forgot; because it wasn't easy to forget the only angel your Father physically made a mistake on when creating him. When the angel turned to me, one blue eye and one green fixated on me from under narrowed brows. Of all the angels in Heaven, he was the only one ever created with mismatched eyes.

Outside of that one imperfection, he was the embodiment of angelic perfection. Taller than most angels, he came very near to having to duck under the door frame to enter the house. His blond hair was just long enough for it to be held in a half tail and he wore some kind of suit with an over vest.

"General Remiel," Phenex bowed low at his waist. "I — I wasn't expecting you here so soon."

General Remiel; one of the premiere generals of Hell who reported directly to Satan himself. And he was standing right in front of me. Great.

Remiel ignored the other demon's statement but tilted his head to him in recognition. "Phenex." He turned to me, one eyebrow lifting. "And this would be?"

"Sire, he is just a lowly demon of the bottom feeding ranks. Hardly worth your atten—"

"The name is Alastor," I declared. "Demon extraordinaire, slayer of spectral serpents, banisher of Loa and vanquisher of harpies."

Phenex glared at me.

I smirked at him and winked.

Remiel walked into the kitchen and glanced at the destruction scattered about as well as the cracked window glass. "This is the base of operations you secured for me, Phenex?"

"Yes, sire. Although there was a small, ahem, complication. But that has all been taken care of so there is no need to—"

"What complication?" The general's tone was flat, devoid of all emotion; but the tremor of a threat was hidden within it.

"Well, umm," Phenex wrung his hands with worry as he glanced at me and back to his superior. "A small, minor really, oversight on my part about filing specific papers for the home's procurement. The property fell through to a secondary buyer but I was able to rectify the matter and—"

"Hold it one minute!" I turned on the other demon, grabbing him by the hem of his robes. "You're telling me that you put me through this whole mess because you forgot to sign a stupid paper and turn it in on time?"

"Have you ever bought a home in this market? The process is insane!"

I grit my teeth. "I should throttle you for what I've had to go through the last week! You used me to clean up your mess."

"Would you have rather I left you in your hole?"

"Instead of almost being eaten by a dinosaur-snake, burned to death by a priest and kicked around this house by two Loa? Hmm, let me think. Yes!"

A sharp snap sounded behind me, akin to the sound of someone snapping their fingers. One moment I was grabbing Phenex and the next both he and I were thrown against the nearest wall; some invisible force pinning us there.

Remiel stood across the room from us. I expected him to be glaring and displeased, but to my shock, he was smirking. Stuffing his hands into the pockets of his coat, he strode slowly over to us. "Do you two think I only just arrived here? I've been watching the two of you for the last hour."

Next to me, Phenex audibly gulped.

"I understand now what has taken you so long to do your job, Phenex." He pointedly looked at me for a moment. "Nevertheless, I'm displeased with how you took care of the matter. How can you continue to be my right hand demon if you can't even perform such a simple task without incident? My future aspirations won't tolerate deviations from the plans set in place. We'll speak of your punishment later. Until then, perhaps cooling your heels inside your friend's cell in Hell will give you the fortitude and cunning I viewed him using."

"Sire, please! It was a small error. Only a—"

The general lifted his hand from his pocket and snapped his fingers again. Phenex disappeared from beside me. That sent a shiver of fear down my new physical spine. Not many angels were able to teleport other angels against their will.

"Alastor, was it?"

I rolled my eyes at him. "Oh, just get it over with,

will you? I really can't stand anyone flapping their gums at me; telling me what I did and didn't do right. I never would have left Heaven if I liked that torture. Frankly, if memory serves, that was why you lot and the new governing body of Hell threw me into the pit in first place. Rebelling is acceptable so long as I'm not rebelling against you, hmm?" I spat on the ground and scrunched my eyes closed. "I won't ask you to make my death quick. Just stop talking."

The pressure holding me against the wall eased off. I dropped to the floor, nearly falling to my knees. I looked up at the general who towered over my smaller stature like a titan.

"I could use someone with your skills," Remiel said. "How would you like Phenex's job?"

My mouth must have hit the floor and kept rolling. Perhaps the shock also shot my brain out of the room, for in that moment of stupefaction, the angel (who had been remarkably silent throughout all the drama) muscled his way forward and took control.

"It would be my honor, sire."

What are you doing? I mentally screamed at him.
You promised!
What are you talking about?
You said if I helped you, that you wouldn't sin for fifty years. Well, we survived and it's your time to pay up! So I say, we start with helping our general.
You arrogant ass!

"Good," Remiel said. "You can begin your service to me by cleaning this place up. The other generals will be here tomorrow."

Both the angel and I stalled in our argument to look at Remiel. "Other generals?'

"Phenex didn't tell you? This house was never intended to be home." He moved out into the entry. "This will be a secret gathering place for the other powers of Hell to meet and formulate our plan."

"Plan, s-sire?" The title was forced out of me by the angel. "What plan would that be?"

Remiel turned back to me, the smirk he'd been wearing spreading into a feral grin. "We're going to overthrow Lucifer and take over Hell. You are looking at your future Satan."

You moron, I told the angel, *you just sold us to someone who is going to start a civil war in Hell.*

Author's Note:

Dealing with Demons takes place 1 year before the main story in *Fallen Saint*.

When this project was first proposed to me by Kira Shay and Megan Vaughn, I was determined to challenge myself by writing a dark, demonic, haunting tale. I did my research, outlined numerous plot points to add in and was prepared to go all Steven King on this one!

Sadly, I'm one of those authors that can plot out things, but when it comes to writing, well the characters just take over and do whatever they please. That's what happened as I wrote *Dealing with Demons*. Al showed up on page one and took over at the keyboard. So, in the end, I come out of the high jacking with a comedy. Doh!

Fear not, Alastor and Remiel will appear again in *Fallen Saint.*

Dear
Diary

Dear Diary
by
Kira Shay

12/05/98

Dear Diary,

After twelve hours stuck in the backseat with
Nicholas, we finally made it. It wouldn't have been so
bad if my CD player hadn't run out of batteries halfway
through the trip. Dad wouldn't get me new ones at the
gas station either. He said I needed to spend more time
with the family and not with my music. Ugh family. I
need my own money.

The house is old, like 70's old. No one has bothered
to update it. The carpets are this mustard yellow shag
and the walls have wood panels. Mom calls it "quaint." I
call it ugly.

They gave me the room with glitter on the ceiling.
Seriously, there's glitter embedded in the popcorn
ceiling. I can only assume something tragic happened to

one of the unicorns from the movie *Legend* in here. As far as I have seen, this is the only room in the house with the stuff. This just confirms the fact that my parents still think I am five years old.

Nicholas loves it here. There were some kids playing outside that were around his age when we pulled up. The little brat didn't even help unload the truck before he went running off. Mom and Dad let him too, which meant I was stuck moving boxes on my own.

Stupid little brothers.

The only good thing is that we don't have to go to school yet. Mom says we can wait until next semester, which is cool, I guess. But if I had my way, we wouldn't have left Topeka.

Ugh. Mom's screaming for me to come down for dinner. Gotta go. I bet I get stuck with dishes again.

12/27/98

Dear Diary,
Something weird is happening in this house. Things keep moving around. I left my backpack in the living room and it somehow wound up in the garage. The cereal found its way into the oven. Mom thinks it's me and Nicholas goofing around. But Nicholas swears it isn't him. It's not me either.

I also get the feeling that something is watching me at night. I haven't slept very much in the last few days. When I do sleep, I have these horrible nightmares about a girl in a white night dress, all bloody. Her eyes are completely black.

When I wake up, I'm drenched in sweat. It's to the point where I'd rather not sleep at all.

01/07/99

Dear Diary,

Tomorrow I have to start school. Mom took me to get signed up for my classes today. The place looks like a prison. Regardless of what I think about the place, I have now officially enrolled in Trenton High School. I am (and it pains me beyond all belief to write this) a squid.

Yes, that's right. Trenton's mascot is a squid and it makes ZERO sense. New Mexico is nowhere near the ocean. Hell, there's not even a lake nearby.

Even my schedule is weird; instead of seven classes, I have four. But they last for 90 minutes. Seriously. 90 minutes in math class is going to kill me!

I talked to my best friend, Cassie today. She says everyone on the team misses me. Except for Elise. Elise is thrilled to be the new catcher this season.

For the millionth time, why did we have to move? There was nothing wrong with where we were. My life was going great! I had friends! I was doing great on the softball team! Just because Dad got offered the same job in a different town did *not* mean he had to take it.

I can't wait until I can legally make my own decisions. I would leave this place in a heartbeat. I don't even have to go back home. Anywhere else would be better than here.

01/08/99

Dear Diary,
I knew today would suck, but I didn't realize

exactly how much. The Trenton High Squids are jerks, every last one of them! Apparently, there's some sort of superstition about the house we moved into, I guess. No one at school will tell me what it is about either. They just whisper about me and try not to look at me too much.

In my first class, a girl named Lizzy introduced herself. I thought she wanted to be my friend. Instead she asked me, "Are you the cursed girl that moved into the Stanton house?"

I didn't know what to say to that. Hell, I still don't know how to react to that question. What did she mean, cursed? She was a total bitch, too! When I didn't say anything, she made some lame joke about how everyone better watch out or I'd do something horrible to them. I don't know what she was talking about. It's a really weird way to greet a new student, if you ask me. To top it all off, Lizzy started spreading around that I was cursed and dangerous. I know that because afterwards, everyone stared at me and whispered behind my back. I only caught bits, but the word I heard the most was "cursed."

I don't know what the hell is wrong with all of these people. The only way I am cursed is that my family had to move here and I have to deal with their stupid superstitious idiocy.

01/26/99

Dear Diary,
I think that Lizzy girl has made me an outcast on rumor alone. No one at school will talk to me. Well, except for this one guy, Dave. I'm not sure what his deal is yet.

Nicholas doesn't have the same problem that I do. His new friends think the house is really cool. That's where I got the story of what happened.

It took a little . . . persuasion, but I got the story about the people who used to live here. According to my little brother's friends, there was a girl about my age who was into some strange things. She swore that a ghost visited her all the time. The popular opinion was that she was just crazy. Like her meds needed to be adjusted or something. I guess her parents walked in on her doing some sort of satanic ritual one night. She went into therapy for a few months after that. When she came back, everything went back to normal.

Except it really didn't.

The boys said she ended up murdering her parents and then committed suicide in the house. In the room where the bodies were found, there was a curse written in blood.

They couldn't say what exactly the curse was, but at least now I know why everyone is avoiding me at school.

Why would Mom and Dad buy a house where not one, but three people died? It creeps me out just being here now. I wonder if this was the room she offed herself in. How horrible it must have been to have that damn glitter ceiling as your last sight.

As for the curse, I don't believe it one bit. I mean, really? The girl was obviously deranged and just because she scribbled something on a wall in blood doesn't mean she could curse someone. It just meant she was psychotic.

So how do I live down an imaginary curse from a dead girl?

03/08/99

Dear Diary,

Something crazy happened today. Everyone was out running errands today and I was left home alone.

I put my Foo Fighter's CD into the portable radio in the bathroom and started up the shower. The water heater must be on the fritz because the water went from hot to freezing in seconds, but that wasn't the crazy thing.

As I was washing my hair, there was the weird sensation that someone was watching me. Several times, I peeked my head out of the shower, but there was no one there. Then, the CD skipped forward three tracks and then back two. I thought maybe my family had come home and Nicholas was trying to annoy me, but there wasn't anyone around. So I went back to washing my hair. The feeling that someone was watching me didn't go away.

This time, the CD didn't just skip, the entire CD changed! Foo Fighters was taken out and replaced with No Doubt. I didn't even have the No Doubt CD in the bathroom!

Someone had to have been messing with me. I turned off the shower and wrapped myself in a towel. I stepped out of the tub and called out, "Who's there?"

That's when something grabbed my hand and lifted it to the mirror. Using my finger, whatever it was spelled GETOUTNOW.

I can't even tell you how badly I freaked out. My voice is still hoarse from screaming so much.

The family came home about then. I tried to explain that the place was haunted, I mean, how else would you explain what happened? Mom thinks all of this is just me acting out because I want to go back home. Well, I do want to go back home, but I'm not freaking out because of it. I wish she would just listen instead of assuming I am making this up. There is something in this house and we have to get out of here now before something terrible happens!

03/30/99

Dear Diary,
I haven't been able to sleep. Every time I try, the nightmares come. I've never felt so terrified and alone before.

Then there are the noises and the things moving in the night. At least I think they are. The shadows in my room move on their own accord and in the morning things aren't where I left them the night before. I don't have any explanation for it and I am terrified.

I've been blacking out recently too, I think. It's hard to tell. The episodes aren't very long, but I still notice the missing time. It's the weirdest feeling when you think you are in your bedroom and then the next moment, you blink and you're in the living room with no recollection of how you got there. Hours have passed, but you don't know where the time went.

Maybe the kids at school are right. Maybe I am cursed. This house isn't helping matters. Even the glitter in my ceiling is starting to look sinister.

I think I just need. . .

GETOUTNOW! GETOUTNOW! GETOUTNOW!

TOO LATE...

04/09/99

Dear Diary,

I think my brother got a hold of you and wrote all of that before. He won't admit it, but I know that he did.

I'm still not sleeping at all. The sounds at night keep me awake. It's like something is talking to me, but I just can't make out the words quite yet.

Have I mentioned that I hate this place? School is unbearable, this house is obnoxious, and I miss my friends.

The kids at school still won't talk to me unless they are openly teasing me. I don't even know about what. They say I am evil, but they don't even know me! How can they say such horrible things if they haven't even spoken to me? They avoid me like I have a disease or something. It's to the point that they stare and call out insults at me as I go past them.

The only person that makes an attempt at normal conversation is Dave. Today he held the door open for me at the end of English and he smiled at me. But I am not sure why. I hate that I suspect everyone's motives like that. But, honestly, I feel like I have to. I've seen the movie *Carrie* too many times to trust anything these people say or do.

Sometimes I dream of running away and going back to where I belong. I could make it on my own. I could get a job, a small apartment or something. The sky is the limit.

So, why am I still here?

04/28/99

Dear Diary,
Something scary happened today, but I can't
exactly say what because I don't really know what
happened. I remember sitting in class listening to Mr.
Andrews talk about the Revolutionary War and then
everything went blank. I don't know what happened.
The next thing I remember is seeing my toes inches
over the edge of the school roof and the dizzying height
of three stories up.

I froze, too terrified to move. What if I made a
wrong move? What if I fell? It looked like the whole
student body was out there watching me. Some of them
even shouted at me to jump already. I couldn't stop
trembling. The school must have called the police
because they showed up a few minutes later. How long
had I been up on the roof?

The authorities spoke at me from a bullhorn. I
couldn't understand what was happening. Firefighters
arrived shortly after and brought me down from the
roof. They kept asking me what I was thinking and why
I would do such a thing. I tried to tell them that I didn't
remember and that I wouldn't really do something like
that.

The strangest part, though, was when the EMT's
examined me, there were all these cuts on my arms and
legs. They weren't random cuts either. They looked like
words in a language I didn't understand. I have no idea
how they got there. I sure as hell didn't cut myself, but
the EMT's didn't believe me. Neither did my parents
when they came to get me.

So now I am confined to my room. My parents don't know how to handle me. Do they punish me? Do they support me? I can see the questions and the fear all over their faces.

I heard Mom on the phone. She's made an appointment with a doctor. I am scared to go (what if they lock me up in an asylum or something?), but I am more scared to not do anything at all. Dad got mad at her for making the appointment. He thinks I'm just going through a phase. Is that all this is? Does everyone go through this?

Nicholas is avoiding me. He isn't even trying to bug me like he usually does. I would be relieved if I wasn't so scared.

I don't know what is going on, but I really wish it would stop.

05/01/99

Dear Diary,
People are acting even more strange than usual. The insults from the other kids at school have stopped, even from Lizzy. Instead, they all watch me like I'm about to attack someone. You would think it was an improvement from the insults, but it isn't. I'd rather have them teasing me. This silence and fear is much, much worse than some stupid comments. Even Dave has backed off a bit. He will wave at me in the hall sometimes, but he won't come up and talk to me anymore.

Even my parents are being weird around me. I mean, I guess it is to be expected since my rooftop stunt, but it still hurts. I can almost hear my Mom counting down to the doctor's appointment. It can't come soon enough for her. Dad agrees that I need to be seen by someone.

What I can't stand is how they watch me. They look at me like I'm something other than their daughter. It makes me angry, like REALLY angry. So angry that I want to poke their eyes out so they would stop looking at me like that.

What is wrong with me?

05/06/99

Dear Diary,

I don't know how much more I can take of this! I hurt Dave today, really badly. He was trying to talk to me and walk with me to my next class. It's the first time in days that someone has spoken to me at school. I was happy. I was relieved. Maybe I wasn't so much a social leper. He touched my arm on accident. I don't know what came over me, but when that happened, I lost it.

I don't know how— my memory of the whole thing is really fuzzy—but the next thing I knew, he was on the ground and I was on top of him, my hands were around his throat. Some of the teachers pulled me off of him. Somehow in the madness, I stabbed him in the hand with a pen. I know how this sounds, but the blood fascinated me. It was all over the place. Some spatters got on me and I found myself staring at the drops, wondering what it would taste like. God, I am going insane!

I wasn't in control. I didn't want to hurt him. He was the only one that was nice to me. Why would I do such a thing? I can't stop crying about it.

My parents, my teachers, the police; all of them asked me why I did it. I don't have any idea because I can't remember exactly why it happened. All I remember is anger and this overwhelming desire to make someone suffer. There is no explanation, none that I can think of.

And now I am responsible for hurting the only person who was nice to me in this godforsaken place. I am so sorry, Dave! I am so sorry!

05/07/99

Dear Diary,
I can't take it anymore. All of these thoughts, these feelings… I hate them! I hate all of the things I've done, especially the ones that I can't remember. My family won't even talk to me anymore. They called some facility and they are on the way to come get me. I don't know what's going to happen. My parents are ashamed of me. I'm ashamed of myself.

I give up. I can't live like this anymore. I can't…

SHE'S MINE NOW

How to Deal with Death
by
Megan E. Vaughn

Chapter One: Acceptance

His lungs burned as the water blocked out all of his senses. Pinpricks traveled up his skin as he tried to focus on the slow, panicked thuds within his own chest.

Breathe.

Breathe!

Eventually, the pain vanished and he was able to once again open his eyes. Within two deep inhales and exhales, the vision of drowning left him and replaced with sunny surroundings as he stood on a wooden porch amongst a group of people. Some took photos of the heavy oak doors in front of them while some looked mildly bored as their companions 'ooed or awed at the Victorian architecture. He knew the doors in front of him and focused upon them, etched glass panes acting like friendly eyes welcoming him inside. He hadn't been there since elementary school when he'd convinced Kiki Gold that there was a ghost touching her shoulder.

The door opened and a woman dressed in a cheap replica of a nineteenth century servants' clothes greeted them. She couldn't have been more than twenty-two, yet her eyes illustrated a strict no-nonsense attitude that went beyond her age. "Welcome everyone to the Van Sloan house, the oldest house still standing in downtown and reportedly one of the top five most haunted houses in America."

At the word haunted several members of the group made silly faces at one another.

"I'm Daphne and I'll be your guide today. Before we get started and enter the house, there are a few ground rules to cover. Please, no using your flashes in the rooms with the curtains drawn. These rooms have light sensitive items and we would like to keep them preserved. Second, please stay on the carpets and rugs. Do not walk on the wood floor itself. Also, please only touch the items I pass around to you. Again, everything in the house in very fragile and many of the rooms are decorated with items belonging to the original Van Sloan family which they have graciously loaned out to us.

"Lastly, I know many of you have questions about the ghosts. Please hold them until we reach the garden at the end of the tour." Despite her stern eyes, each word flowed from her with pleasantness and cheer. "Are there any questions before we get started?"

He raised his hand. "Yeah. Any idea how I got here?"

"No?" she said after looking directly at him. "Then let's begin. Now, this house was built by Martin Van Sloan in 1877. Van Sloan was a great business man who opened the first large department store in this area. As his business grew, he decided to have this home built for his wife. He was very interested in politics so he bought land just down the road from the courthouse and city hall. He also started a trend of the upper class setting their backyards and carriage houses right alongside the banks of the river."

She pointed down the road to a whitewashed wooden relic with steep steps leading to a high door. Then she waved another hand in the direction of the river winding around the edges of the city. A couple of people in the group took pictures of the carriage house automatically, without even really listening to what it was.

"Within a few years the couple gave birth to two children, Marilyn born in 1882 and Martin Junior three years later. The house itself became a central hub for societal life here in downtown. Mrs. Petunia Van Sloan was the head of several committees and funded a great deal of charity work. Anyone who was anyone frequented the Van Sloan house."

Daphne stepped to one side and offered for the group to file into the front hall. He followed obediently, nearly bumping into an overweight man slowing trudging alongside. "Sorry," he muttered. The man did not answer.

The guide shut the door and pointed at the rooms around them. "You are now within the downstairs hallway. To your left is the door to the dining room and to your right, beside the staircase is the front parlor. This was the room where Mrs. Van Sloan entertained guests." She ushered them into the room. The parlor was fairly standard for a Victorian house. Fireplace with screen. Faded red sofa and two matching chairs. A round table at the center from which tea could be served. Only one item seemed out of place: a bisque faced doll had been haphazardly left on the floor in front of the piano.

"Now in 1922, when a grown up Martin Jr. sold the house to a banker named Byrons for $12,000 dollars, the new lady of house used this room to throw lavish parties." Daphne continued her teachings, not paying any mind to the one discombobulated tourist slowly realizing he didn't remember how he'd come to the old house.

"Miss, I think I'm supposed to be somewhere..." He trailed off as his thoughts escaped him.

Still, the tour guide ignored him.

"As this was during prohibition, Mrs. Byrons was very nervous about the fact that City Hall was within walking distance of the house, even though many of her party guests were politicians."

Daphne lifted up a floor board at the center of the room. "Convinced that someday the city's top judge would bust up one of her parties, Mrs. Byrons had this trap door put in. If there ever were a raid her guests could simply toss all of their alcohol into the cellar. She was not the most practical of women; she never thought to put anything in the cellar to catch the bottles and glasses. We are still cleaning up glass down there from one of her more paranoid moments. More on Mrs. Byrons later."

The adults chuckled at the tale, thinking of how silly prohibition was. A little boy at the front of group interrupted the jovial moment by pointing at the misplaced object on the floor. "Why is there a doll in here?"

"That—" Daphne glanced down in surprise at the toy and scooped it up, "actually isn't supposed to be in here. Children usually weren't allowed in this room as it was for company." She set the doll upon one of the chairs. "This doll is one of the few toys we have which we know belonged to the Van Sloan children. In 1889, Marilyn came down with scarlet fever. She fought off the disease for much of her short life until finally passing away in 1894. She was only twelve years old and her death was devastating for her parents."

"I hate how she always says finally as if I should have given up sooner. You really have no tact, Daphne."

He turned towards the source of the girl's voice, finding a thin child of twelve standing behind him in the parlor doorway. She wore a white pinafore over a gingham dress with long puffed sleeves. A black ribbon kept the sides of her brown hair swept from her face.

She grinned at him. "Hello there. What's your name?"

"Ned," he whispered with uncertainty. He glanced over at the tour guide to see if she would scold them for talking over her.

"How do you do, Ned?" The girl peered around him at the group of people. "You know, you don't have to whisper. They can't hear us."

He glanced again at the tour guide, then back to the girl. She did not seem too concerned with his confusion.

"You must be the man whose car flipped into the river yesterday. You have my sympathy."

"You. . . What? My car didn't—" Ned's brain flooded with images of headlights coming at him, his foot pumping the brake pedal, squealing tires, crashes of waves against glass, and the feel of the steering wheel flying through his fingers in the opposite direction he had wanted to travel in. Without another word to the girl, he broke the "stay on the carpet" rule in order to edge around the tourists. He faced Daphne and waved a hand at her. "Miss? There's some kid back here and she's. . . Look, I don't know if she's part of your staff, but I don't like these kinds of jokes."

Daphne ignored him once again and told the group to take a moment to look at the room while she passed around a stereopticon they could take turns squinting through. The overweight tourist Ned had almost bumped into bounded towards the fireplace, yelling to his wife to get a picture of him with the "booze hole" in the floor. His sandal clad foot stepped down directly through Ned's tennis shoe. Ned jumped back, fell through a chair, and onto the floor.

"Don't worry. I'll help you," the girl called and crossed through two women in order to reach him. One of the women shivered while the other hadn't even noticed. She pulled on Ned's arm and brought him back to his feet. "You need to focus on having a body. I mean, you don't really have one anymore, but if you pretend you have some weight it'll keep you from floating or sinking."

He barely listened to her as he wildly reinspected the room. "Why can't they hear me?"

"I told you; you're dead, you silly goose." She adjusted the ribbon at the back of her head distractedly as she asked, "What did you say your name was?"

Still stunned, he heard himself say "Ned" as if on autopilot.

"Dead Ned. That's funny." She did not giggle at her own joke, only offered him a pitying smile. After flicking a banana curl over her shoulder, she held out a hand to him once more. "Come on, I'll show you around the house. I promise to do a much better job than Daphne." As if the living tour guide could hear them, she added in an exaggerated whisper, "She's new."

Ned felt his head nod while his thoughts begged to be awoken. The word "dead" stayed trapped in a reality just beyond his reach.

The girl motioned for him to follow her back into the front entrance and pointed at the hat rack beside the door. "You know this isn't from my day. That awful Mrs. Byrons thought it looked quaint and vintage. She put it here." The girl spoke with distaste and realized she had gone off track. "Sorry, I should be telling you about the porch, but I—"

Her eyes fell upon his slack jaw. He watched her short fingers grace his arm. He felt nothing. "Hey. It's okay. Everything is going to be alright."

Ned's shoulders tensed. "How? You just told me that I'm dead."

"Exactly. The hard part is over. Now you just get to sit back and enjoy the show."

"Wait, wait. Shouldn't I be getting a moment to freak out or something?" Ned had never been the sort to panic. He believed in assessing the situation first and dealing with the anxiety later. He assumed this was a dream. It had to be dream. What was proper reaction to finding out you were dead within a dream?

"Why? That sounds like a waste of energy. Honestly, as long as you're with me you'll be just fine."

"What does that mean?" he muttered without expecting an answer.

"Come on. I want to tell you about—"

The girl was interrupted by Daphne bringing the tour group back into the hallway. She rolled her eyes as the young woman further told the information starved tourists about the Van Sloan family. "After Marilyn died the family did continue to live in the house. Their son married and moved to San Diego after serving in World War I. After a couple of years, Mrs. Van Sloan passed away and Mr. Van Sloan moved to San Diego to live with his son's family."

Ned chased after the group, giving a quick look back at the little girl. She was mimicking Daphne as the woman recited facts.

"There were about three years in which the house lay empty between Mr. Van Sloan leaving and the younger Martin selling the property to the Byrons."

Ned followed Daphne, waving a hand at her

frantically and screaming, "Can you hear me?" at the top of his lungs. Daphne pointed to the next room the tour group was about to enter. Her hand cut into Ned's chest and out the other side. He stumbled away from the offensive living limb and rubbed at his tee shirt, absent mindedly checking for damage.

Marilyn nudged him into the dining room gently. "If you need to shout, go ahead. It won't bother most of them. C'mon."

He stared at the girl desperate for answers, however, still followed obediently as Daphne went on with her facts, un-phased by the presence of the two entities.

"Despite this, the family did leave a number of furniture pieces for the new owners including the table, china hutch, and sidebar you are about to see in the next room. These pieces were very important to the Van Sloan household in that Mrs. Van Sloan wrote in her diary that she had purchased them from the estate of an earl in England who once hosted a dinner party for Queen Victoria herself upon that very table."

The child giggled outright. "Are they still falling for that one? When is someone going to do their homework and realize that Mama made that up?"

Ned's shock fell away briefly. "She did?"

"Of course. She inherited that furniture from her maiden aunt, who was Swedish by the way. Mama just liked to tell stories that would one up the women in her sewing circle."

Ned's head whipped back and forth between the tour guide and child. "Okay, not to be rude. . . but what the hell does any of this have to do with me?"

The girl clicked the heels of her black, button-up shoes once. "I think you need some time away from the living. Let's try to avoid Dolt Daphne for a little bit. Why don't I take you upstairs and introduce you to everyone? It will give you some time to calm down. Mama knows you're coming."

"Mama?" Her words slowly sunk in as Ned trailed after the girl up the stairs. He remembered those stairs creaking when he toured the house as boy. Now they stayed silent. Pausing on a step, he shifted his weight back and forth, willing for the obnoxious sound to come.

"Oh, forgive me. I just assumed you figured out who I was. I'm Marilyn Van Sloan." The girl watched him attempt to make the stair squeak, realizing she did not have his full attention.

His feet pounded against the carpeted wood and he squeezed his eyes shut. At last, a small squeal came from the old board underneath him. Ned released a satisfied and relieved breath. Ghosts can't jump on stairs. Ghosts can't sigh.

"You were remembering something," Marilyn commented. "You've been here before? Let me guess, school group?"

He nodded, opening his eyes. With new determination, he told her, "This is a dream."

A shadow crossed her face and another pitying half smile caused her brow to crease. "Come along. I'll take to you to meet Mama first."

The upstairs started as a sunny, quaint hallway which split off to a second, more shadowy hallway halfway down. All of the doors stayed open, ready for the trains of tourists to traipse through. A long ornate rug ran from the top of the stairs all the way towards the other end and had been covered with protective plastic. Ned recalled once trying to shift his weight on the plastic in order to watch the fiber of the carper change direction under his feet. The tour guide from when he was a kid must have just adored him.

Marilyn clicked her heels together again, but the

patent leather made no sound. She pointed at doors in a rapid motion and listed labels: "Way down there is my room. Marty's room. Guest room. Down that hall was mine and Marty's playroom. The stairs to the attic are down there as well. This is Mama and Papas room, later Irma's room." She started for the door closest to their left.

"Who's Irma?" Ned followed her obediently, but his eyes continued to wander, trying to pick up on other small details he remembered from his last visit to the house. The more which came to mind, the more he convinced himself that he would wake up soon.

"My friend. You'll meet her later."

The master bedroom was furnished with a mix of Victorian and Art Deco designs, the result of former owners leaving behind their possessions. The clash between the gaudy, paisley cushions and the geometric glass lamps revealed how desperate the museum was for any kind of antique. The headboard of the wide, short bed was a heavy oak that formed a triangle above the pillows. Small tables on either side of the bed held various little trinkets to give the illusion that someone still lived there.

A vanity with a marred looking glass faced the bed against one wall. Old powder boxes and beauty supplies covered the tabletop. A plastic box with a hole in the top sat at one corner of the table which Ned remembered as being a hair catcher. Women would keep the hair they cleaned out of their brushes to weave into arts and crafts projects. It was one of those things that grossed out all of the little girls he went to school with, so of course he remembered. The thought passed swiftly and he tried to focus on keeping his chest rising and falling. If he could keep breathing, everything would be okay.

Three windows along one wall gave the room such a cheerful feeling that Ned almost missed the woman in the rocker sitting beside them. Her face focused on him. She was pretty, somewhere in her early thirties, with her hair swept up into the loose bun which he'd seen models wear in Victorian ads for soda. A sewing basket sat upon her cinched lap, occasionally colliding with the embroidery hoop between her fingers. She wore a plain, yet clearly expensive, high-collared dress. The dress managed to show off her figure while still giving her the air of a wife and mother.

Marilyn grabbed his hand in hers for a brief second to keep him from walking too far into the room without invitation. He had he slightest sensation of cold pressure against his palm. "I felt that!"

"Well, yes. You're settling in." The child turned to the well-dressed lady. "This is the lady of the house, my mother." She then leaned to him and whispered, "Be as respectful as you can be. She'll be impressed."

The woman motioned for him to enter. Marilyn skipped over and hovered beside the rocker with a beam. Ned stood awkwardly less than a foot away and continued to breathe too heavily. Despite having convinced himself this was a dream situation, Ned instinctively thrust out a hand to the woman. Her warm smile resembled that of her daughter as she accepted his fingers within hers. Another uncomfortable cold sensation ran up his arm and the exaggerated movement of his chest slowed.

"Mama, this is Ned. He's new," Marilyn explained as she sat down at her mother's side.

"A pleasure, Ned. Welcome to my home. I am Petunia Van Sloan. Make yourself comfortable and consider this your home as well now." She set the embroidery hoop down atop the basket to show him that she could not be distracted.

He stared, rudely and plainly, trying to will himself to see out of the window behind her. He thought of turning and running down the stairs until he was back on the street outside of the house. He remembered a photo he'd seen of Mrs. Van Sloan when he'd taken the tour as a kid. The picture must have worked its way into his dream for she looked exactly as he'd remembered it.

The moment was broken by Daphne and the tour group entering the room. Mrs. Van Sloan shook her head slightly as if the young guide's mere presence were a horrible inconvenience. Marilyn set her hand on her mother's shoulder and asked, "Can you see them today, Mama?"

Mrs. Van Sloan haughtily returned to her needlepoint. "Of course, I can see them, Marilyn. Why wouldn't I see them?" In a lower tone she murmured. "Does she think I wouldn't notice complete strangers trouncing through my home. It's disgraceful."

Marilyn glanced at Ned, giving him a silent, pleading look followed by a half shrug. He recalled a similar look from his buddy when an embarrassing aunt showed up at their anatomy class "for a surprise visit".

"Here we are in the master bedroom," Daphne explained as the people clicked away on cameras. "This bed was purchased from Mr. Van Sloan's own store after Mrs. Van Sloan had seen a similar model from the Selfridge Catalog, one of the most successful department stores in England. This bed became one of the most popular pieces of furniture sold through Van Sloan's store across the West. It mixed the elegance of Europe with the sturdiness of Van Sloan's own woodworking company found right here in this town."

Mrs. Van Sloan sat forward in her chair and allowed her needlework to slip off her lap. "Martin found the woodworking company? Why, I like that. It was my idea to use the Clarke Woodshop. I discovered them while out walking with Mildred. You remember,

Marilyn?"

"Yes, Mama. But Daphne always gets that wrong. Remember?"

"Judy manages to remember. What is the matter with this young woman that she can't seem to give me some credit for the good I did for my husband's business?"

"Mama, she doesn't—"

"I was a suffragette, for pity's sake. I helped your father with his business to the point that I was considered a partner in his firm. Does this young nit ever remember anything about me beyond what I bought?"

"She always remembers the public feud you and Mildred had that time in front of the courthouse about what school Marty should go to," Marilyn stated, then realized a moment later that she was not helping. "Mama, can't you just ignore Daphne, just this once? She's a silly girl who can barely remember to button her blouse before she leaves the staff room. You shouldn't focus too much on what she says."

The damage had already been done. Mrs. Van Sloan melted into her chair, tears forming in her eyes. Her face darkened and the lines of her years began to deepen. "Is this how I'm to be remembered? Just some ninny housewife who spent her days shopping and arguing?"

"Oh, Mama, please, don't take it so hard—" Marilyn started, but her mother's crying cut her off.

"No. No. This all that is left of me. Marilyn is dead. Marty is always away. All I have left are my memories of my younger days." The gray in her hair lightened. Within seconds, the vibrant young woman turned into a bitterly frowning old woman.

Ned took a step away, nearly running into the same overweight tourist from earlier. "What's happening to her?" he asked in alarm.

"She's having a bad day," Marilyn stated quickly as she wrapped one arm around her mother's shoulders. "Mama, you need to stop taking it so hard. You're here with me, remember? You aren't alone. Papa and Marty are long gone, but I'm here, Mama. We still have the house."

"Yes, the house," the older Mrs. Van Sloan sneered. "The house which is being ransacked daily by these disrespectful oglers!" She pointed a wrinkled finger at Daphne who continued to prattle innocently. "Your father never stood for behavior such as this, Marilyn. Especially not to have that girl upset me like this week after week."

Ned turned his attention to the tourists. One woman within the tour group and the young boy both shivered a little, as if they could sense Mrs. Van Sloan's dark mood. The sight of the boy rubbing his arms brought Ned out of his stupor. Dream or not, he needed to be useful.

He knelt down by the rocker. "Mrs. Van Sloan? Mrs. Van Sloan, are you listening to me?"

"What?" She glanced down at him, having forgotten his presence a moment earlier. "Who are you?"

"I'm Ned. We met a second ago. Mrs. Van Sloan, I think you need to take a deep breath and calm yourself down."

"Don't you tell me what to do, young man. I have a right to be upset in my own home!"

"Yes, you do. But you're also upsetting the kids." He pointed at the little boy. Petunia Van Sloan's face softened instantly. She did not go back to her youthful beauty, but the angry lines resembled more of a kindly grandmother as she focused on the child.

She then smiled up at her daughter with embarrassed roses in her cheeks. "I am sorry, darling.

But I do wish Judy would fire that girl already. If she worked in this house when I was alive, I can tell you she would have been out on her ear within the first week without references."

Marilyn offered a relieved expression to Ned as she answered, "Yes, Mama. Will you be alright while I show him the rest of the house?"

Petunia Van Sloan looked one last time at Ned, again appearing to have forgotten him. "Awe! Yes, of course. You two go enjoy yourselves." The soft skin of youth melted back into her features, her hair darkening and spine straightening. "I must get back to my sewing anyway. Lovely to meet you—"

"Ned," he offered. "It's Ned."

They entered the hallway, leaving Mrs. Van Sloan to her embroidery. Marilyn did not give Ned words of gratitude, but her eyes shined at him now with childish hero worship. Within seconds, the look was gone and she went back to being the proper hostess. "Well, I suppose you should be introduced to Byrons next, but I know you won't thank me for it."

They crossed into the room at the opposite side of the hallway. Although sunlight filled the room just as it had in the hallway, Ned felt strangely stifled as he entered. A shorter version of the same wooden headboard he'd seen in the master bedroom drew attention to the center where a man in a wrinkled, sweat stained suit lay sprawled.

The balding head barely lifted as they came in. "Oh. The child. Go away, girl."

"You know that's not how this works," she stated smugly. "I go where I please."

"And I don't?" he scoffed. "I could leave this room any time I chose. . . if I chose to."

The girl's nostrils flared. Ned thought he saw one of the heavy curtains flutter in response to her anger.

"You leave this room and upset my mother again and I will toss you into the garden myself!"

The sweaty man sat up, bleary eyes reacting to the light as though they had just flung open a window. "You don't have the strength!"

"Dare me!"

The man relaxed his shoulders slightly and shrugged. "No. I already know what you'd do. You'd try to make that pathetic soldier and your brainwashed friend drag me out. You'd never go near that garden."

Marilyn looked ready to make a rather loud comeback, but the man turned his squinted gaze to Ned. "I think that one can see us," he grumbled hardheartedly.

"He's not alive, you numbskull. He's a new resident. Ned, this is Mr. Byrons. You don't have to be polite if you do not wish."

Ned almost laughed at her annoyance. "Um. . . hi."

Byrons sniffed at him. "How?"

"How?" Ned repeated the word with a stammer. The more he stared at Byrons the more he felt himself squirm.

"Yes, old sport. How did you get done in? Killed in the alley down the road? Shot by a jealous girlfriend? How?"

"That's his business, Byrons," Marilyn insisted with a shocked tone.

Ned found himself mimicking the actions of the living boy in the tour group, his feet desperate to turn back towards the door to the open air of the hallway. Byrons's bloodshot eyes challenged him and he stayed put. This was his dream. He could play along until he woke up. "It's okay. Um. . . Car accident, I think."

"Dull." Byrons grunted as he swung his legs over the side of the bed. He waved his hand to the empty bedside table. "I tried taking poison, but it was a very slow, painful process."

"Poison mixed with a whole bottle of gin," Marilyn corrected. "He didn't have enough poison to kill rat. He made the most awful sounds all night after he took it though."

"I shot myself in the end," Byrons stated almost proudly.

Ned knew who this was now. Byrons was the banker who owned the house after the Van Sloan's, the same one whose wife built the booze disposal hatch in the parlor floor. He'd lost everything in the stock market crash, his wife already having left him directly before that due to a gambling problem. Fearing his debts to a series of unsavory characters, the man took his own life. Ned had never been good at history, but this story was burned into his brain.

Byrons's death was the one every school child who passed through the house always remembered. Morbid curiosity and the horrifying thought of someone committing suicide in a room you were currently standing in made every little girl shudder and every little boy awe. "Yes. I know," Ned said, not sure of how else to respond.

"Yes. You've been on the tour, I'm sure. But what I'm sure they did not tell you was that I was not found for three days! What do you think of that?"

"I think you would've smelled pretty bad by then. The average human body starts to lose rigor mortis and tissue with decay within seventy-two hours of death. Fluid will actually form a methane gas that comes out of the lungs through the nose and the—"

"You're a rude little bastard, aren't you? Suggesting that I smelled. I am telling you the story of my death! Show some compassion."

Marilyn was giggling happily by then. "Why should he pay you courtesies you never pay to anyone else?"

Byrons turned the full force of his anger upon her. "What do you know of it, you little bitch?"

"Hey!" Ned lost his words beyond his one syllable protest. It amazed him that someone from the golden past would use that sort of language around a child.

The word did not phase Marilyn who rolled her eyes and set her hands on her hips. "Just for that, the tour group is not coming in here."

The drunkard's face fell. "What?"

Without a word or motion from Marilyn, the guest room door swung shut just as Daphne and her followers crossed the hall. "That was weird," they could hear the young woman say through wood. "Must be a draft. These old houses, you know. . . "

The brass handle jiggled and wiggled violently for nearly a minute. Daphne's flustered voice spoke up again as the murmurs of questioning tourists started to grow louder. "It must be jammed. Sorry, folks. I guess we'll have to skip this room for now. I'll talk to the custodian about it when we're back downstairs."

There were one or two disappointed groans from the people who must have been looking forward to going into the "suicide room". As the shuffling of feet echoed away and Daphne jumped back into her memorized speeches, Marilyn gave Byrons a smug smile.

"No audience today," she said with a wiggle of her fingers at him. She turned and walked directly through the wooden door, leaving Ned staring at the angry Byrons.

The man on the bed started to throw a tantrum. He growled and snorted while tugging at his shirt. He mussed what little hair he had and pounded his fists against the bed. A pillow shifted slightly without him touching it.

Ned backed towards the door, trying to follow the

girl and muttering, "Nice to meet you, I think." His hand collided with the wood.

On the other side of the door he heard Marilyn humming. She paused her tune in order to call to him. "Can't you get out?"

"The door is shut," he answered as he watched Byrons's face darken to a shade of crimson.

"So? Imagine that it isn't shut. You don't have a body anymore. Doors can't stop you."

"Oh yeah, then what's stopping the hot head in here from following me?" he hissed angrily as the room's stiffing atmosphere started to swallow him.

"Me. Now come along. You have more people to meet."

Ned started to press his hand against the door once more. Still solid. He heard the girl repeat, "Come on." With both eyes shut, he stepped towards the door, thinking only of the hallway. A heavy wave crashed against him then subsided. He opened his eyes again when he heard the girl say happily, "See? It's easy."

"Right." Ned took three steady breaths, realizing for the first time that he did not feel any tickle of air against his lips. "Just breaking every law of physics. No big deal."

Marilyn twisted her torso so her petticoats fluffed around her calves. "Be glad. That is Byrons's good behavior. He likes to make Private Sterns cry."

"Who's Private Sterns?"

Marilyn pointed over her head. "You'll meet him later. First, we need to talk to Irma."

Falling in compliantly behind the girl, the two of them traveled down the hall to a room which had been made to look like a Victorian nursery. Crisp, white linens adorned a brass bed. Old toys had been strategically set about, looking more like a museum than a playroom.

A slender woman in her sixties was rushing around, her hands outstretched in front of her with an anxious twitching. She wore an outfit which was smart, nevertheless semi-casual; a pencil skirt and button-up blouse. Her complexion was a darker hue reminding Ned of the Greek student at his university. Her chocolate brown hair was pulled up in a high ponytail whipping back and forth as she bounced around the room. Strands of silver managed to catch the sunlight, revealing more of her age.

The woman excitedly turned to Marilyn. "Good. You're just in time. Daphne is doing the tour today. What shall we do to her? I was thinking of shifting the dolls, maybe making them tremor ever so slightly? Make her think she's seeing things—"

Marilyn glanced at Ned with shame. "Sorry, she gets excited about our little pranks." She then turned to the woman and grabbed her hands. "Irma, we have a new resident. This is Ned."

Irma instantly lost her childish zeal. Her expression stayed friendly and warm as she extended a mature handshake to him. "Welcome, Ned. I'm Irma."

"Irma's adopted father owned the house during the second Great—" A quick look from her friend cause Marilyn to correct herself. "Second World War. She grew up here."

Ned's brain searched what few things he knew of the house's history, grasping at how this woman had been produced as part of his dream. "Your dad was the German doctor. The one who rescued all of those Jewish refugees."

"That's right!" Irma's face lit up. "He rescued nearly two dozen people, including me. No one ever remembers that. All they ever care about is Byrons and his pathetic, selfish end."

Not sure how to explain why that detail stood out

in his mind, Ned shook her hand one last time and released. He awkwardly tapped his thigh and wondered where the conversation was supposed to go from there. "You lived here till you. . . " He tapered off, suddenly wondering if the word "died" was insensitive after seeing Byron's reaction.

Irma gave Marilyn a secret sideways glance, the sort of look shared between two old friends. Again, Ned saw the child-like excitement hidden in Irma's eyes. "Till I passed away? You can say it. Yeah. I lived here with my father and then my husband and this is where I died." She moved her hand around the playroom and did a little jump. "And this is where we are going to make our stand against that feather-brain, Daphne and those tourists. Are you with us, Ned?"

Marilyn giggled and ran to an edge of the room, her hands hovering upon two dolls. Her giggle was sweet and eerie at the same time, a sound from the past desperate to live on. "Very well, Irma. I'm ready."

Irma waved her hand at Ned expectantly. "What do you say, Ned? Ready to stretch those ghostly muscles?"

He looked at Marilyn's expression lighting up the room. He herded the tour group coming down the hall, the young guide's voice dripping with fake cheerfulness. What could it hurt? This was all a dream. "Okay, what do you want me to do?"

"Most excellent!" Irma positioned him at the small tea table. She squatted him down at eye level with the painted porcelain cups. "Set both hands on the edge."

He did as she said, his hands passing through the rounded edge of the wood. Ned released a frustrated sigh. Marilyn bounced slightly on the bed, making the springs squeak. "Concentrate, Ned."

Narrowing his eyes at the table, Ned tried to imagine the feel of the cherry wood and the rattle of the china as he applied pressure. Still, his hands faded through the table. Irma stayed nearby, hovering over him with an encouraging whisper. "You heard her, Ned. Just concentrate. Pretend. That's all this is. It's all pretend."

"What? Pretend I'm alive again?" The thought seemed extremely strange. After all, who played pretend in a dream?

"If that's what it takes. You want to be in control. It's all in your mind. That's all this is. That's all we are. We're make-believe." She set one of her own hands on the table and a vibration ran through the toy dishes. The gentle tinkling seemed like a mighty roar and Ned desperately wanted to make that sound through physical means.

She edged away to give him space, retreating to a corner of the room where a teddy bear and a red haired rag doll kept their fabric hands crossed together.

Ned flexed his fingers, thinking of something else to concentrate upon. He started to list the bones in his hands under his breath, starting at the distal phalanges and ending at the carpals. After that, he moved onto the names of the muscles, imagining each of them flexing as he joints gripped the edge of the table. He imagined it all, the smooth texture of the finished wood and the warmth of the sunlight streaming through the window to cast rays upon the china's painted pink flowers.

Daphne entered with her group in tow. "This is the nursery. When the two Van Sloan children were older, this was turned into a playroom. Later, when the house was used as a World War I hospital, this tiny room held up to seven cots for wounded shoulders."

"It was four cots and they put an iron lung," Marilyn corrected even though she knew the woman could not hear her. She pointed down at a faded pair of wheel tracks partially hidden by a rug. "See. They ruined the floor."

"Focus, Marilyn. We have the tourists' attention. We just need for Daphne to turn around." Irma watched the tour guide who walked backwards into the room. Her followers shuffled in, each one barely mindful of the person in front or beside them. Their eyes darted around the room, the women enjoying the pinks and frills. The men only peered around, mildly interested and awaiting the next room.

As Daphne spoke, Marilyn began to bounce a little in order to give the room a gentle squeak. She wiggled the toys atop the bed. The boy from earlier pulled at his mom's sleeve. "Did you see that?" he started to whisper, but the woman shushed him as she continued to listen to Daphne.

Irma shook the teddy bear and doll, causing them to topple. A man with an oversized camera jumped slightly and Daphne faltered mid-sentence in order to turn and look. She then picked up again with several stutters, having forgotten what she'd been saying.

Ned continued to whisper the parts of his hand to himself, watching his joints tense. He gripped the table and shoved it three times.

A couple of people in the group took a step back. Daphne stumbled on the hem of her dress. With a recovered smile, she turned to the crowd. "Happens all of the time, folks. Old houses tend to settle. So. . . let's move on to the next room."

The group vacated swiftly, the tour guide being the last to go. She gave one final, disgusted look about the room and gave a decisive shake of her head. Marilyn hopped up and started to dance around. Irma let out an unlady-like whoop. It was so small, but to the girl and the woman it had become a triumph. They had once again left their mark on the living and made their presence known.

When the celebration ended, Marilyn took Ned's

hand and dragged him up to the third level of the house. He yelled a goodbye to Irma, still caught up in the moment and forgetting his internal mantra that it was all a dream.

As they walked, she explained, "You and Irma can talk more later. We have the tour to continue. During the Great War, this place became a back-up for the hospital down the road, just like Daphne was saying. Many men passed on in the house at that time."

"Your mom must not have liked all of those gurneys and equipment being moved through her house," Ned realized aloud.

"Mysteriously, the doctors could not open the main bedroom door the entire time they were here," Marilyn answered with a giggle. "Anyway, of all of the men who passed away, Private Sterns is still here. He's a very nice young man."

The attic was full of wires and broken furniture. At one end of the space, under a low beam was a broken cot. A man lay very still in the darkness with a magazine across his lap. He sat up slowly, grunting as he greeted his visitors.

"Good day, Private Sterns," Marilyn said with a quick smile. "How is the leg?"

A faded green tank top clung to the young man's thin frame. A coarse blanket covered one of his legs while the other bandaged limb lay exposed. He pulled at a leather cord, the string going taut against the skin of his neck. At the end of the cord hung an aluminum disk stamped with the name Sterns and series of numbers. Ned could tell the man was younger than him, perhaps seventeen or eighteen years old.

Marilyn ran her fingers across the air, motioning to the edge of the white cloth surrounding his injury. Sterns looked pleased, nevertheless worn as he answered her. "Much, much better. I think they'll send me home soon."

"That's wonderful. I'm sure they shall." Marilyn pulled Ned over to the bedside. She held up their clasped hands. "Ned, this is Private Sterns. Private Sterns, this is my new friend, Ned."

The soldier held out his hand, dropping the dog tags against his chest. "Nice to meet you. Where do you hail from?"The sight of the injured ghost allowed dread to creep back into the edges of Ned's mind. He focused hard on the previous sense of joy and tried to think of ways to wake himself up. "My family lives in a fly over state. I moved out here for college," Ned answered. "What about you? Where's home?"

The light in the man's eyes instantly dimmed. "Where?" The question seemed foreign.

The little girl quickly changed topics, her voice soft and upbeat. "Never mind, private. Maybe you better get some rest. They'll never send you home if you don't heal."

Ned pointed at the leg. "That happen recently?"

The private sheepishly grunted and moved the blanket a little further. For the first time Ned noticed that below the knee, the bandage tapered off. The young man's left foot had been left somewhere far away and long ago. "One last battle on the day before I was supposed to ship out; I got hit by some shrapnel. Doctors did their best, but couldn't save the foot." He shrugged and added, "Got off easy, honestly. Most boys saw much worse. Did you serve?"

"Serve?" Marilyn nudged Ned and he added, "Uh, no. I was. . . wasn't selected."

"Waiting to be drafted, huh? I wish I had done that. I volunteered. Couldn't wait. Me and my bud. . ." Suddenly, Sterns's face fogged over. He stared down at the place where a foot should have been for a long while and started to repeat the word "buddy" under his breath. His shoulders tensed. After a full minute, his breath quickened. "Where am I? What is this place?"

Marilyn set her hand on his shoulder and started to rub as if he were the child, not her. "Shh. It's alright, private. You're safe. You'll be home soon. Why don't you rest for a bit? The doctors will be in later."

"Doctors?" he repeated.

"Yes. You've been ill and in pain. But it won't last forever. Remember?" The young man's quiet panic echoed through the attic like an overwhelming haze. His behavior did not phase Marilyn.

The soldier rubbed at his head and pulled again at his dog tags. At last, he laid his head down upon the cot and snuffled to cover a sob. Marilyn continued to rub his back for several minutes then slowly backed away when she decided he was calm.

With a finger upon her lips, she motioned for Ned to follow her downstairs. When they were back upon the second floor, she chewed on her lip. "Sorry. He's not always like that."

"What was wrong with him? Doesn't he remember that he lost is leg?" Ned could hear the callousness of his own voice. He did not have the energy to hide how the soldier's muttering still ran through his ears.

"The private forgets sometimes that he's dead." She brightened. "Most of the time, he's very hopeful. We like to play checkers."

"Did he die of the wound?" Ned though back to old medicine and mistakes that were made.

"Not exactly. Infection. It wasn't treated in time. He doesn't remember everything about his life anymore. He's too far from anything he knew and I'm sure the head injury he had before he died didn't help any." She paused, her nose going up into the air like a bloodhound. "Do you know what time it is?"

He didn't hear her. The scream of car tires and the

cold of the river shocked Ned's senses once again. He sat on the floor, his arms flung across his knees. Every bone in his body seemed far away. The darkness settled heavily on his mind. "I am dead, aren't I?"

Marilyn stood next to him with her toes pointed at his limp legs. "Yes. I told you were."

"But I'm young. I am–was a careful driver. How did this happen?"

"Things just happen. I know it's hard at first, I was young too."

Guilt outweighed his shock as Ned look at the girl as she bashfully folded her hands in front of her apron. "I. . . I'm sorry. I. . . just—"

"You can cry if you need to. Most people do at first." She held out her arms like a doll. "Or I can give you a hug if that will help?"

The clouds lifted in his mind enough for him to appreciate the girl's efforts. "No. No, I'm going to be alright...I just. . . What now?"

She pulled him back to his feet. "The best thing to do is stay busy. You can be part of my routine for a while."

"You have a routine?"

"Most ghosts do. Except Byrons."

Glancing back at the stairs, Ned realized he wanted to be like the little girl. She preoccupied her own mind with taking care of everyone else in the house and no one really seemed to worry about her. Still, the panic of the soldier sat in his chest. "Is that going to happen to me? Am I going to forget myself?" Ned stopped in his tracks, the hallway stretching out in front of him like a death row mile.

The girl flipped her hair and tried to keep the same upbeat voice she'd used with the World War I soldier. "I don't know. Depends, I guess. Our memories are just like the living people's memories. You have to keep reminding yourself and searching your mind in order to keep them fresh. The difference that for us it's what keeps us here. We keep remembering and hope that someone will remember us." She squeezed his hand. "And we help each other. You remember me and I'll remember you. You're part of the house now."

Ned felt gray and thin. He wondered if he could simply vanish right then and there. "When do I leave?" he wanted to know as a wave of nausea swelled across him.

"Leave?"

"Yeah. Move on to another level of existence or something like that?" He waved a hand at the ceiling as if Heaven were literally just above the attic.

"How would I know that? I'm just a little girl, Ned." Marilyn knew her answer disappointed him. He assumed she had made the same comment to each new specter within the house and did not push the question. She clapped her hands decidedly and added, "This is what I do know. The living can be very suggestible."

"Meaning?"

"Meaning do you want to help Irma and I set up a tad of red paint along the banister. The tour groups simply go mad for it. You'd think they'd just seen proof of the abominable snowman with the way they snap pictures and carry on."

Ned understood suddenly that this was the only comfort the child could offer him, minor distractions at the expense of the living's sense of wonder. It felt almost cruel. The living would know the truth soon enough. Still, he found denying the kid her fun was the last thing he wanted.

"Sure, but shouldn't I have a mourning period or something?"

"If you want." She released his hand and closed her eyes.

Ned closed his own eyes. He did an inventory of his life. His family, his friends, his professors, even the cute girl at the pizza place he and his buddy went to every Thursday. His friend was probably the first one who found out about Ned's death. After all, Ned had been driving his car at the time. He really hoped his friend missed him more than the car. He knew it was an awful thought, but hey, it was a nice car.

Ned felt the cold on his arm. Opening one eye, he looked down at Marilyn. "Are we done mourning yet? Not be insensitive, but I really want to go play."

Unable to make his voice work as he held back a choking noise, Ned motioned for her to lead on.

Chapter Two: Depression

Marilyn took Ned back downstairs. "Who else is here?" he asked as they wandered through the dining room. China had been laid out for a party that would never happen, carefully dusted each day to keep away the sense of a haunted room.

"Judy technically runs the house, but she's rarely here anymore. I think she works out of some office down the street for the historical society. She only runs tours on weekends and on Daphne's days off. There are also the volunteers, but they come and go so often, I can never keep up with their names." Marilyn paused at the dining room table, running her hand over the lace cloth and attempting to stir the fabric. She nodded at Ned to try mimicking her.

"No other ghosts?" he questioned, his own hand going directly through the tablecloth.

"Not at the moment. Other than when this was a hospital, not *that* many people have passed on here. We might be a haunted house, but we are still respectable." She frowned at his transparent hand. "Concentrate. Do like you did upstairs."

Ned did not care about his hand or the table. He squinted down at the girl in confusion. His feet ached to check out the river for clues of his afterlife. "If what you're saying is true then I should be haunting the river, not be trapped here."

"The house must like you. We've had spirits come that the house didn't like very well. I was surprised that we never ended up with any spirits from the courthouse down the road. Although, Judy once bought a vase from the war between the States to put in the parlor. There was this rather disagreeable woman who came with the vase. I don't remember her name, but I remember she wasn't here very long. She caused a lot of trouble. That's one of the reasons I keep Byrons's in the guest bedroom. When ghosts spread trouble, the house does not run as smoothly."

"Don't you and Irma cause trouble?"

"Oh no! We just have a little fun, but we don't ever truly bother anyone." Marilyn playfully ran her fingers over the silverware, causing a soup spoon to collide with a desert spoon. She heard them clink and she giggled in satisfaction.

"Where did she go?"

"I can't recall any longer. I just know that when she was here the house always felt dark and lonely and a lot of the tourists would complain." The subject matter forced Ned to shift uncomfortably. Despite the tale she weaved of a ghost even worse than Byrons, Ned could not help but see a just normal little girl in front of him.

"Were you a ghost when your family was still living here?" His voice softened with concern.

The question did not bother her. "Yes. I stayed to look out for them and to play with my brother. He was so little when I died."

"But they all left, except your mom."

There was a shrug of the puffed sleeves. "It was not bad. They had their lives to continue. I wasn't lonely, if that's what you're worried about. Even when Marty forgot I was still here and didn't believe in ghosts anymore, he at least brought his family here. I got to see his wife and his three children. The littlest one was named after me."

"But he didn't even see you or talk to you when he was grown up."

"The living aren't supposed to be preoccupied with the dead. We are dead much longer than we are alive. Better to spend that time with other living people. That's why I've never completely understood all of the ghost hunters who come here. Sure, they are fun to trick and they make things interesting, however, I do get tired of them bringing in weeping mediums constantly calling me 'poor child' and telling me to move on. It's really none of their business." As she spoke, Marilyn found her way out of the dining room and into the entryway of the house. She sat upon the stairs, facing the front door.

Ned followed, sitting a step below her. Outside, he heared Daphne preparing her next tour group, staring her speech about flash photography all over again. "Do all ghosts feel that way?"

"No. Especially not Byrons. If he had his way, he would always be down here trying to get the living to notice him. There was a team of those paranormal researchers writing a book about local ghosts that came here last month. Byrons made a complete idiot of himself, screaming at them and trying to hit them. They even got his voice on tape telling them he wanted out. They interrupted it as him telling them to get out. . . which they did. Shame really, they never finished. I bet Harry could have bought the book for me to see after it was published."

"Harry?"

She jumped up in a panic, the hem of her dress twirling around her calves like mist. "I think it's noon!"

"So?" Ned tried to keep his attention on Marilyn, but Daphne had entered with her new group. He could not help being distracted as the particularly large crowd shoved their way into the foyer, careful to avoid touching one another in the small space.

"So? That means Harry is on break! Come on!" Marilyn waved her hand and rushed back into the dining room, giggling joyfully as she passed through tourists. Ned followed with more caution, avoiding the unpleasantness of touching. He hated the sense of a living person brush through him. Each time it rocked his reality. Only once he had been trapped in the center of a group. He had three different human hands, a foot, and a shoulder all passing into his nonexistent form. He wanted to yell, to be angry at the reminder that he no longer had a body. Marilyn had pulled him out and scolded him. "Just ignore the living. You'll be better off that way."

A few people seemed to notice them or at least notice something. A fleeting sense of the past, of something dark and sad crossed into their innocent reality. Then their expressions would relax as they forgot again.

Marilyn ran through the room with a gleeful "wee!" and skipped up to a door reading "staff only". She melted through it. Ned paused before the closed door, hating the look of his hand disappearing through the wood. With a deep breath, he entered the room and shook the phantom limb that was his incorporeal form.

The room was tiny with a high window, modern refrigerator, and table with two chairs. The contemporary feel made Ned want to sigh in relief. Having been surrounded by antiques all day, the modern contraptions filled him with joy. It may not have been much, but the square television with rabbit ears standing awkwardly atop a rickety stand relaxed him.

"This used to be the butler's pantry. That was what

they called it, but we never had a butler. Now they use it as break room where they like to complain about the tourists." Marilyn pointed at the door one second before it slowly opened. Harry entered and Marilyn clapped as if he were the costumed entertainment at a children's party.

Harry seemed to be nearing retirement age. He moved with slow purpose, still strong enough to get the job done, however possessing enough ache in his bones to know his limits. He wore the usual coveralls and sweat of a maintenance man. "Hello," the man said under his breath.

"Hello, Harry," the child answered.

Ned whipped his head between the pair of them. "He can hear us?"

"Who? Harry? No. But he's worked here long enough that he usually senses when we're around. He's very nice."

Harry sat in one of the chairs with a weary groan. He shuffled off his work boots and propped his feet upon the other chair. He reached across for the dial and switched the aging TV between stations. "There's a movie playing on channel three. I think something with giant lizards eating New York." Marilyn pouted. "Or there's that kid's show about the boy and the dog. Which one do you want to watch?"

"Oo! The kid's show, please," she answered with enthusiasm.

Marilyn planted herself onto the floor. She pat the ground beside her and Ned also sat.

"I thought you said he couldn't hear us?" Ned stated as he watched the older man grunt with a certain amount of disappointment and switched channels to a sticky-sweet program staring a generic looking "pretty" girl.

"He can't. I told you. Harry is just nice."

Harry rested his shoulder blades against the back of his chair again and muttered, "Tomorrow we watch what I want, kiddo."

"He's just teasing. Tomorrow is his day off. He always watches something he knows I'd like, except when he wants to watch the news."

"But he can't hear you or see you? Why does he turn on the TV for you?"

"Because he believes in ghosts and, like I already said, he is nice. Honestly, Ned. Keep up."

Ned studied her watching the moving picture flicker across the screen. Her eyes glowed and she reacted with all of the emotion a director would have wished for. She booed the bad guys, cheered the good guys, and gasped at the predictable twists.

"You like TV, huh?"

"Mostly. Although I have trouble focusing on it at times. When I forget that I'm passed on, I lose track of some things in the house. The television is usually the first to go. I don't think my mother has ever noticed it. She only sees her things and where they've been moved to." She glanced up at Harry in admiration as he struggled to knock a rock from his boots.

Ned recalled running through a stairway covered in plastic when he was a Marilyn's age. "I wonder what ghosts in old houses that change a bunch over time see. My best friend used to live in an old colonial and his parents were always 'fixing it up' as they called it. They knocked down walls and added in modern everything."

"I think that if they noticed that would drive the spirits mad. My mother and Byrons hold absolute wailing sessions over a single vase being moved. Do you think that house was actually haunted?"

"Nah. I mean, we thought so when we were kids and of course my friend told everyone it was haunted because it made him seem cool. Ten year old boys are super impressed if they think you live in the house from a Vincent Price movie."

"Who?"

"An actor. He. . . you know what, never mind. What's next?" He glanced at the door where Harry had entered from. "Are you going to give me a tour of the outside too?"

Marilyn thrust her hands at him. "No! You mustn't go outside!"

"What?" Ned leaned away from her wildly protesting hands. "Why?"

"Because. . . we're house ghosts, that's why. The front porch is okay, but that's about it. Understand?"

"I guess—"

"Please do not guess. Please tell me that you understand."

"Okay. Okay. I understand." Ned thought about going through the backdoor, just to see what would happen. The urge to rebel swept his mind with a strange hope. The thought to run away from the girl and the house and go find out more of what had happened to him gave him a renewed energy. And yet, there he remained upon the floor with the ghost of young girl happily humming along with cartoons, already forgetting his mention of the dreaded outside.

As the strangeness of the situation sank in, he thought about his mother and his father receiving the news of his accident. He wondered if the friends he had been on his way to see the night he died found out right away or not until that next morning when he was still missing. He fumed over the number of insensitive cars which must have grumbled in traffic held up by his accident. Ned debated over how he felt over the accident itself. It wasn't fair. He never even had a chance to save himself.

Energy ran swiftly through him, a dark surge of

tension started to rebuild the heavy nest within his chest. Why did he have to die? Why didn't the universe go after someone older, who had lived their life? The TV flickered as he wanted to blame someone, anyone for what had been taken from him.

Marilyn frowned. "You're upsetting the electricity. What's wrong?"

Ned started at the fuzzy picture upon the screen. "I'm doing that?"

"What's the matter?"

A rant poured from Ned as Harry escaped from the steadily suffocating room. "What's the matter? Marilyn, I died. I'm dead. I can't reverse or tell anyone that I'm okay. . . in a manner of speaking. I want someone tell me why I had to die. Why me? I want to know whose fault this is."

She pulled her knees up to her chest, but was un-phased by his yelling. "What exactly did happen?"

"My friend called me to drive his car out to the party he was at. He'd been drinking and was using at an excuse to make me take a break from studying. Then, I had trouble with the brakes and the road was wet and then the car was in the river. That's all I really remember."

"Do you think it was anyone's fault?"

"No. It was just an accident.

"Then being angry won't do you any good. You don't want to turn out like Byrons, right?"

The uneasy hostility of the upstairs room had lingered with Ned. Even the idea of returning to Byrons's room any time in the near future filled him with dread. He had never been a harsh or antagonistic person. To become like Byrons would be like losing his living self. "No. Absolutely not."

"Then forget about it. Focus on your time here in this house, not what brought you here." When she knew she had him calm, Marilyn went back to watching her program and Ned went back to studying her.

As they fell into a comfortable silence, the show ended. Marilyn broke the reverie first. "Ned?"

"Yes?"

"I'm glad you're here."

She turned to him. The child's smile refilled him with warmth and chased out the last of his wrath. "Thanks."

She climbed off the floor and shook imaginary dust from her petticoats. "Television time is over. I think I know what you need."

She took him to the front porch and sat on the top step. Each time Ned tried to ask what they were waiting for she shushed him. She had him silently wait as three more tour groups were greeted and left.

As the last of the tourists left for the day, the sun dipped below the old courthouse at the end of the street. The light dimmed, painting the clouds in pinks and oranges. The living walked down the road without taking note of the simplistic beauty.

"Pretty, right." Marilyn pointed at the sky. Her smile rivaled the dazzling colors.

"Yeah. Petty." Once more, Ned's mind wandered to his life. He thought about his dad, holding him up on his shoulders when he was a toddler so he could be closer to the fireworks. And his mom keeping one hand on his back as he sat there with his hands wrapped around his dad's chin. It was before his brother or sister was born and it was one of the only memories he retained of being an only child. Before he'd moved away, he'd done the same thing for his cousin, setting the kid upon his shoulders while his sister and his aunt taught the kid to squeal each time a rocket burst overhead. His guts tied in knots and a spot somewhere in his chest began to weigh against his ribcage.

Ned rubbed his face and the lump returned. Marilyn said nothing as he wept. He cried for the lives which his brother and sister would live and that he never saw. He cried for the time he spent away from them and thought of how he should have invited them to visit him at college.

His tears were quiet, rolling into the collar of his tee shirt. Ned did not sob. He just allowed the slow trickle to escape his eyes as he continued to stare at the sunset. His stomach twisted and turned. The sky darkened quickly and his mind filled with the single thought that his life was over. His limbs twitched and ached, ready for a fight, but still stood upon the porch crying. Exhaustion began to seep into his every thought.

As the world lost more of its light, his brain flicked with ideas he'd never had before. He could curl up into a ball and hide his face. He could stay there and sleep until all the other ghosts forgot about him. He was all alone and he would stay alone until the day when his own friends and family finally came to get him. Despair could offer sweet release, a break from trying to sort out what had happened. The universe had screwed him over and he didn't have to take it. He could simply forget everything and rest.

Little fingers pulled on the edge of this tee shirt and a girl's voice urgently asked, "Do want to have a tea party?"

Ned's thoughts broke. The sunset lit up the sky once again the balloon his in chest relieved in his surprise. "Um. . . a what? Now?"

"Yes. Why? Did you have something else to do?" She refused to release his shirt, watching him carefully as he inspected the world for the darkness which had tried swallow him up.

Rubbing his eyes and finding they were completely dry, Ned replied, "Sure. Do I have to dress up or something?"

She grinned at him and took his hand in hers again. "No dress code required, although I have some rather flowery hats if you would like to wear one."

"Only if we can find one that matches my shoes." He held up his worn out sneaker and felt the last of his sadness vanish as the child giggled.

Chapter Three: Bargaining

Time to the dead was a funny thing. Ned tried to watch the seasons and the clocks, but he soon realized that no matter what he did, days would sometimes go missing all at once. He wasn't sure if he'd just forgotten those days. He'd think of his family, depression weighing upon him for only a few minutes, and then suddenly remember that he'd had similar thoughts before.

The others were not particularly concerned. He learned to let it go. His afterlife thus far was filled with much of what it had been the first day. He played tricks upon tourists and Daphne with Irma. He had surreal "let's pretend we're still alive conversations" with Mrs. Van Sloan and Private Sterns. And of course through all of this, Marilyn was by his side, convincing him to play dolls and skip rope with her. Somehow, he kept forgetting to be sad or to miss his life or to even to create his own plans. Routine became his second best friend after Marilyn.

Nights were different. He had always imagined ghosts to be more active in the twilight hours, rattling chains and having skeleton tap dances. Instead, without the living around to observe the others became rather quiet. They acted more as they would when they were alive. Mrs. Van Sloan would lie in her bed and fan herself. Irma and Marilyn liked to peer out of windows at the still streets.

At times, Ned would go up to the attic. He played cards with Private Sterns while looking out of a round window at the back of the house. The high window was the only one in the house able to see over the garden fence and view the river behind. The current seemed slow and steady, calm waters gently pulled debris out to sea. The violent battering of splashes and rushing waves that had kept him down the night he'd died felt like a completely different river. When he watched the water, he felt the icy pin pricks filling his lungs to bursting.

Then the private would call out, "Gin!" As he suggested they play another game, Ned would turn away from the window and forget again about the river.

If Ned had been able to calculate accurately, he would have realized that only a month had passed before Marilyn set him free to explore the house on his own. Still, doll tea parties became a norm and he found himself drawn back to the playroom every few days.

One day in the early morning hours when the house was painted with the blues of sunrise, Ned found himself once again heading in the direction of the nursery.

"You don't have to do everything that little brat wants you to do, you know," grumbled Byrons from his bedroom door.

Ned paused to stare at the sweaty man who hovered at the edge of the room, not daring to pass the threshold. "She's just a kid. She's not trying to be bossy. She just wants someone to play with."

Byrons chuckled. His laugh was low and dark, the sort of noise typical of a haunting. "You think so? The house likes her best. Haven't you noticed that? It responds to her better than to any of the rest of us."

Glancing up at the striped wallpaper and inspecting it carefully, Ned shook his head. The sense of gullibility and insecurity ate at his brain. "The house? The house is. . . it's just a house."

"Right. And we are just figments of the imagination. Maybe we're all just parts of her imagination." Byrons dared to take a single step into the hallway. He whispered into Ned's ear and the young man was amazed that whiskey still clung to the air around the spirit. "Maybe she's the one keeping us here? You ever consider that?"

Scowling, Ned took a dramatic sidestep away. "You ever consider that the gunshot to the brain scrambled things up there?"

As he continued his trek down the hall, he heard the unpleasant chuckle once again. "You are a rude, little shit. You know that." Ned shook away the comment as he practically ran for the playroom.

Marilyn had been expecting him. The dolls and bears had been set up around an empty seat. She always knew he would show up.

"Ah! Mr. Ned. You have come at last. Mrs. Roosevelt was just expressing her concern that you would be late and your tea would get cold." Marilyn poured out air from her toy china pot as she nodded at the cloth doll with the bisque head.

Ned stared at "Mrs. Roosevelt's" blank, painted eyes. He wanted to make a joke or to respond with a tone of mocking, upper class wit. All he managed to do was stare. Byrons's words had crept within him, infesting his brain.

"What's the matter?" The girl set down the teapot. As she straightened her back, she looked more of the age she had died at, not the small child she preferred to portray.

He felt Byrons's words squirming. "You said that

the house chose me. Is the house alive?"

Her expression warmed. "I like to think it is, but I really don't know." Her tone, so casual and innocent, instantly eased the squirming. Of course she liked to believe it was alive. She was alone in the house for many years before her mother died. The house was her guardian, her constant.

He pushed the squirming to the back of his brain and sat himself down. She was, after all, just a kid. She was not some dark and powerful force holding him there against his will. He accepted his tea and played the usual game until they heard Judy and Harry unlock the front door.

Marilyn liked to follow around Judy as if she were the woman's assistant. Judy had all of the earmarks of an old fashioned librarian; glasses hung on a chain around her neck, silver hair always pinned up in a bun, high collared blouses, and a stern mouth. She ran the proverbial tight ship and dismissed volunteers for blunders as quickly as she trained them. Where Daphne tried to mimic her boss, folding her hands in front and frowning at each historical inaccuracy brought up by the tourists, Judy was the genuine history aficionado. She had the ability to recite the background of every dish, chair, and hairpin within the house. Her least favorite topic was the hauntings.

She understood that the idea of ghosts was good for business, therefore she allowed the occasional private séances and Halloween ghost hunts for a lovely extra fee. She knew it was the first thing her superiors and local government officials encouraged. People liked ghosts. They also liked the youthful Daphne, the young art history major she had hired, against her better judgment.

When she had arrived, Daphne decided very quickly that she desperately wanted to be like Judy. She mimicked the older woman's facial tics for an air of seriousness. She attempted to pull her layered, cheaply dyed hair in a bun. She even tried on one occasion to wear Judy's nametag through her entire shift. One disapproving look from Harry put a stop to that one.

Daphne claimed not to believe just as her mentor did, yet became unnerved by every minute noise in the house and fed the tourists stories of each trick Marilyn preyed upon her. Whether the young woman admitted that she honestly thought that the ghost of a child was targeting her for harassment was beside the point. She knew how to make the tourists happy and thus Judy made no fuss.

Judy simply refused to discuss the matter. "I have not, nor shall I ever experience anything unusual in this house. It is just a house. If you want to know about ghosts, you may purchase the brochure in the gift shop." The gift shop had once been the Van Sloan family carriage house Daphne would point out on tours.

Nevertheless, Marilyn followed Judy on her weekly rounds and responded each time the woman spoke to herself.

Judy inspected the dining room with a clipboard. "Hmm. This tablecloth needs to be washed. I wonder if the blue one is still in storage."

"No. You took it to your office and never brought it back." Marilyn read the clipboard over Judy's shoulder. "Oh! But can you please take care of that low hanging curtain in the nursery. The tourists keep stepping on the hem and it's turning black."

The boss moved into the parlor and Marilyn chased after her. "Or we can check the fireplace in here first."

Irma and Ned watched the pair with amusement. "You know she can't hear you," Irma chided with her arms crossed over her chest.

Marilyn wrinkled her nose at her friend. "That does

not mean that Judy does not value my opinion."

With a good natured sigh, Ned left the ladies and moved back into the employee breakroom. Harry had been repainting a slat from the fence, the victim of local graffiti and a violent kicking. Having returned it to the expected white, Harry cleaned up the painting supplies.

The T.V. had been left on to keep the eerie silence at bay. Upon the screen, Ned saw a news team doing an interest story about a group of college students volunteering in the community. They had been cleaning up trash or built a new swing set or some other activity which would look good for anyone playing to go into politics. Their deeds did not interest Ned. A young woman had been what caught his attention.

With her hair piled atop her head in a carefully crafted mess, the young woman forced a smile for the camera. As she spoke of her selfless deeds into the microphone, her gazed stayed raptly fixed beyond the face of her interviewer. Ned knew that gaze.

The young woman had been one of his roommate's conquests, one which did not take his "love 'em and leave 'em" policy as a truth. Her bitterness at their breakup was felt by all of their friends. Hers was not the only heart broken by Ned's friend who he had to deal with, she simply stood out. Her intense, indignant stare stood out.

Tearing himself from the screen, Ned thought again about his roommate. The guy had never been a great human being overall, but he had never failed to be a good friend. Ned no longer worried over whether his friend had wondered about his death or felt guilt. He just wanted to know how he was doing. Was he still partying every weekend or did Ned's untimely demise finally give his life the wakeup call it needed?

Byrons's words squirmed again as Ned watched Harry gather the piece of fence and tools. The ghost thought about how long he had been within the confines of the old house. Harry opened the backdoor with his hammer and the piece of fence easily balanced in his thick arms. The outside world glowed with the sunshine, bouncing off of the plants and the aged steps leading into the garden.

Ned followed Harry out in a rush. He paused on the back porch, wishing desperately for the sense of heat on his skin or the breeze passing over his arm hair. He heard knocking followed by a panicked little voice calling his name. He turned to see Marilyn at the kitchen window, her eyes wide. Her bottom lip trembled. "Ned! Come back inside!"

He gave her a half smile. "It's okay," he mouth and waved at her.

As he took his first step off of the porch onto the grass, he heard her palms beating wildly at the window. Harry went about his yardwork without notice. A part of Ned wished the old man could see and hear the little girl, guessing that the workman would know how to calm her down.

"I'll be right back," he called over his shoulder, hoping his voice penetrated the window glass.

Her pounding became more fervent. "Ned! Ned, please!" Tears started to roll down her ivory cheeks. Ugly winkles scrunched up her eyes and a red flush tinted her whole being. The house seemed to panic in response to the girl, the curtains in each window fluttering wildly. Wood creaked loudly and Ned wondered if the building would suddenly grow an arm and pull him back inside.

Deciding to ignore Marilyn, Ned strolled through the backyard. It was a pleasant garden with an iron bench sandwiched between a trellis of grapes climbing the back gate and a tree with thin, over-reaching branches. Ned never did learn about different flora and fauna, but he assumed it was a birch. The back of the house also featured an old water pump and a nineteenth century wheelbarrow strategically placed near a rock garden. Ned neared the welcoming sight of the pinks, yellows, and blues of the patch of earth. He'd have to ask Marilyn's mother if she'd once had a garden in that part of the yard or if the historians had once again misplaced a part of her life.

Ned focused his energy on a peony, watching the stem bow beneath his fingers. He managed to pick the flower, the effort giving him a sluggish feeling. He dropped it again instantly. It fluttered to the ground, landing petal side down. He thought of trying again, of bringing the flower in to Marilyn as a peace offering for upsetting her.

The cold came on suddenly. Ned barely had a moment to think as a chill engulfed him and darkness dimmed the garden. Smoke wrapped him in a blinding black, despair pulling out his ability to run. He fell to his knees, sensing something watching him as he suffocated in a physical manifestation of sadness. As Ned started to give in to the feeling, all of the pain and terror of his death returned to him. The water poured into the windows of the car, his hands slipping over the wet door handle as his lungs filled.

As his brain screamed, "I'm going to die! But I can't die!" a set of hands pulled him up by the arms and dragged him through the backdoor of the house. They dumped him on the floor and Ned looked up at his rescuer – Byrons. The drunken ghost collapsed onto the tile beside him, trembling. Marilyn wrapped her arms around Ned's neck and continued to cry.

An eternity passed before any of them were calm enough to speak. Byrons pushed himself back up and snapped, "There! He's safe. Now you both better just stay out of my way from now on!" He still shook, walking in a wavering line back out to the dining room.

Marilyn untangled herself from Ned and squeaked out a reluctant thank you to the man. His response was a grunt which he offered in passing to Irma as she ran into the room.

Her first move was to the window, staring out at the garden with heavy breaths. "It has retreated back to the side of the house I think," Irma explained as she sat down on the floor beside Marilyn. "You never told him about it?"

"I didn't want to scare him." Marilyn hung her head guiltily.

"What was that?" Ned asked, surprised at the calm sound of his own voice.

"We don't know." Irma's frankness was suddenly comforting, presenting the words with clinical logic. "It keeps us in the house. If any of us try to step off the front or back porches, it attacks."

"I told you there used to be a few more of us in the house," Marilyn added, "some faded on their own and some. . . some tried to leave."

"You made it sound like they left on their own or just vanished. Not that they were attacked."

Marilyn responded to his comment with another guilty drop of her chin. "When I was a little girl, my dad had a patient who came to live with us, this disgusting old man that chewed tobacco and was always saying lewd things to the nurses or secretaries. He died of a heart attack." Irma glanced at Marilyn as if checking if her memory was accurate.

"You knew he was a ghost in the house when he died? I though you only ever saw Marilyn?" Ned asked as he sat up straight. He was determined to collect up any dignity left to his sorry existence.

"No. She told me about him."

"Compared with him, Bryons was a teddy bear,"

Marilyn recalled sourly. "He wasn't here long. He kept accusing my mother and me of holding him hostage in the house. One day, he ran outside and within minutes the thing in the garden took him. I'd seen it once before to one of the soldiers from when we were a hospital during the Great War. The soldier went peacefully though, like he was embracing the darkness. The awful man struggled and screamed. The thing in the garden started to shake him back and forth. It was terrible to watch. Then, he just. . . vanished into the smoke." Her eyes glazed and she stared into her lap as if the moment were something she needed to feel guilt over.

"Do you remember it being here when you were alone here?"

"I don't know. I never went further than the porch. Why did you even go out there?"

"I wanted to see how my life is doing—"

She cut him off with a confused scoff. "Ned, your life is over."

"Yes, but things that made up my life are still going on. I want to know about my friends, my family." He turned a desperate gaze upon the girl. "Please, Marilyn, I just want to know."

Her perplexed expression deepened. She glanced at Irma who shook her head. "Ned, we don't know to leave the house," the woman explained.

"But you both have been here for years. Hasn't anyone ever done it?" His eyes continued their pleading and Marilyn whimpered.

"The thing in the garden always attacks anyone who tries to leave. Always."

Ned lay back down on the tile Cond sighed. "Okay, Marilyn. That's something you need to tell someone about when they first get here. Kind of important."

"I'm sorry." She whispered the two words to him.

"It's fine, it's fine," he muttered quickly, wanting to

alleviate her guilt. "Just leave me here to get stepped through by tourists for few hours and I'll be right as rain."

"How will that make you better?"

"It'll remind me that I'm dead and that I can't die again from a heart attack." He rolled over onto his side and a memory of his life created a pinprick at his racing heart. His roommate used to dare him to take risks.

"You're studying medicine, Ned! You, of all people, should appreciate the health benefits of an adrenaline rush," his buddy would chide. And Ned would always reply how he'd rather play it safe and keep his heart beating. Funny how things worked out.

After a couple of weeks, no one spoke of the garden incident again. Byrons steered clear of Ned when he tried to thank the man for helping him. The simple show of gratitude upset Byrons more than any insult Marilyn could dish out. Ned assumed that it spoiled his bad mood. The ghost liked watching the tour group entering his sanctuary with instant unease. He thrived on their reactions to the distinctive atmosphere he radiated and acts of heroism simply did not fit well into his routine.

Ned started to form his own routine, conforming to the house and each quirk death presented. He continued the tea parties and pranks acting as if nothing had changed for him. Yet the thing in the garden still gnawed at him, still filled him with suffocating thoughts. He had to resign himself to the idea that he would never leave the old house.

One morning, just after Daphne had arrived to begin readying the house for the mass of tourists, Ned wandered downstairs to see a change in the system. Mrs. Van Sloan sat in the parlor, her hands folded in her lap and her eyes upon the window as if she were expecting company to arrive on the porch.

Without fully entering the room, Ned asked her what had brought her downstairs.

In a tone that mingled annoyance and sweetness into a perfect mix, she answered, "It is my house. I may go where I like."

"I didn't mean anything bad by it." He glanced backwards at the front door. "Are you waiting for someone?"

She guiltily tore her eyes from the window. "Well. . . yes. My husband."

"Your. . . Ma'am, you do remember that he isn't here, right? I mean. . . you do know me right now, right." He entered the room slowly, terrified of setting off a meltdown.

"Yes, Ned. I know who you are and I know that my husband is not currently present. Why else would I be waiting for him?" The woman waved her young, slender hand to a chair and he obediently sat down. "It's our wedding anniversary."

"Congratulations?"

"Thank you. I am waiting for him to come. I know it will be only a short visit, but it is better than nothing." Another short peek passed the curtains and a secretive smile forced Ned's next blunt words.

"Why do you think he's coming?"

She tilted her head at him and for a brief second he saw the same sparkle in her eyes which he saw in Marilyn's whenever she had full awareness that she was the smartest person in the room. Ned read the expression carefully. "Has your husband come to visit you before?"

"Indeed. A couple of times."

"Hold on a second. He leaves wherever he is and comes here and then leaves here without any problems?" Ned did not realize that he had moved to the edge of his seat.

"No. It isn't something he has control over. It just. . . happens. And it might not happen this year. I just would rather be prepared." Her hands smoothed down her skirt and checked her hair.

"Marilyn never said anything about this—"

Mrs. Van Sloan laughed with silver bells in her throat. "She always forgets. It's not a bad thing. I know I forget things occasionally."

"What about Irma or Byrons? Do they see him?"

"You know, they never have. Isn't that strange?"

"If he does come, do you think I could speak to him? Maybe he has some idea of how I can go visit my own family."

"I assure you he does not. I am sorry, Ned but as I have said it is a rare treat. We have no control."

"I'm starting to see that. I get why they call it Purgatory."

"Your dramatic phrasing is not appreciated."

"Sorry."

Mrs. Van Sloan pivoted her head back to the window and Ned knew the conversation was done.

He left her to her gazing and wondered to himself if what she said was even true or just some idea she'd created throughout the decades.

He slipped through the closed dining room door, nearly running into Irma.

"Whoa! A little distracted today?"

"Can the dead haunt each other?" He asked himself aloud.

Irma, assuming the question was for her, replied, "That sounds counter-productive. Why would we haunt each other? That doesn't really keep us remembered?"

"It forces us to remember each other, doesn't it?"

"Is that why you're barreling through doors. There are better ways to try to frighten me, if that's your goal,

Ned." As she spoke, she carefully stooped down and tried to pick up Daphne's keys which she must've slipped onto the floor. "Speaking of haunting, where should I have these mysteriously wind up."

Realizing that Irma was not the sort to engage in existential questions with, he pointed at the top of the china hutch. "Why don't you put them up there?"

"Perfect!" The room, satisfied with the new position of the keys, grew just a little brighter. The air gained freshness, a flowery scent meant to convey a renewed contentment.

Ned and Irma returned to the entryway and the steps facing the front door. Irma sat down with a groan, despite the lack of ache in her body. She offered Ned a friendly smile. "How are you holding up?"

"I don't know. I'm not sure how I'm supposed to be so I have no basis of comparison." Ned passed his hand through the banister, watching the tips of his fingers vanish into the wood. "You said your dad owned the house right? Why isn't he here?"

For the first time, Irma looked her middle-aged years. Wrinkled eyes offered him glittering amount of understanding. "I think he had other plans. Whereas I, I chose to stay."

"You did?" The idea sounded like the most ludicrous rambling Ned had ever heard. He stared at Irma with a mixture of betrayal and astonishment. "You were able to choose?"

"I don't know if I was able to, I just always knew I would end up here." Her smile grew at his shock. "When I was a little girl, I was sick quite a bit and there were rarely other children in the house to play with."

"But you could see Marilyn," Ned remembered aloud.

"Yes. And she was my very best friend until I started school. I couldn't see her as easily as I got older until eventually she stopped appearing and I had school chums to occupy my time. The older I grew, the more I brushed her off as having been my imaginary friend, the result of a lonely little girl's pretend games. It wasn't until I was married and my husband started to see and hear things in this house that I ever started to suspect that maybe Marilyn had been real."

"If you didn't think she was real, how did you always know you'd end up here?"

"When I had cancer, I eventually stopped responding to treatments. Instead of going in a hospital, I wanted to be at home where I had everything around me that I reminded me of the people I loved. My husband's reaction was. . . less than favorable, but he caved and brought me here. That's when Marilyn started to come back and see me again. She played games around the room and mimicked my husband behind his back without him knowing. She did everything in her power to make my last living days as amusing as possible."

"And you remembered everything from when you were a child?"

"Yes, especially how lonely I always thought she must have been. I figured it wasn't such a bad way to spend eternity, playing with your best friend and staying where you had been the happiest."

As she finished her story, he nodded although he was not completely certain he understood. The story did not apply to him. The house held no value to him and his attachment to the little girl started after he was dead. One part of the woman's story still nagged and he asked without worrying if it was rude. Afterlife tact had grown exhausting. "What happened to your husband?"

"Ronald? The house was in my name and he never wanted it, so he left. I managed to find out that he did remarry towards the end of his life, another out of practice, but good Jewish woman."

Ned tried to read her expression. Her features were such a blend of nonchalant and cheerful, he felt like Irma was speaking of a stranger. "Don't you miss him? Wouldn't you have liked it if you could be wherever he was?"

"Of course, Ned. But the way I see it, Ronald and I had our time together. And it's very difficult to keep a marriage together through a lifetime, much less eternity." As an afterthought, she added, "It is bizarre journey marriage. I'm sorry you'll never experience it."

The comment caught him off-guard. "I guess." Marriage had never been high on his list of goals. Of course the thought of its unattainability added to the pang of loss. He pushed it down. "Hey, I haven't seen Marilyn in a while. Any idea where she is?"

Irma pointed at the front door. "She's been very quiet today. Maybe you can cheer her up."

No more words were spoken between them as Ned passed directly through the old door. Marilyn sat upon the porch watching the people go by. Children her own age, or the age she had once been, ran by without taking notice of her. Ned took a spot beside her.

"What's wrong?" he asked, nudging her sleeve with his shoulder.

"I miss my street. I miss what it used to be like. It's too busy now. Too loud." Two boys were hassling one another, one heatedly jumping around the other and threatening with mock scorn.

Ned adjusted his sitting position. "Really? You didn't have annoying kids on this street in your day?"

"Well, boys can always be irritating, no offense," she replied as she suppressed a smile.

"None taken. I accept my role in life." He pointed at two women each pushing a stroller and exchanging parenting tips. "And moms didn't stop to talk in your time?"

"Yes. . . they did that," Marilyn answered thoughtfully.

Two cars nearly collided bumpers at the nearest intersection. Despite the accident having been avoided, both drivers exited and began to sling swear words back and forth.

"And the honking, the shouting, the traffic? That was all your time, right. Just in a different way."

"I suppose." She rewarded him with a smile. "The language adults use now when they yell is more. . . colorful."

"I doubt that. I think they were just more careful about shielding you from it back then." He placed both hands over her ears. "There. That better?"

Her whole body giggled as she shook him off. Rising, she pointed to the door. "Very well. I am done moping. Tea party?"

"Um. . . yeah. Sure." Ned winced a somewhat at the thought of yet another pretend tea party. "Give me just a second."

She passed through the front door and Ned stood atop the porch, stretching his neck to inspect the bend in the road which rounded the house. He could spy the very edge of the river at the curve in the street. How long had the road been blocked up when the car had flipped over into the water? How long had traffic been backed up as they retrieved his body from the wreck? Were flowers left near the edge of the bridge in his honor near where he'd lost control of the wheel; where the brakes had given way beneath his foot and he'd heard the awful skid of the tires?

He had always been such a careful driver. Was the road just too slippery? Had he taken the curve too sharply? The events were a blur which played at his brain like a melody on repeat, but he couldn't grasp the lyrics.

He took two steps off of the porch, still straining to keep eyes on the river's edge and the road. Within an instant, the black cloud blocked his path. Ned fell backwards against the stairs as the thing from the garden hovered over him, daring him to take another move away from the house.

Scrambling back with panic tensing his limbs, Ned retreated to the safety of the front door. The shadow stayed fixed in the yard barricading him onto the porch. The idea of being a prisoner frustrated the ghost. He heard a growl enter his voice. "What do you want, huh? I'm already stuck here for eternity! You can't let me just look outside? What are you?"

As he shouted, the shadowed stirred. It moved slowly closer to the steps, however never moved up them. Ned laughed in triumph. "Well, at least that's one thing. You can't come in."

Tourists came and went as always, but that night had a change. After the house had been locked up, a man in his early twenties knocked upon the door. Ned followed Marilyn in a rush to see who it could be. Daphne, dressed in jeans and a low cut blouse, answered the door's summons. She let the young man in and they exchanged embraces.

"Must be her latest boyfriend," Marilyn grumbled. She trailed after them into parlor.

"Is bringing her boyfriend in here allowed?" Ned whispered, even though he knew the couple could not hear them.

"No. She doesn't do it often. I think it's just when she's been here more than not here, if that makes sense. That way she doesn't look like a workaholic. . . that's a term, right?" Marilyn watched the pair curl up on the sofa, arms entangling each other. "It's rather disgusting."

"Maybe we shouldn't be watching this—"

"I am not leaving them alone in this room. He looks a vagrant!" The young man wore his hair purposely messy and had carefully planned holes in his jeans.

"I don't think Daphne is going to let him steal anything," Ned explained, trying to gently pull Marilyn backwards.

"She's different when her boyfriends are around. She even more . . . you'll see."

The young man reached out for a lamp. "Do I have to light this with a match or something?" He pulled out a lighter, his thumb repeatedly flicking over the top.

At first, Daphne panicked. "No! We have electricity. Put that away!" When he scowled at her, she giggled, a contrived sound she intended to seduce the young man beside her. "You're so bad," she said after a second when he did not respond.

At the phrase, he leaned over and kissed her. The action was deep and hard, his tongue forcing its way into her mouth desperately. She returned the action, her arms wrapping under his coat. It wasn't until his own hands scurried beneath her top and fumbled with the clasp of her bra that she gently pulled back from him.

"What are you—?"

"Come on, Daph. Don't tell me you've never thought of doing it on one of those big, old beds." He half whispered the words as he nibbled on her neck.

She leaned into the kisses and sighed. "I'll get fired," she tried to argue, yet she allowed his hands to wander down her back side.

"We can play a little pretend," he coaxed, his pelvis rubbing against her jeans almost comically. "You'll be the lady of the house. I can be the lowly stable boy come to tempt you." His hands moved again to her bra.

Daphne waved his hands off, nevertheless stayed leaning against him. "Knock it off. It's not happening. Not here."

He moved off of her almost instantly. His hands waved angrily. "Oh yeah. Then where? You're roommate is always around and my parents are home." Ned thought about his roommate feeding some of same phrases to his many girlfriends. A part of him wanted to cheer his roommate on. After all, he was young, in college, and living every man's dream when it came to have his pick of the ladies. Still, each time Ned wanted to tell the girls to run. He wanted to do the same for Daphne. He wanted to warn her against such phrases and such boyfriends.

The young man went on. "You know, I'm starting to think you don't love me—"

"I do," she squeaked, tears entering her eyes. "Sarah won't always be around. She's going to visit her uncle next month, I told you."

"I can't wait till next month." The anger drained from the boyfriend's face and his lips zeroed again against her chin. "Besides. Why wait when we have this whole place to ourselves."

"I said no," she weakly repeated.

"Baby, no one will ever know," he cooed. His hands reached again, fumbling against her back.

She allowed the clasp of her bra to come undone, before she jumped back, the first tear rolling down her cheek. "We can't. I like this job."

Her boyfriend's arms pushed her back, not enough to cause her to tumble, but enough to create a mortified expression and the tears to pour forth at full speed. "Fine!" he snapped. "Find your own ride home!" He stormed out of the room, his feet scuffing the wood. The door slammed behind him, coinciding with a choked sob from Daphne. At first, she stood at the middle of the room, her feet moving her back and forth between running after him and the safety of the sofa. At last, she sunk down to the floor, her shoulders shaking. Another second passed and she followed him at a sprint. They could hear her yelling for him to wait.

Marilyn ran to the door and out onto the porch. "Wait!" Ned shouted for reasons he wasn't sure of. From the safety of the top step, they saw Daphne groveling to her boyfriend through the windows of his muscle car. They could not hear her words, yet they could see her winning him over. Soon, the two were making out.

As Daphne climbed into his car, Ned tapped Marilyn's shoulder. "Let's go back inside."

The child numbly did as she was told. "Ned, why would she go running back out to him?"

"I don't know." She gave him an accusing expression. "Honestly. I don't know. I guess she loves him."

"But why? He didn't seem very lovable." They passed through the front door and Ned worried that Daphne would forget to return to lock it before leaving. He wasn't sure he and the other ghosts could fight off intruders unless the burglars were struck terrified by objects moving slightly from where they originally had been. "Ned? Ned, explain it to me. She's wasting her life. Why would she do that?"

He took his mind off of the door and pat his little friend awkwardly on the shoulder. Concern and frustration shined through her eyes and realized she was comparing Daphne which her own imaginary version of the life she should have led. If Marilyn had lived to be an adult, her boyfriends would have been upstanding gentlemen who called upon her in a traditional manner. Someone to fit all of her Edwardian ideals while still adhering to her childish fairy tale notions of love to meet her parents and walk her down a church aisle. The young woman in the car making out with the delinquent mess went against every idea the child must have had about what dating should have been.

"Maybe. . . maybe Daphne doesn't have that many people to love." It was all he thought to say and it was enough.

She leaned against his side. "I wish you could get back to people who loved you. Still, I'm glad your here."

"It's okay. I'll make a deal with you. Why don't you cut Daphne a little slack and I'll help you keep Byrons in line. Or we can come up with some new ways to creep out the tourists without bothering her as much. I think she needs some good luck."

Marilyn pulled at his arm, swinging it instead of shaking hands. "Very well. However, I think we need to come up with something extremely spooky for the tourists."

In the weeks which followed, Marilyn and Irma stopped picking on Daphne as much. The eye rolls and the muttering criticisms never stopped, but the young woman's tours ran much more smoothly from then on.

Chapter Four: Anger

Outside the weather turned crisp and more field trips and book clubs showed up to the house. The latest tour was a group of kids from a private school. Teachers chaperoned while parent volunteers hung at the back of the group chatting.

"Blaaaa!" Ned wailed at them with his arms over his head. "Boooooo."

Not a single human acknowledged him.

Marilyn laughed. "I'm sorry, but you are simply not scary."

"Oh yeah? I've never seen you actually terrorize anyone."

"I make my presence known."

"Yes. But have you actually ever scared the pants off anybody?"

The girl's mouth twitched back and forth thoughtfully. "Very well. Come with me."

The two of them hung at the edge of the wall at the spot where the hallway turned. Marilyn started to whistle a tune, something old and childish. Her whistling turned to humming. As the field trip stood in the hall, listening to Daphne explain about Marilyn's brother, one boy alone noticed the sounds. His sneakers carried him away from the group at a snail's pace; however no one noticed his absence. Marilyn motioned for Ned to duck into the attic stairs and she did the same.

"Hard times, hard times, come again no more," she sang down the stairs. Her haunting voice was rewarded with the squeak of rubber soles passing the "staff only" sign and heading up the steps.

Ned moved himself away from the entrance, wiggling his eyebrows at Marilyn in order to break her concentration. Her focus was entirely on the boy. He could not have been more than ten. His hair was shaggy and blonde reminding Ned a little of his own mess atop his head. The boy paused at the top of the stairs.

Marilyn, her hands outstretched in front of her, stepped into the light. For the briefest of moments, the boy could see her curled hair and pressed dress. She tilted her head and asked him in a whisper, "Have you come to play with me?"

The boy's yells bounced through the attic and rang across the house, filling each human ear with his terror. He almost tripped down the stairs, still crying out and grasping at what he had seen.

The girl turned to Ned in complete triumph. She swished her skirts back and forth, beaming up at him. "See. I told you I can be scary."

"You win. You are the master of horror," Ned declared. He glanced over at the small window at the edge of the attic. The soldier had climbed from his cot and hovered at the glass. "Hey, Stern. You're out of bed!"

Instantly, Ned marched up to the one legged man. Marilyn hung back, her victory waning as she watched Sterns fingers working at the window.

"I need to go," the private muttered as his nails scratched the glass.

"Go? Go where? Come on. Come back to bed and we'll have nice quiet game. Maybe I'll go easy on you this time."

Sterns pushed Ned away when he offered him an arm. "Get away! I don't know you! What is this place? How did I get here?"

"You were wounded in the war, remember, Sterns?" Ned wanted to be like the little girl, able to say just the right thing in order to calm him.

The private turned to him wide-eyed. "What war? Who is Sterns?"

The question was a new one and Ned looked at Marilyn whose own gaze glistened. Then, she let out her own scream. The thing from the garden hovered at the window, blocking out the light. Sterns continued to claw and strain his fingers, trying to open the sealed pane.

"I have to go. Don't you see? I have to go," the soldier muttered. "It wants me to go."

Ned struggled and fought the private, the two young men becoming an entangling of violent pulling and swearwords. Finally, he forced the soldier to sit upon his cot. The black cloud at the window slowly descended. As the sun warmed the attic, Sterns started to cry. He laid his head on the pillow and Marilyn stroked his brow until she felt he had composed himself.

Ned and Marilyn left the attic with a balloon of distress hovering over their heads. They nearly ran into Judy as they reached the second floor hallway. The older woman kept pulling upon her sensible, Edwardian jacket and staring at the wallpaper.

"What's with her?" Ned wanted to know.

Judy's lips thinned then parted. "That little boy was very upset," she said to the walls. "I've always let you alone and respected that this is your house."

Ned and Marilyn did double takes between the historian and each other. The little girl's eyebrows did a dance of shock as Judy continued.

"Today. . . I was disappointed in you. You did something base and you stooped to a level I never thought you were capable of. I know you are just a little girl, but you have never been mean. What did that little boy do to deserve to have you frighten him like that?"

Marilyn's shoulders sunk and her hands fell to her sides limply. "She is scolding me."

"Yes, she is." Ned watched Judy walk away, carrying her stern expression with her. He did not know whether Marilyn needed comforting or affirmation. She numbly trailed through the hall. By the time they had started down to the first floor, her mood already had brightened.

"I am going to focus on the good news. Now I know that Judy believes in me," she explained as she skipped down the stairs.

"Aren't you worried about the private?"

"I told you, he just gets like that sometimes. He will be back to his usual self in a few days."

"Marilyn, the thing in the garden was coming after him! It was calling to him! Doesn't that worry you in the least?"

"What are you talking about?"

Ned gaped at her, trying to read her smiling eyes. "Are you kidding? It just happened. You were there—"

The front door interrupted them and a man in his early twenties made his way into the house. He was separate from any tour. His only companion was a young woman in a tight sweater and jeans.

"I don't think we're supposed to wander around on our own," she explained with worry.

"We won't stay long," he answered, giving her a dashing smile. His confidence calmed her, yet she hovered in the entryway as he poked his head into the parlor.

Marilyn started to bristle. "The nerve of some

people!"

Ned circled the young man, inspecting his good looks and leather jacket. "Hey! I know him!" So much shock weighed upon those words and as Ned realized that he had remembered something, something he didn't realize he'd forgotten. "This was my roommate."

"This?" Marilyn wrinkled her nose at the young man.

"Yeah. I was driving his car. I was on my way to pick him up from a party when I. . . He was pretty good friend to me. Stop making that face, Marilyn."

"Who's she?" Marilyn pointed at the young woman as she crossed her arms over the university motto printed across her chest.

"I think she was in my Intro to Bio Chem class," Ned replied with a shrug. "I never thought she'd date a cad like this guy. Maybe he finally smartened up his taste in girls." He looked the roommate in the face. "You always did have a way of pissing off the wrong women. Maybe you've finally grown some brains."

"I don't think I like them." Marilyn wrinkled her nose and stood protectively close to Ned.

The roommate stuffed his hands into his pockets and peered around the room. His girlfriend's lips turned upward with sympathy. "How do you feel being here?"

"It's weird. You know, Ned mentioned coming here when he was kid. It was always this passing thought. . . and he. . . I mean, it was right around the corner, you know?" The roommate chuckled. "I told him that we'd need to do a double date here. . . since chicks dig history." He laughed quietly and his girlfriend rolled her eyes. His face fell and he breathed inward sharply to keep back a sniffle. "I just thought, maybe I'd keep the bargain." The face he wore was the most sincere expression Ned had ever seen upon him. His roommate was ready to cry. He never cried. He made fun of men who cried. It was the only tactic he never used to pick up girls.

The bio chem student went to his side, rubbing his arm and pulling him back. "Come on. We better go before we get in trouble."

Her boyfriend sucked in more air and choked a little. "I just—I don't know what to do. It was my car, Mary."

"And it was raining and the roads were slippery and so many other factors played in." She touched his chin and gave him a soft peck. "Breaking and entering into museums won't fix that. What would he say if he saw you here right now?"

"He'd yell at me and tell me to go buy a damn ticket.

Ned looked at Marilyn and explained, "Yep. That sounds like me." He watched the pair leave and for the first time he desperately wanted to be seen. He wanted to pat his friend on the back and give the proverbial "everything is okay". His hand went directly through his roommate and before he tried again they had wandered out of the door.

Satisfied with their departure, Marilyn dropped the guarded attitude. "What was his name?"

"What?"

"That man. What was his name?"

Two blank saucers stared at Marilyn. The void engulfed his brain and he thought it might swallow him. He ran up the stairs to an empty room without another word. The name was gone, vanished with so many other parts of his life. He paced throughout the night, running pictures across his mind's eye. The slideshow of memories became a chant, similar to his memorization of bones. He chanted where he had been born, his parents' names, his childhood pets, his first victory, and even things he had lost.

When the sun rose, he emerged to find the little girl sitting on the steps leading down to the foyer.

"Larry. My roommate was Larry."

Marilyn did not answer. Her eyes faced steadily frontward. Ned looked down the stairway at the door. "Are you waiting for Harry? It's been a while since he's been to work. Hope he's okay."

"I'm waiting for Papa to come home. He has a surprise for me. He promised." Marilyn wrinkled her nose in his direction. "You're supposed to be in bed, Marty. Mama's going to yell at you."

This was not the first time in the last few weeks that Marilyn had mistaken Ned for her brother. The first few occasions unnerved him and he went on the defensive that he was not her replacement for a long dead sibling. It was rare that she lost her sense of death and the first few times he'd experienced it, he had panicked. Irma assured him that flying off the handle did no good. He learned to take a deep breath and calmly bring the child back to reality.

"Nope. I'm Ned, remember? Your brother died in San Diego."

She looked through him, and then adjusted her gaze. "What did you say, Ned?"

"I asked where Harry was. He hasn't been around in almost two weeks."

"Has it been that long?" She hopped up and pointed as the front door's deadlock clicked. "That sounds like him now."

The door swung open and Judy entered first, followed by Harry and Daphne. All three were cheerless. Daphne moved away from her two superiors and hung at the side of the staircase with her eyes refusing to lift from her tennis shoes.

"Harry, you didn't have to come to work today," Judy insisted. She hugged him and whispered, "I didn't have a chance to see you at the funeral. It was a lovely service. I'm so sorry. You know how much I loved your wife."

He nodded, his head seeming like a brick his old neck could barely hold up. "Thank you. I just—it was Heather's time. I'm just glad the kids and I were all—" He brushed his thumb against his eyes. "I think I just want to get back to work for now."

Judy nodded with understanding. She walked away with her gaze still upon him. When he passed Daphne, the young woman avoided his eyes, uncomfortable with her own ignorance to his loss. She only knew the heartbreak of the young, the dramatic loss of first love and quiet nostalgia of fading childhood memories. She managed a "good morning" in his direction before escaping up the stairs with a lame excuse.

Harry did not seem to mind and continued to the butler's pantry with his usual trudging. Marilyn and Ned trailed after him, watching as he precisely went about his routine. He kept a red tool box, rusting at the corners but otherwise well cared for, atop a shelf which had held soup bowls in Marilyn's day. His stiff hands paused in mid-reach for the box. His shoulders buckled and he nearly sobbed.

Marilyn hung in the doorway, looking at the old man and studying the crumpled wrinkles of his anguished face. He took the toolbox with him as he staggered to one of the chairs. He arched his back and rested his head on his empty hand, the other hand hanging the toolbox down between his knees. Ned watched as tears rolled down Marilyn's face. He thought to protect her from the sad sight; to give Harry a private moment. He pulled on her shoulder, but she moved into the room without a word.

Sitting down on the floor as she always did when they watched TV, Marilyn focused all of her energy on the nice man. She thought of the grandparents she'd last seen decades ago. Her whole body tensed with a mixture of empathy and jealousy. The anguish of saying goodbye to a husband was never destined to be hers and despite the pain on Harry's face, she sensed all of the good things he was going to miss. She set her hand on his elbow.

Ned took another step inside, mesmerized by the sight of the girl in her play apron and banana curls attempting to comfort a man who had seen more of life than she ever would.

Her fingers pawed at the air around Harry's sleeve. Her eyes intensely studied him as they both cried, together yet apart. The old man lifted his head and looked directly at her. He seemed a little shocked, still said nothing. Marilyn gripped the arm of his shirt fiercely. Her lips mouthed out "It will be all right", however her voice failed her. In that moment, she was solid. She had real fingers holding on for literal life. Her tears splashed upon his knee and Harry still said nothing to her, his jaw falling open on a broken hinge.

The second passed and her hand fell through his arm as it would normally do. She moved away from Harry as he recovered himself. He stayed silent as he dried his face with a handkerchief. As he started to leave, toolbox in hand, he paused at the TV. He flipped the switch, found the kids' channel, and went upstairs to fix whatever had broken in absence.

Marilyn turned to the television set. She spread her skirts around her and got comfortable. She pat the floor, as always, insisting Ned sit with her.

He stayed where he was, the memory of a beating heart racing against his brain. "You touched him."

"Yes." Her word was cut as short as she possible. She did not look at him.

"He saw you that time. Marilyn, he saw you."

"Yes. Sometimes they see us. You know that."

Ned pulled at his hair, for the first time in a long time remembering what exhaustion felt like. "Damn it, kid. Just give me some answers."

She narrowed her eyes squinting at the television. "I can't."

"What do you mean you can't? You know what's going on. I don't. Why don't you just tell me so I don't find out in some horrible way later?" The volume of each word grew. His body tensed as he awaited her reply.

"I tell you things," she muttered.

"Only when I beg!" The lights in the room flickered.

At the snap of his voice, she set a glare upon him. The curtains rustled and the house creaked with her annoyance. "What exactly do you want to know?"

"Why did Harry see you?"

"I don't know that?"

"Were you trying to get him to see you?"

"No."

"Did you even want him to be able to see you?"

"I don't know!" She hopped to her feet and walked around him. "I don't know everything. And sometimes I forget things. The things I do know I had to figure out all by myself. If you really want answers, I suggest you do the same!"

In the following days, Marilyn returned instantly to her games and Harry to his work. Ned tried his best to stick to the parts of his routine which did not involve the little girl. He sat with Mrs. Van Sloane as she embroidered. He followed around a tour group with Irma, watching the subtle way she ran her hand down the backs of people and watched them shiver involuntarily.

Then came the day he went to have a chat with the

private. He entered the attic and felt stifled by a feeling he could not name. Ned pulled at the collar of his tee shirt and slowed his steps. The attic felt empty. The soldier had vanished leaving the attic in a state of nothingness.

Ned walked across the expanse of dust covered floors where Marilyn awaited him. "Where's the private?"

"Gone." She sat upon the cot, her legs pulled up against her chest. Ned wondered if her depressed form created an indent in the fabric visible to the living.

"Gone where?"

"Just gone. I don't know where."

"He has to be in the house, right?"

"I don't know, Ned." She stared straight ahead. "Maybe he died."

"He was already dead."

"Yes, but he was such an old ghost and he had so little to keep him here. Maybe he just let go."

"Let go? That's it? We can do that? We can just fade away? Talk to me Marilyn! Tell me what is going on."

"You're cross with me again and I can't fix it. Sometimes I just know parts of rules, parts of reasons. I told you everything I know."

After a long, irritated sigh, Ned reminded himself that she was just a little girl. The words were becoming as much of a mantra to him at labeling the bones in his hand or listing the names of his loved ones. "I'm sorry."

"I'm sorry as well," she whispered.

She was running her knuckle back and forth across the cot's worn down mat. Guilt swept away the last of his anger. "What can I do? Is there anything I can do?"

The little girl cried for only a minute, one brief minute of sobs. It took her no time to stop the tears. "Just say goodbye, Ned."

"Goodbye, Ned," he replied, earning a giggle from

Marilyn.

He left her in her grief and wandered directly through a couple inspecting the hallway wallpaper. The man shivered. The woman did not. Ned did not stop until he was out on the front porch. At first, he paced. Darting from one edge of the wooden railing to another, Ned kept the corner of his eye on the corner of the garden. He put courage into each forceful step, building up enough resolve to move to the bottom step. The thing from the garden appeared almost instantly, hovering just in front of Ned.

At first, he moved back a single step to gain a little height. The smog towered over him still, wavering back and forth in place.

"I'm not trying to leave so calm down. I just want to know why."

The thing hovered menacingly. Ned stared down the shifting smoke, remembering how being engulfed by the thing had felt.

"Why the private? Did you take him? He never bothered anybody." Ned did not expect the fog to answer, yet his questions began to bark with a growing rage. "What are you? Why would you want Sterns? Do you eat us? Eat our memories? Why do you keep us here?"

The thing continued it vigilance, guarding the final porch step from the shouting spirit.

"Answer me!"

The front door rattled open with a start at Ned's outburst. He spun around to look, expecting to see Daphne preparing for more tourists. No one, living or dead, appeared the doorway. Grinding his teeth, he turned back to the garden monster, but it had vanished. Weakened by his emotional outburst, Ned slunk onto the porch and rested his head in his hands.

Chapter Five: Denial and Isolation

Irma was the only other ghost in the house to mourn the private's disappearance. Her answers to Ned's questions about the soldier's fate were same as Marilyn's – changes in subject and insistence that they would work hard to remember the young man well.

Time dwindled away lazily. The house buzzed happily with the energy of the cooling seasons. Ned reveled in it, breathing the sense of rebirth and using it to keep his mind active. He wandered aimlessly, removing himself from the tedious schedule and spending his hours chanting his own life back to himself. He also kept a close watch upon the world outside of the house.

One day, he peered out the dining room window, parting the curtain just enough to see through. The tour group stood oblivious to the thing leering behind them. The great black smoke stayed just at the edges of their group, engulfing the people at the back in its dim light. His fist struck the window once, creating a large thump. Several members of the group faltered and glanced at the window with alarm, yet did not see him.

"Back off!" he shouted through the glass.

The dark thing floated just to the left. The tour group still tensed its' shoulders. Some people gave each other accusing looks. All the residual unease from the thing showed in their biting expressions. A millisecond passed and with it all evidence of the shadow. The tour group's eyes returned to the vapid amusement of people who were not certain why they paid to hear old objects.

"What are you doing?" Marilyn asked from behind Ned.

The young man leapt up, the curtain fluttering in his hand. "Don't sneak up on people like that! You almost gave me a heart attack!"

Marilyn giggled delightedly. "No I didn't." She glanced at the window, but kept her distance. "What are you doing?"

Ned took a deep breath. "Watching the thing in the garden."

"Why?" She began stepping back, holding out her hand as a cue to follow her.

Ned stayed put at the window. "I don't know. I just— Don't you wonder what it is? Why it's out there? It doesn't seem to bother the living unless it's right on top of them."

"I don't pay that much attention to it and you shouldn't either," the girl answered smugly. With her arms swinging, she skipped away from him calling, "Now, come see what Irma and I did!"

Ned followed her into the kitchen, silently reflecting on how much of his afterlife he spent following her. Irma was placing a pot atop a tower of chairs they had built around an over-turned table. Other objects had been placed in various nooks and crannies of the structure.

"What do you think?" Marilyn said proudly. "Think it'll scare someone?"

Irma frowned. "I hope so. It took an eternity to drag the dining room furniture into here."

Ned eyed a notebook reading, "Expenses" at the center of the mess. "Are you sure this is a good idea? It's going to take them a while to take this apart without hurting themselves."

"We just want to watch some tourists gasp," Irma explained. "We've done things like this before. As soon as the group is rushed away from here we put it all back."

Marilyn placed her hands on her hips, admiring the structure. "I think we should leave it up a little while. There are three more groups scheduled today, one right after the other; we can get a lot of use out of this."

Ned circled the tower. "Why so many?"

"It must be October. We get a lot of foot traffic around October." Irma sat at the edge of the steel sink, waiting for the living to witness her art.

"Byrons loves this time of year. They all want to hear about him and his temper tantrums," Marilyn added.

Judy and Harry ran into the room, barely noticing the stacked chairs.

"I can't believe this! Who approved this?" Judy ranted as she shuffled the papers in her arms.

"Someone from the city council thought it would be a good idea," Harry grumbled. "Are we going to reschedule them?"

"I tried that. They won't leave and they have a permit to be here today. This is so infuriating." Judy set her files on the sink beside Irma and gathered herself. "Here's what we do. We give them two hours. That's it. Daphne can do some her storytelling outside in the garden, after they interview her, and then rush the groups through afterwards. It's not an ideal situation, but it'll have to do."

"I guess I'll go help them unload then." Every wrinkle in Harry's face frowned as he marched through the house.

The three ghosts shadowed, running to the front windows. The world outside of the house was a sunny postcard full of smiling people gathered near the porch. Ned noticed spectators pointing and whispering excitedly about the house. "What's going on?"

The front door opened and shut multiple times. Mrs. Van Sloan came to criticize. Even Byrons had been permitted downstairs to observe the cause of all of the commotion.

Irma pointed into the parlor. He saw a film crew setting up lights and winding long cords from hand-held camera along the baseboards. Judy and Harry were running around the room frantically, begging the men not to set heavy electronics atop the antique furniture. Daphne stood uselessly in a corner, grinning like an idiot as a stranger applied a little extra make-up to her face.   At the center of all of the trouble, a plump woman in a light linen dress and a shawl silently looked around the room. She stared off into space. Every few minutes, she would turn herself around jerkily as if she'd heard something startling. The Bohemian pattern across the hem of her dress swished back and forth in a mess of colors. On her middle-aged cheeks rested the metal rims of a pair of glasses. She squinted unattractively through the thick lenses, wrinkling her nose and showing off every line of age gracing her face. Atop her head rested a mess of frizzy peroxide blonde.

"Who is that?"

"A medium, or so she says," Marilyn's mother sniffed with disgust. "Every few years they bring one of those shysters into my home. It's disgraceful."

"The filming equipment is new," Irma noted. "Maybe it's for a television program this time?"

Marilyn huffed. Her shoulders stiffened and she angrily tossed a stray curl off of her face. "Either way, we are not going to help that woman make money. Everyone remember no contact and no moving anything. Byrons, you especially—"

"Oh, come now. What if this one is real? I could tell about—"

"They're never real," she answered between tight lips. "Byrons, go back to your room. Irma, will you take down the furniture tower. Maybe after you're done, you can go upstairs with my mother?"

Mrs. Van Sloan's tone withered. "I will not, Marilyn. You cannot tell me where I can or cannot go within my home—" Wisps of gray began to paint her hair. The corners of her eyes began to wrinkle.

Marilyn took a deep breath and replied quickly, "Very well. Mother, you can stay wherever you like. Ned, you stay with me."

Despite her protests, Mrs. Van Sloan and Byrons went upstairs while Ned and Marilyn watched the film crew give Daphne her fifteen minutes of fame. She stuttered and fidgeted and forgot her story halfway through the telling. Once finished, the mortified young tour guide escaped outside to detain her next group until the film crew was ready to move upstairs.

Harry had already gone up in order to secure any breakables. Only Judy stayed to observe, refusing to speak on camera.

Ned and Marilyn stood as sentry at the door. "Does this happen a lot?"

"About once or twice a decade someone writing a book about ghosts or psychics will bring a medium here. They touch things and squint their eyes a great deal. Then they walk around the house saying that they feel the great depression of my mother and the despair of Byrons—"

"He must love that."

"Yes, you will want to avoid him for the next week

or so after this. The attention gives him airs." The girl looked on worriedly as Judy chased a member of the film crew off of the arm of a Cherrywood chair. "They've never brought cameras before."

"Judy doesn't seem too thrilled by all of this," he observed.

"She agrees to it whenever the city threatens to shut down the house as a tourist attraction."

"If it's not making money, what's the point, huh. I'm surprised that you and Irma don't' want to mess with this woman like you do with the tourists."

"And make everyone think she truly is psychic! We have our pride, Ned."

"I get it. So what are we going to do?"

"Keep an eye on her and try to keep her from upsetting anyone."

Cameras rolled as the blonde woman squinted at the room. "This house has a strong aura. There is comfort, but also loneliness. I feel many a presence here."

"They always say that," Marilyn explained. Then, much to her surprise, the woman directly faced her.

At first, Ned thought she saw them until she called out, "Come forth, spirits. Make yourselves known."

The psychic continued to stare in Marilyn's direction. The pair of eyes made the ghost uncomfortable. She glanced down at her patent leather shoes and adjusted the hem of her skirt.

Then, the hippy tilted her head and adjusted her glasses. "Poor child," she whispered.

Marilyn's chin shot up. At first, her eyes were full of shock. Then the medium added, "You just wanted to grow up. I'm so sorry."

This time, the young girl's eyes blazed red. "You don't know anything about me. Go away."

"Poor child," the woman repeated even more

quietly, as if it were a secret between her and Marilyn. She then turned to the film crew and sighed, shaking herself back into her over-dramatic flair. "I think we are done in this room. Shall we move on to the kitchen before the upstairs? Then we can be done for the day."

The men all shuffled out of the parlor after her. Marilyn stared at the spot where the medium had been, her jaw clenched and her eyes misty.

Ned set a hand awkwardly on her upper back, right between her shoulder blades. "You okay?"

"I hate those fakes coming into my home and trying to make a reputation off—" She balled her fists. "She's wrong. I'm not a poor child." She growled and as she did the rocking chair across the room toppled over. With a meek sob, Marilyn glanced at the fallen object, then at Ned, and dashed away up the stairs.

Instead of chasing her down, he went to the dining room where the crew had swiftly readjusted their lights and microphones. Judy guarded the china hutch with her stern glances. The cameras rolled once more as he entered.

The medium turned towards Ned automatically. "I sense another presence. This essence is strong and curious. They are so curious about why we are here. Who are you, spirit?"

Ned realized that this was his chance. He could tell the psychic all about himself and she would tell Daphne. His name would be a part of the tour. He would be one of the ghosts they tried to summon on Halloween and he would not fade away as Private Sterns had done. It was his chance to keep himself together, his mind with his spirit. Maybe his family would hear the stories of his haunting and fly out to investigate.

His excitement waned. His mother would be devastated to think of him trapped there. His father would claim the house was using their grief to add to the tourism. He would be harming them through reputation alone just by planting the simple idea; Ned is a ghost.

He almost imagined his reflection within the medium's glasses. The woman continued to squint in his direction while the cameras rolled. "Marilyn is not a poor child," he told her calmly. "She takes care of everyone in this house. She is responsible and strong. She has helped a bunch of clueless adults who don't know what their place in the universe is anymore. She is the mistress here and you have insulted her. You should leave."

Whether the woman understood his words or not, she sensed his meaning. She frowned and tuned to the camera. "There is hostility here. It isn't anger or a want to create fear. I think it's protective. I think the spirits are protecting this house. I feel they want us to know that we are safe here if we are respectful." She paused and the camera stopped rolling. Her shoulders tensed and her tone turned stiff. "We need to do some shots upstairs in the suicide room or this thing will be a dud."

Judy sneered at her. "It's a bedroom. Not the suicide room."

The medium removed her glasses and wiped them on the edge of her blouse. "No offense, but plain old bedrooms don't get people to watch television. But bedrooms where men shot themselves and I claim never left the house. . . " She trailed off to give Judy a sleazy smile. "You'll be thanking me for how much money this place is going to make after my show airs."

Ned stood beside the fuming Judy as the camera crew tromped up the stairs. "Don't worry," he told the historian, "Byrons will make her wish she never came to this house. . . just by being Byrons."

A few days after the psychic had come and gone,

Marilyn continued to keep to herself. Her only contact with anyone was a series of nasty tricks she played on different tourists she judged as "deserving it". She spent an entire afternoon moving around Daphne's water bottle, hiding it in cupboards. Ned left her alone for several days until he decided it was safe.

He found Irma in the parlor reading. The sight never occurred to him before. She looked natural there in the light with the book hovering in front of her dark eyes. She looked alive.

"Where's Marilyn?" Ned asked the older woman.

Irma set the work of fiction in her lap and looked out of the window intently. He glanced out and noticed a young woman paralyzed to the sidewalk staring back. He laughed as Irma waved.

"Having a tea party in her room. You know, I'm always tempted to wave when someone sees me. Just completely break with ghostly mystery and tradition."

"Another tea party? Was is it normal in her time for twelve year olds to still play with dolls and marbles."

Irma sat back. She could no longer be seen through the window. "I'm not entirely sure. But you have to understand that she was sickly most of her life. Her parents babied her and playing was important especially when her brother was still young. Besides, I think it makes it easier not to dwell on the growing up she never got to do." She gave him a grin and he saw that she was missing teeth towards the back of her bottom jaw. "Why? Are you growing sick of tea parties and marbles?"

"Not quite, but if I have to do this for eternity, I'm going to be." He rubbed his brow. "Irma, do you ever feel yourself forgetting things?"

"What sort of things?"

"Your life."

"No. I'm surrounded by the memories of my life.

This house was my father's, then it was mine. I can still imagine him or my husband sitting here." She set the book back on a shelf where it belonged. "The furniture was different then, of course."

"I'm starting to forget," he blurted. "What should I do?"

Irma's eyes wandered back to the window. "I would talk to Marilyn about that." The woman returned picked up a different book, signaling his time to leave.

Ned went to the master bedroom where mother and daughter enjoyed a companionable silence. Marilyn sat upon the small stool at her mother's feet. Mrs. Van Sloan looked as she always did when she was happy, a middle aged woman with young, worn eyes. She worked diligently upon her needlework with perfect posture and her only head tilted downward. Every strand of hair was perfectly folded up to meet the bun atop her scalp. She put every turn of the century postcard to shame.

Ned tried to remember his own mother. He always thought of her as young. She'd married when she was seventeen, managing to lie on the certificate. When he was growing up, she liked to play with him. Not just watch him or make some halfhearted effort of bouncing a teddy bear around his face. She wore an eye patch and told him their beat-up station wagon was a pirate ship. As they'd run errands, she declare war upon nicer vehicles.

Ned's dad was a warm man. He worked long hours and was doted upon by his wife with a nightly beer or shoulder rub. He never took work troubles home with him. He demanded full accounts of Ned's day starting with breakfast and ending with the moments before they'd started the conversation.

The facts of his family were whispered to himself and to the hallway. When people die young, a common phrase said by the grieving is how they remember "how full of life they were". Ned always thought of his parents that way, two people who never let the problems of the world lessen their small, stolen moments of happiness. They always had energy and imagination. Ned, personally, always considered himself rather dull. He liked books and documentaries and his mother used to call him the Professor.

What had she said to him the last time they'd talked on the phone? "Don't work too hard, Professor. Stress is a killer." Her heart must have been broken to think of her last morbid joke to him after she'd received the news. A selfish part of him hoped she kept that sense of humor through it all, from the moment she heard of his accident to the moment she had to come home after his funeral. Other people always drew strength from her. He hated the thought that she was unable to do the same for herself.

The child noticed her friend mumbling to himself and hopped off of the stool. "Ned! Do you want to play?" She pulled him into her nursery and set him into his usual chair.

He shifted his weight and held his breath. She smiled at him with all of the innocence of the young. He had to remind himself that she was technically much older than him. "Marilyn, you never ask about my family. Or very much about my life. You know everyone's background, except mine."

"My mother always taught me that it is far too forward to ask personal questions," Marilyn replied as she offered him a cup of tea. She then set another cup in front of her doll.

"No, thanks." Ned waved at the cup at stood. "Shouldn't I be talking about it though? I think I'm starting to forget things."

The girl sighed with annoyance. "Very well. Tell me

about your life."

"I—" He searched his mind for living days, days of feeling the sun on his face and the wind in his hair. The thoughts of his family slipped away again. His first thought was of the car wreck, the moments before the wheel had slipped through his fingers and water surrounded the windows. "I was on my way to a party at my college the night I. . . that night. I was in college, you know, out-of-state. My family lived here when I was a kid. We left when I was in high school and I came back for college."

Marilyn's interest was piqued. "Do you think your parents held your funeral here or where they live?"

"Probably where they live. It's where my uncles and aunts and cousins all are. The day I— I had heard from my high school girlfriend. She's a teacher. She told me that my littlest cousin is turning into the biggest tattletale who ever lived."

"You were in love?" The girl asked her question without jealousy or sympathy, just pure interest.

"No. I mean. . . I guess she was close. We were good friends, but we really didn't last long as a couple which might be why we stayed friends. She's married to another of my friends now."

With a clinical nod, Marilyn replied, "I never had a chance to be in love either, but from what I've seen it's a mess. Especially since Daphne started working here. Every week she has her heart broken. She always brings her. . . young men to the house and they are always just awful. You saw the last one. They always want to kiss her a lot and then mess with things in the house." She paused to blush. "Daphne was extremely cross with one a while back. He tried to toss around my grandmother's Italian vase like a football."

"She was worried he'd break it?"

Marilyn nodded once more. "The second he was

alone, the private and I took care of him. He ran out of the house yelling like an infant and Daphne came in the next day crying that they were no longer together." Her last sentence filled her with pride.

"I thought you don't like Daphne. Why save her from a guy?"

"It's embarrassing. My mother says that staff like Daphne represents this house and thus represents us. I would never have been with such a low and crass man if I'd lived to Daphne's age. She should be more careful with her life."

Ned leaned on the back of a chair, focusing his mind on the thought of the wood and the weight of his own arms. "But it is her life, Marilyn."

"Then she should take some pride in it." The girl's nose flew upward and she sniffed with the attitude befitting her twelve years.

"Is that what you think of everyone? That they don't live the way you think they should?" He tried to make the question

"Of course not! Daphne is such a special sort of aggravating in how she. . . conducts herself." Marilyn sat up in her chair, returning to her usual younger behavior. "Tell me more about what you remember. Maybe. . . we've never talked very much about the crash."

"The car was my roommate's. I was meeting him at the party. He'd gone early to stop some jerk from being alone there with his girl. I was driving because I don't drink." Ned stood up with a sickly green tinging his cheeks. "Funny, huh. He left me with the car 'cause I was the safer driver."

"Can I ask? What did happen? Why did the car go in the river?"

"Pair of kids on their bikes. Nobody's fault. We were just all in the wrong place at the wrong time and I have to swerve to avoid them. The road was wet and the brakes weren't fast enough. . . something must have been wrong with them. No one's fault." He turned to leave. "Sorry for interrupting your tea party."

Marilyn jumped from her chair with such insistence that she managed to knock the furniture over. "Ned. What were you studying in college?"

"Medicine. I wanted to save lives." She knew she should have asked more. Instead, she picked up one of her dolls and fussed with the yarn hair. Ned studied her. "Are you ever going to just let go like you think the private did?"

Marilyn's smile waned. "Why would I? I like it here. My mother is here and Irma too. This place makes it easy to remember my father and brother. I have no reason to leave."

"What about what you never got to do? What if leaving the house means you have another chance at all that or seeing your dad and brother again?"

Her mouth twisted in annoyance. "You need to learn to understand that sometimes life was just what it was. I was sick a good part of my life and I always knew I'd never be able to be courted or go to my first dance or even wear long skirts. But I liked the life I had and I like this afterlife." With a heavy smile, the kind which seemed like an act of God upturned the corners of her mouth, she added, "And I can't leave Mama or Irma and they aren't ready to go."

Ned's own expression caved and he gave one last attempt to sway her. "You're twelve years old. You don't have to take care of everyone else."

"You need to understand," she said again, "I never got to take care of anyone when I was alive. This is my turn."

His frown rivaling her pasted on smile, Ned escaped her room. Byrons stood in his doorway. He leaned in with a sway in his shoulders, drunkenly squinting upon Ned with disgust. "You still don't get it. We are not anything. We are a fraction, a shadow left by a corpse. The majority of what you were is rotting at the bottom of that lake or in the ground, assuming they fished you out."

"What's your point?"

"The point is that there is no point. So stop asking the kid questions even she doesn't know the answer to."

Ned scoffed. "You can't make up your mind, can you? One day you're trying to convince me that Marilyn is running this place and the next you're trying to tell me to stop bugging her with questions."

"She has control. That I know. But do you really think she would have wanted that pathetic soldier from upstairs to go away? If she knew the secrets to leaving this place, you know exactly who she'd kick out first." He bowed his head proudly to Ned.

"Why do you stay? Why don't you just let go and try to leave?"

Without replying, the drunk maneuvered clumsily back through his door. A second later Marilyn appeared in the hallway. "I'm sorry. I didn't mean to seem insensitive to your questions. Let's go watch some television with Harry and then you can tell me more about your mom and dad." Her little hand slipped into his. "I want to know more, I really do."

Soon, they were in front of the rabbit-eared TV. Harry and Daphne were eating an early dinner. The young tour guide had risen to adjust the picture quality as the afternoon news began to blur.

Daphne sunk back down into the chair as soon as the wavy lines had vanished from the screen. "Harry, did you see this?"

The old man looked up from his potato chips. "What's that?"

She excitedly pointed at screen, her movement shaking the floor slightly and causing the rabbit ears to shift. "You remember that car that flipped into the river behind the house almost a year ago?"

Harry frowned deeply, saddened by the morbid light in her eyes. "Yes. That poor young man drowned didn't he?"

"Yeah! Well, it turns out that the police found tampering with the car's brake line and had opened an investigation. The car belonged to the guy's roommate who was a major heart breaker. The police actually tracked down the roommate's old girlfriend and she confessed to putting a hole in the brake line. She thought of just scaring her ex; maybe have him end up in a little accident. She never meant for the other guy to die." At her excited words, the TV started to blur.

Moving solemnly across the room, Harry fixed the antenna and waited for the wavy lines across the screen to focus. The news had already moved on to the weather. "Poor young man," he repeated under his breath. "Did they say his name?"

Daphne focused on fixing the hem of her cheaply made Victorian reenactment dress. "Um. . . Edward something. . . I really didn't pay that close of attention to that part."

The frown lines of Harry's face sunk further into his cheeks. For half a second, he looked ready to have a serious talk to the young woman. Returning to his lunch, Harry suppressed a sigh. "Did you set out the donation flyers by the front door?"

"Not yet."

"You better do that or Judy will be on you about it for the rest of the day."

She set herself upon her feet reluctantly and shook out the cotton skirt. As she left the room, she casually stretched her arms over her head and gave an unladylike groan. "Bring on the tourists."

Harry waited for her to leave, then rose to switch off the television. Setting a weary hand to the back of his neck, he repeated one final time, "Poor young man" and returned to his work.

Ned teetered beside Harry. He tried to steady himself on the table, but his hands sunk directly through. Anger surged up and down his limbs. It had not been a random accident. The accident had been because of some stupid girl who acted recklessly. He had died because of a pointless revenge prank. The texture of the wood was fresh against Ned's palms as they collided with the table. An animal-like growl he did not recognize ran through him. Then he shoved. He pushed the table and the contents tumbled over. A buzzing filled his ears. The electric lights in the room zapped. Fuses blew with loud pops. Smoke curled from the T.V. set.

Ned did not care. He wanted it all to break. He wanted the house to fall apart, to rumble and shake until the foundation cracked and the roof caved in. Marilyn must have been there with him, but he did not see her through the tunnel vision of anger.

The last tour group of the evening entered the house. The last group was always the largest as by that time the sun was nearly set and the house was bathed in a perfect eerie glow for morbid thrill seekers. Ned realized that he wanted to tell them a ghost story.

Cameras clicked and children whined. He stepped into the dining room. Ned thought only of his tense muscles and the darkness set upon his brain. The room went black and stale air invaded the senses of the living. Several members of the tour group screamed including Daphne.

She quickly composed herself and told the group, "Not a problem, folks. Old houses sometimes have electrical problems. I'm sure our maintenance man will have things up and running in no time. Please do not try to move around the room until the lights come back on."

As she spoke, she scrambled to the china cabinet at the edge of the dining room. Within a drawer, several flashlights and batteries had been stashed for just such an occasion. She fumbled in the dim light, checking each torch until finding on which would switch on.

She shined the circle of the light at her group and told them with relief, "See. Well, if the lights do not come on in a minute, we may have to cut the tour a little short."

"Maybe it's the ghosts," a man joked and wiggled his fingers up the back of his girlfriend's neck.

She laughed and shooed him off. "Daryl, cut it out. You know I don't believe in ghosts."

Her flippant laugh in the face of his anger cut into Ned. Racing at Daphne, he put all of his will into his hands and forced the flashlight from her fingers. She yelped as she lost he grip and the object was flung though the air at the laughing tourist.

The woman and her boyfriend ducked. "What the hell?!" they both shouted at different times.

"I am so sorry!" Daphne started to spout, a tremor in her voice. "It just slipped from my hands—"

In another instant, Ned pulled at the table cloth. He did not manage to spill over any of the antique dishes, but yanked several place settings together. As the silverware clattered against the soup bowls, the tour group released a collective gasp. He thought of toppling the crystal decanter when Daphne stretched her arms towards the table, trying to shield the group from the strange occurrences.

Irma and Marilyn stood to the side as Ned lifted a pair of serving tongs and managed to fling them through the air. The group of humans ducked and huddled together.

Marilyn's curls bounced as she watched Ned pace. "You're scaring me!" Tears rolled down her cheeks. Her sorrow rivaled his anger and the house felt every moment of it. Curtains fluttered and the room's temperature dropped even further. The tourists rubbed the goosebumps from their skin.

Irma wrapped her arms around Marilyn and the girl encircled her friend's waist. She gave Ned an expression of fear and disapproval. "Honestly, Ned. You've gone too far. Stop this before someone gets hurt."

"We can't get hurt, remember," he grumbled under his breath.

He stomped amongst the tourists, many of them gasping as a rush of ice cold air passed through them. One child started to cry that she felt someone push her. After a minute, Ned moved towards the door.

"Where are you going?" Marilyn chased after him.

"I'm done! It isn't fair and I'm done!" He ran through the front door, wishing he could push it down.

The girl pulled on his hand, her heels digging into the porch. "Please, Ned. Come back inside."

He shook her off and hopped over the side of the railing. His feet landed in the grass and Marilyn's voice went shrill. He had to shout over the top of her. "Okay, thing! You come get me if you want, but one way or another I am leaving this house!"

The thing in the garden rounded the side of the building. The edges of the black cloud blurred and focused in a steady rhythm. It hesitated, eerily hovering as a tourist having a look at the outside of the house walked directly through it. The woman had no way of knowing what had happened to her, but she showed the effect of the cloud instantly. She scowled and knit her brow, her mind trapped somewhere between rage and anguish.

"You want to do that? You want to make me feel like I shouldn't exist?" Ned accused, squaring his shoulders for the one-sided wresting match. "You want to fill me with despair? I hate to break it to you, but right now I couldn't get much lower."

Accepting the challenge, the thing lunged forward. The smoke surrounded Ned, suffocated him. He caught glimpses of the house through the swirling winds that pulled at him. He sensed the house watching, the building itself taking on a new persona in his mind. It had been his prison keeping away what was left of himself after his life had been taken. The nostalgia he'd experienced the first day on the porch was gone. The memories of scaring little Kiki Gold turned bitter. What if the house had chosen him from that moment? Maybe the building always meant for him to end up there.

Ned could sense himself slipping away, the blackness latching onto his soul and drowning him. And he was allowing it. He wanted things to be quiet, to be easy to answer. Mysteries were overrated.

As the smoke forced its way into his ears and mouth, his rage and depression intensified. The house held him hostage. Ned would not sit around and wait for his own memories to fail him. He thought of Byrons, of all the hate and bitterness locked away in a single room. Ned imagined himself in that existence, living forever with the obsession of his own death.

The idea of Byrons created a pinprick in Ned's pain, a tiny hole allowing in a minutest amount of sunshine. From the porch, Marilyn watched with her palms cupping her mouth to keep her from shrieking, her dark eyes peeking over the top of her round cheeks. Within her expression, the pinprick reflected with her last remnants of hope that somehow Ned would escape the oblivion engulfing him. She fought for him in the only ways she could. She kept him grounded and existing. She remembered him and made his presence known.

The urge to battle back returned, this time powered by the pinprick as it grew into flashbacks of the past year. He'd never truly grieved his own death. Marilyn never allowed grieving. His fears were screamed into the blackness.

"You go ahead and try feeding off of me, but you know what? I'm not just some memory! I'm not just the result of an accident! You can't just take me away and you can't just make me forget! If you're going to swallow me up, you better be ready to choke, because I am not going without a fight!"

Both eyes focused on the house and saw through the black and through the unhappiness. The smoke thinned, making his vision clearer. The crushing pressure against his head and chest release him.

He took the opportunity wrestle back. Chanting the names of the bones within his fingers, Ned latched onto the thing from the garden. The smoke entwined with his arms and he dragged up the porch stairs.

Marilyn waved her arms. "Ned, don't!"

"I'm going to find out what this is and I am going to find out why it keeps us here if it's the last thing I ever do!" Ned did not know why he yelled. He swayed as he kept the shadow in place. It shifted against him, determined not to go into the house.

Her hand waves and tears pouring down her face, Marilyn screamed out, "It is trying to protect us!"

Slowing the struggle, but not releasing his hold on the thing, Ned stated harshly, "This is not a nurturing being, Marilyn."

"Not that. The house. Unless the thing from the garden is part of the house. I've never been sure. All I do know is that the house is trying to keep us safe. That's all it ever wants."

Nerves still trembling within him, Ned slowly realized why the house favored Marilyn. It was not simply because she was the first to die there. The house understood her. It understood her need to take care of others. Underneath all of her confidence and years of afterlife experience, she was still just a child who had no idea of what she was doing. And the house empathized with that.

Moving through the front door, Ned respectfully bowed his head with his arms still wrapped within the garden creature. The smoke had begun to shrink down, retreating within itself to be the size of a pillow. It was Marilyn's turn to follow Ned and she did so from a safe distance.

"I get it now." He addressed the house without taking a second thought to the darkness which still filled the rooms and the clustered tourists being calmed by Daphne. "You tried to do what you thought was best. But you can't scare and force people to stay someplace, even if you are trying to help them. If all we have left are our memories, then all we have left are our choices too. Irma chose to stay. Private Sterns did not and now he's gone." Straining his neck as if the ears of the building hung from the ceiling, he added, "You have to let some of us go if it's time for us to go."

The boards beneath the rugs settled to the ground with pensive sounds. The parlor drew Ned's attention with a rustle of curtains and the sound of wood scraping against wood. The bootlegging trap door lay open. The cellar beneath Mrs. Byrons's booze hatch was darker than Ned remembered. Holding his arms over the pit, he released the thing from the garden. It dissipated into the black, taking the last of Ned's bitterness with it. The trap door slam shut and the house lit back up with the smell of sparking electricity.

The young ma celebrated with a surprised, "Huh. I did not think that would work."

Marilyn edged into the room. "Wonderful," she weakly replied, her arm desperately reaching for him. "Let's go upstairs and play."

Ned's jaw went slack. "Aren't you glad? It can't scare you anymore. It won't upset the tourists or lurk in windows." Marilyn gazed at the trap door. "I get it. You wished it had taken Byrons before it left, huh?"

The comment made her smile, but the joy faded quickly. "Let's go find Irma and plan a prank. Come on. I think you need cheering up."

"Marilyn, I'm sorry I scared you."

With one hand on the doorway, her fingers twisted a little further out in hopes that he would take her hand. "You had a shock. It'll be alright now. We can go play and just forget about it. Well, we can. I don't know if Daphne will—"

"But we can't."

Her hand dropped to her side. "Why not?" Her eyes sparkled with fresh tears. "What happened to you. . . that was awful. But you can't let it rule you."

"I know." The next sentence was difficult, hanging within him like a lead weight refusing to be pulled up. "I know and that's why I can't stay."

The girl heaved a sigh. "No!"

"It's your turn to understand, okay. I get it now. You stay here so you can hold onto to who you were when you were alive. I need to go someplace where I can remember my own life. I want to find my family. I can feel myself getting lost."

"Like the private," she stated in a whimper.

"Yeah."

"Marilyn, I need to go. Will you say goodbye to everyone for me?"

Her tear stained eyes continued to gaze at the trap

door. Worrying that if he waited much longer that the house would trap him again just to make the child happy, Ned walked out the front door and down the porch steps without a another word.

Her patent leather shoes trailed silently after him, still not daring to move from the very edge of the bottom step. This was the furthest she had been from her house since her death. Her arms wrapped around his middle with all of the veracity expected of a young girl. The hug was everything he ever remembered a hug to be. The warm muscles in her little arms tightened around him and he returned the embrace. For the first time, his senses were aware of the cotton of her sleeves and the curl of her hair. In that second, they were both real and he wondered if the living were looking at them, assuming them to be alive. Ned almost didn't want to let go.

"Why are you crying?" she wanted to know with her signature giggle when they at last pulled apart.

He didn't know that tears had left his eyes and he found it a wonder that he could still cry. "Just because I'm leaving, it doesn't mean I'm not going to miss you." He gave her one final pat upon the head and thanked her again. With a shaky breath, he looked onto the spot where the road bended into the bridge over the river. Taking the first step to the edge of the sidewalk, he paused to look back at her. "Wish me luck?"

Marilyn set her hands behind her back and swung her knees slightly. With a decided smile, she called after him. "You know the best way to deal with being dead?"

He blinked his tears away and awaited her wisdom.

"You don't want to be just another wailing soul tormented by the past. The best thing to do is to just forget." And at that, she grinned at him. It was the same semi-pitying yet childish smile she'd offered him when she'd first told him he was dead.

"No. How about no more forgetting? I'm going to take the torment with the tea parties." He rolled his eyes at his own words. "Okay, cheesy I know. Maybe you should consider it. Sometimes it can be good to remember the things that make you sad."

Her eyes sparkled at him and she waved him with thoughtful approval. "Goodbye, Ned."

As Ned turned away, he concentrated upon his own feet. A moment of dread and excitement mixed within him. The soles of his shoes met with pavement and continued to walk away.

About the Authors

**Sidney Reetz
"That red-headed
Devil woman."**

Born and residing in
Phoenix, Arizona, Sidney
started writing in the
fourth grade for her own
enjoyment. The stories
penned back then were
during her high fantasy
period and involved a lot of
dragons, elves and magic.
She was ten years old.
Needless to say, they were

horrible and will never see the light of day – but were fun to write and taught her a lot about discipline. In elementary school she entered the 'short story' competition and baffled the organizers when she dropped off a 150-some-odd page manuscript. They must have liked it; she won second place.

When not transcribing the Devil's words, Sidney is an avid crafter and all around nerd. She likes watching anime and making themed playlist far too much.

Kira Shay

Kira has been telling stories for as long as she could talk and writing them down as soon as she could hold a crayon. While her chosen writing implement has matured, she still enjoys weaving stories that both entertain and make people think. She is one of the founders of FSF Publications. Kira currently lives in Arizona with her husband, Will.

Megan E. Vaughn

Megan E. Vaughn became a writer to distract from the fact that she does not know how to read. She has been locked in an epic battle with dust bunnies ever since she moved from Wisconsin to Arizona as a child. Beyond that, she has earned her degree in history, traveled to many historical ruins in various places, and forced her friends to pretend to be impressed by historically significant rocks. Currently she lives...right behind you! Ha! Made you look.

www.ingramcontent.com/pod-product-compliance
Lightning Source LLC
Chambersburg PA
CBHW061011120726
47910CB00006B/1877